eric koppitz ★ fallen leaves

Life will haunt you.

To the angels in my life,

I wanted to make the few of you proud.

You all know who you are.

Thank you.

As an American raised on red meat, I exaggerate. Sometimes there has to be blood. I'm a fiction writer, not a journalist; I have the right. Journalists would make great fiction writers because they exaggerate for their agenda's appetite. I lament saying that The Media have succeeded in deciding how the world is supposed to think because you might just believe anything that you read. Just the same as my having to publish and promote this book independently, I want you to start conducting your own investigations and empowering yourself, if you already haven't. Then one day we can start electing people for the practitioners that they truly are, not because we are mesmerised by the pretty blue bow that The Media gift-wrapped them in. So, for love and for truth, I write the following:

If I really knew a girl like Felicity in high school then I would've never wrote this story. Jason and Jim, some of the pages in here may remind you of those days and agree that we actually knew a lot of characters that could've been in this book. I'm glad it's just fiction, but I shudder to think that it all could've happened.

Chad, I'm sorry I couldn't give Ethan a brother in this one. But it's high time you write your own novel. And Dad, we get along fine these days, don't we? I mean, what else can I say? We weren't perfect, but there was no violence in our home. None. No family is perfect but we tried to be as good as we could when it counted. But Mom, you *were* perfect.

The birthday parties end. Youth slowly shrinks from its Jupiter-size to just that one sparkling pebble on the river bank that might remind us of what being a teenager used to feel like. Every kid wants to scream loud enough for the whole world to hear them. Seventeen is tough. <u>Fallen Leaves</u> is my scream, half my life later.

-   *Eric Koppitz*

23 July, 2012

Life has haunted me,

And time never stops.

The ghosts spoke through my demons,

Until hope shined through fall's death.

One demon remained,

And he was my son.

I kissed him upon his brow,

And prayed he'd wait for me in peace.

the face of a porcelain doll

What's that sound?

<click-clack, click-clack, click-clack>

It's coming from outside the window. I toss my warm blankets to the side and rise from my uncomfortable bed. My alarm clock mocks my misery in bright red digits...

3:07am

'Why can't I just *sleep?*'

Because you hate *this town. High school sucks. You want to kill your father...*

'Stop...please.'

You want to die...

'Just kill me then.'

No, Ethan, that's your job. One of these days you're going to grab Dad's shotgun, stick the barrel in your mouth and...

'Shut up!'

You can't sleep, Ethan, because you talk to yourself. Just like you're doing right now. Don't worry, though. You're just going a little insane.

1

I peer between the half-opened drapes that shiver in the late September gusts. Bataan Drive curves around the sharp suburban bend and bathes in the moonlight. Leaves fall from wicked old oak trees, decorated red and gold. A porch light barely flickers in the distance and parked cars give shelter to stray cats. But my neighbourhood's overnight peace has been cracked...

<click-clack, click-clack, click-clack>

What is that sound, for Christ's sake?

Across the night a glowing white shape approaches from around that bend. But it's not the headlights of a middle-of-the-night drive, it's something else. A little startled, I cower, and then notice a black shape beneath it.

And I'll be damned if it's not a horse!

Its hooves are click-clacking against the tarmac. The white shape is the rider upon it, wearing a flowing gown draped on her feminine curves. From just above the window sill my tired but curious eyes watch the woman approach. *Am I dreaming? Is she real? Why on Earth is she riding horseback at this ungodly hour?*

The horse prances the woman through the confirming street light and comes to a halt on the curb that nibbles our front lawn. Her black locks thrash to the side to unveil her glowing white face, the face of a porcelain doll. As stunning as she is, she's the most terrifying creature I've ever laid my eyes upon!

But even more terrifying is the way she stares right back at me!

I dive down onto the wood floor, out of her sight beneath the window, and just listen.

The distant wind chimes jingle in the gusts. Fallen leaves

rustle as they're blown down the street. But the loudest sound is my heart thumping against my chest.

My curiosity lifts me back up and I peer out again, just over the sill. That woman has dismounted and just stares into my bedroom, through the black tresses obscuring her face. I need to shut this window, lock it and close the drapes…or else this beast of a beautiful woman might…she might…

I cannot imagine.

I collect my nerve and rise from my coil, watching my shadow crawl on the moonlight that has spilled into my room with hope that it will distract me from my fear. But this moment has grown too intense. My room has begun to spin.

'Ee-thaan…' A voice whispers, dizzying me even more.

Between the dancing drapes from just the other side of the window, two white, slender hands slither their long, pretty fingers upon the sill. From out of the corner of my eye those fingers grind their nails into the sill's chipped paint, amongst the dead houseflies.

A sudden gust of wind blasts the drapes wide open…

From just arm's length the woman draped in white stares right at me! Right *through* me!

Her hair, black like a raven's feathers, flows around her snow-white face. Her lips, red like the roses she smells of, open to whisper my name again. Her breath of cinnamon trails, fusing intoxicatingly with her rose fragrance. But it's her eyes that dominate. They blaze green. They penetrate my skull.

How can such a beautiful woman be so horrifying? How can she…?

'Ee-thaan…' she howls. Her voice is angelic. Of a ghost. It fractures into a haunting echo…

'Ee-thaan…'

* * *

3

The morning sunlight bathes me delicately into consciousness and shines upon two tickets to a rock show. Not just *any* rock show. They just rest there upon my window sill.

AN EVENING WITH

The Vampire Bats

<u>THE AMERICAN THEATER</u>

Wednesday, September 29

Doors 8:00pm

Tonight.

I lay my trembling fingers upon the tickets, my trembling fingers that failed to point and click the mouse fast enough on the morning that they went on sale.

It sold out in seven minutes.

These two glossy, perforated stock miracles might as well be made of diamonds and pearls. I begin to spaz out as I consider the demand to see The Vampire Bats in such an intimate venue. Holy shit! Naked cartwheels down the distance of Bataan Drive are in order! *These tickets were sold out, man! Gone! Oh baby, yes!*

But brakes screech in my head. I remember what happened overnight. That woman. *Was last night a dream? Who was she?*

I'd failed to win *The Point* radio station give-away. I couldn't afford to buy them from scalpers, nor could my parents (or would they have). They don't even know who The Vampire Bats are! But as I examine these tickets in the morning rays of sun I know that they are *real*. One for me and one for a friend.

Where did these tickets come from?

That woman put *them there.*

4

the vampire bats

On the edge of the stage, in front of white lightning strikes, the next generation of rock displays the presence of gods, behind dark drumbeats, creepy basslines, and spooky post-punk riffs all laced together with synthesisers. And two thousand people worship them as if they are indeed almighty, chanting the tragic lyrics along with the front man clad in a black kimono…

'The river…refrained…to let her swim.

My angel's…dead on…the muddy brim.

It rushed…against her…into the unknown,

Pulling…her down…into the drowning zone

UNTIL NOTHING AT ALL COULD BE SEEN!

But the BLACK! The SLUDGE! And the MURKY GREEN!

And her LIFE! FLASHING! BEFORE HER EYES!

The river…rushed our…love to demise.'

The Vampire Bats electrify The American Theater as they perform *'The River'*. This heavy, Goth-rock thumper ricochets around the grand Beaux-arts interior. Through the rising fog of the dry ice the band look like ghosts. But the *real* ghosts who built this venue, which opened in 1917, watch from the nooks on the mezzanine, just as they have for the last century.

Girls and boys drink and smoke and slither their tongues into the mouths of the willing. The pit has become a village of Hell, and its fires might be burning this place down for all I know, as I'm sweating my balls off in the human stew boiling in front of the stage. The new concert T I wear is soaked but I'm buzzing hard and chock full of adrenaline. I put the flask of Jack Daniels back to my underage lips and knock the pinball-bodies around the pandemonium circle. I slosh the whiskey around inside to gauge what I've got left. *Plenty*. And already I feel powerful. Confident. Suddenly I'm not worried about my troubles. I'm not at school or in my father's shadow or in my bedroom hiding from the world I live in. I'm not letting life drive me mad. I feel so *alive,* at last!

Now someone re-appears that I thought had long since been devoured by this pit. Perhaps swallowed down into its stomach, pushed through its bowels and shit out in the back by the bar. My best friend, Justin, stands once again at my side, sporting a Death Elvis look that's still somehow very much fresh and in tact. Together we absorb the energy - a fusion of the band's ferocity, the crowd's youth and the spirits of this grand old building.

'Dude, how *did* ya get these *tickets*?' Justin asks.

'I *told* ya!'

'That's bullshit, Ethan! These tickets sold out in eight minutes! Tell me, now. *How?*'

'Seven, actually.' I take another long swig of Jack and grumble through my boozed breath, 'I told ya. A ghost gave them to me.'

'Dude, that Jack's gettin to ya!'

'What's it matter? We're here!'

A renegade from another pack grabs me and says, 'Hey-'

'Hey, fuck off!' I bark back. I'm not drunk yet. Just aggressive. I'm sweating out the alcohol.

'Easy, easy,' the renegade replies. He stands behind a slutty-looking little Goth with his inked-up arms wrapped around her. 'Come to the party tonight!' he demands, bloodshot eyes wide-open, crushed with black liner.

'What party?' Justin asks.

'Our party! It's gonna be wicked! Hey, how much was that t-shirt?' the renegade asks me.

'I don't know. I stole it.' *It was twenty bucks. Ouch!*

'Rebellious, budday!' He cheers, and then says, 'My Cleo here thinks ya look like Brandon Lee!'

Justin chimes in, '*Ethan... Brandon Lee?* Ya mean, *The Crow's* Brandon Lee?'

'Totally!' she slurs.

'*Your* Cleo?' I ask. What is she, your *puppet*, man?'

'What?' peeps the renegade.

'Cleo, DO YOU TALK?' I over-annunciate. 'ON YOUR OWN?'

'Nevermind Ethan here,' Justin says, 'he's on the whiskey apparently. Where's your party?'

'Look,' the renegade says, whipping out his cell phone, 'just come to our party! What's your num-?'

Where did he go? He's *gone!* The pierced mouth and eyes of his girlfriend change into big Os of 'whoa!' Perhaps *he's* about to be swallowed into the pit's stomach, soon to be shit out somewhere near the bar? No, he's being ripped apart and tossed around like a rag doll by the other sweaty animals. The renegade's happy face has suddenly become dark with worry as

9

he realises that he has no control over where the hundreds of claws carry him. He screams helplessly as his shoe is ripped off and thrown onto the stage near the keyboardist. He drifts away to the back of the pit, out of sight, like a ship disappearing into the ocean night. No one knows for sure where he'll end up or how he'll get back to his party with just *one shoe!*

And his girlfriend screams, 'Oh my God!' just before *she's* winched up. Her N.W.O. boots stay on but the snaking hands rip her fishnets to shreds. Every part of her teenage body is being groped and violated. Her thrilled screams are even louder than the deafening band as the beasts of the pit bounce her around like a beach ball.

'It might have been a great party.'

Justin and I take in all the good, wholesome entertainment, wearing evil smirks, savouring our being two of two-thousand, united as one. The wild animals amongst us battle past the thin layer of spirited but out-manned security and take to the stage. They perch onto its edge between the amplifiers while the rest of the pit licks their chops and waits. As the band strikes the first note of *'Tragedy'* the stage-diving commences. One by one, the wild and brave leap into the abyss in hopes of hitting the warm, sweaty palms of hands, not the unforgiving beer-soaked floor. And I'm flying high, hearing my current favourite song *live…*

'The bloody mess,

Was all my stress,

A tragedy…in mosaic…form!

I lost my head,

And now she's dead,

Drenched in the horror storm!

10

As The Vampire Bats scorch it out, one by one the flying bodies are caught. The crowd surfing is rampant and Justin has disappeared again.

'Fly! Fly my little bats!' The front man screams during the bridge. 'Fly into the night!'

My body aches from the surrounding chaos. But as I lay my eyes on a beautiful creature the pain is soothed. With hair like fire, eyes like emeralds, a black split-second poisons my mind that this is all just a wonderful dream and nothing more. But as she rams into me it feels so right! So real! Her heart squished into mine when our bodies hit, like two hormone sponges. Our stars didn't just cross, they *collided.* Her wild smile straightens under her piercing green eyes and inferno of red hair. We gaze at one another as I grab her hand and pull, but she's being pulled the other way by the brute force of the pit. She calls out to me as I struggle to hold on, but her hand slips through my sweaty grip like Vaseline. I can't see her anymore. She's disappeared into the crowd.

Who was *she?*

I turn back to the stage, to the band, to the flashing lights, to find that an airborne, out-of-control silhouette flies straight for me! I'm no better than a deer in the headlights.

'Eeee-thaaan!'

Justin lands on my head and the two of us topple to the floor.

7am deja vu

A maniac rips through my bedroom door

And carries a twelve-gauge across my floor.

My eyelids break free from a restless night's sleep.

Between crusty lashes I stare at the creep.

A tall silhouette stands at my horror's crest.

My heart crashes 'gainst the inside of my chest.

In absolute terror, adrenaline rushes through.

I gasp for mercy from the demon in my view.

It's my suicide-face on the man I see,

Cocking the shotgun and pointing it at me.

He puts the barrel to my suicide-head

And with my own eyes he aims and shoots me dead.

Panting and drenched with cold sweat, I've just woken up from a dreadful nightmare. I'm still alive, and you can't *die* in your dreams, right? Still, my nightmare was so very real. Just like the one I'd had the night before.

How did those tickets end up on my windowsill? My

aching head's in my hands. My temples throb. My eyes are on fire.

Am I going mad? I run my fingers through my sleep-tangled locks and gently rub my temples with my fingertips.

I must be.

My alarm unleashes a scream that would wake the dead, telling me that it's time for school. The reality that I've woken to is much worse than a scary woman on a horse or being murdered by, well, *myself.*

Please, God. Let school be a bad dream, too. Sigh. 'I wish I *would've* shot myself,' I mutter in a cracked nasal tone. Being dead would at least end my misery from this 7am déjà vu. Sometimes my subconscious mind dismisses that alarm as just a crow or a car alarm and I sleep *right through it.* But would I sleep through something a noisy as, say, an F-15 breaking the sound barrier? A fatal car accident right here on Bataan Drive? A tornado? I live in the Midwest after all and perhaps I should contemplate that last one. Nevertheless, my alarm clock is my first taste of the Real World in this life. Without it I wouldn't wake up, I wouldn't go to school, I wouldn't graduate, I wouldn't become…

'I'm your father and I'm warnin ya. If ya don't graduate, ya won't live here.'

I just want to sleep forever.

Back in elementary school my mother woke me nice and easy-like. She'd have cinnamon oatmeal steaming in the kitchen just waiting for me to dig into.

'Breakfast is the most important meal of the day, Ethan.'

16

She'd let me fall back to sleep a little while longer if I wanted but she'd be damned if she'd ever heat it back up.

'Sleepin in means cold breakfast.'

She'd actually *sing* those words. The acoustics in the bathroom were pretty good and all but she could actually sing! Yeah, I loved to fall back to sleep, perhaps slipping back into that beautiful dream on the stream of my mother's lullabies. And, yeah, I'd eaten my oatmeal cold on a few dark winter mornings. Lesson learned.

Mom eventually became a workaholic. She's out the door before the sun rises anymore. No nice wake-up call. No hot oatmeal. The good old days are gone, just like she's been now for over an hour.

The oatmeal steamed

And mother's shadow moved in the bathroom light

That spilled into

The cold hallway just outside my bedroom door.

I was seven

And Bugs Bunny ate a carrot on TV

By the window

From where the crow cawed in the dark winter morn'.

Another day

In Hell waits as my alarm clock screams again...

I'm seventeen.

17

I can't remember how many times I've pressed SNOOZE now. I'm still a sucker for the extra sleep in the morning, when the pillow becomes a euphoric drug that my head sinks back into. But as the pillow becomes softer the alarm just continues to blast off every nine minutes.

'Turn off that god-damned alarm!' my father shouts. 'Every fuckin morning!' *My fucking father...*

Alas, another day at Ritenour High waits. The seven hours I spend there is a whole other brand of misery. I can't tell if they're trying to run a school or a prison. Teachers monitor the hallway traffic like cops. From the fenced in practice field, during gym class, I swear I can see men with rifles and binoculars staked out on the school's roof. Surveillance cameras are planted everywhere and wired up to the Principal's Office. From there Old Man Powers can hawk the campus perimeter, the same as the rifle-wielding watchtower guards. The rumour around school is that he's got an 'eye-in-the-sky' set up, like in those casino movies, except they peer down upon us from inside the smoke alarms.

My Uncle Pete, whom I've met just once, is a pit-boss in Las Vegas. He warned me not to even *think* about getting away with cheating unless I wore a ten-gallon hat or a sombrero. Sporting Western head gear at Ritenour High isn't a good idea, let's face it. Why would I want to take any chances at a school that exposes me to the clichés of teenage society: general confusion, hopeless insecurity, outrageous behaviour in an attempt to *hide* that insecurity, emotional outbursts, fear of leadership, strange self-expression, lack of experience, fear of the future, age discrimination, rabid hormones, hatred of authority, parents embarrassing residue, wild mood swings, relentless appetite, uncontrollable laziness, last gasp of pubescence, cliques running in packs, unapologetic fashion conformity, sad unpopularity, exhausted street slang, false

18

invincibility, teen angst and one's constant need for just a little more sleep…it all sucks.

But I suck even worse. Oh, and yeah, and I have a Physics test this week. A one-legged man in an ass-kicking contest has a better chance. I'm officially doomed…

I've heard those fairy tales about high school sweethearts and game-winning touchdowns. Maybe I should just admit to myself how much better my life would be with a spoonful of High School Glory. It's my senior year, for crying out loud! But I'm chomping at the bit to just *move on* to the next thing. To Nowhere-to-go-but-up City. This school thing has been reduced to a monotonous process in which I just keep my head down when moving through Ritenour's rambunctious locker-lined hallways. I ignore the artificial spirit that will liven up college-bound transcripts. I steer clear of the haters who talk way too seriously about topping the numbers of the Columbine Massacre. What can I say? I can't wait to graduate from this school, and from this depressing part of my life. But I don't know if I'm going to survive long enough to ever wear that cap and gown.

Motivation: Zero.

Not only does school suck but this hangover is getting worse. *Getting drunk at concerts on weeknights is my only joy.*

Ah, but I remember that girl last night. My sore eyes light up. Oh, that green-eyed girl. The one that got away, literally slipping through my fingers. I close my eyes and see her on the backs of my eyelids. She blazes in red, green and white; bright lights of hope against the darkness of the concert pit.

I couldn't even call to her. I didn't know her name.

What if I'd stayed with her? Where did she sleep last night? Where is she now?

Forget it Ethan, she's not real. It's all in your mind.

I glance at the clock. 'Fuck, I'm late!' Ms. Lancashire will

19

tear into me like a lioness with hungry cubs to feed if I'm tardy again. That old hag! As I begin to rush around I notice an issue of *Hustler* lying on my bedroom floor. *Gotta get rid of that.*

As I lunge for it I trip over my black German Shepherd. 'Charlie, God-damn it! Do ya have to sleep right in the middle of the floor?' Charlie just looks up, past his furry face, through barely-opened eyes. 'Oh no, Charlie, don't move. You just stay asleep. I don't want to interrupt your dreams.' As I roll my eyes I accidentally look into the mirror. *'Shit,'* I blurt out. Just a reaction, like a sneeze or a cough, to how *horrible* I look this morning! Whipping myself into something half-way presentable will be a chore...and a minor miracle.

But first things first, that Hustler. Standing on the desk chair, I pull the Doc Martens boot box from the shelf inside the top of my closet, the last sacred place I know of. *My parents will never look up here.* I can't imagine the nightmare of my parents finding my porn. I scoff. There are guys in my class who roll joints in their living rooms with their fathers while glaring at this type of filth. Hash and skin mags in plain view. Shocking, but it's all around us here in North St. Louis County, where my parents made every attempt to raise me in their own excruciating form of a conservative home. Taboo isn't some little country back road in my family, it's an eight-lane superhighway. And the only way my parents drive the road of sex and drugs is 15 mph under the speed limit in the slow lane with their blinker on. If it's embarrassing in front of my parents then it's wrong, and embarrassment is a common emotion for me. I've probably got a lot to hide. And while I drag this compromising humility through North County it's a wash, as the lack of eligible young girls here make it necessary to keep the porn mags around. At least until I finally get the internet in my bedroom, that is.

'Ya wouldn't need this shit if ya had a girlfriend,' I mutter as I put the boot box back on the shelf, 'if I ever *begin* to understand em.'

20

I forgot to ask Justin for a lift but it doesn't matter. Justin was a lot drunker than me when we fell into the back of that taxi. Hell, he was passed out by the time we got on the highway! I damn-near had to carry him to his door! If he makes it to school on time this morning it should make the six o'clock news! And if I…

'The wheels on the bus go round and round. Round and round. Round and round. Yeah, Ethan! Hehe! Haha! Atta boy, sing with Mommy now!'

I blast through the front door and run like hell through the rain for the bus…but it rolls right past. No brake lights, just sludge splashing back from the tires as it accelerates down the street. And life's hammer hits me over the head again. Without a car a two mile walk through the cold downpour stands between me and school. The falling rain swerves my hangover back into ferocity.

That bus is *gone.*

Motivation: *sub-*zero.

Suddenly, retreating to the safe, dry, quiet confines of my bedroom to stare at naked women all day long sounds like a great idea. But instead of allowing a bad morning a chance to start a domino effect into getting kicked out of the house, I decide to brave the weather and get to class. Graduation is near, but so far away. Not until June.

And fall has just begun.

the garage

The ugly dead weather soaks the fallen leaves. *Rain, rain, go away. Please...never come back.*

There's an umbrella in the garage but my father doesn't allow me a key. Still, I know how to get in, lifting the doormat and picking up the hairpin, jimmying it around for a minute...Presto!

I can find anything out here if given enough time. But given less than ten minutes not even Charlie's canine nose can sniff out a specified target. Good ole Charlie. He may be a trip hazard in the morning but he's smart. And right on cue there he is in my bedroom window, watching me with that, 'I'm sorry' look on his face. Charlie knows...

My father's cavernous garage is a cluster fuck of mechanical flotsam and jetsam that would provide a yard sale junkie paradise. Dad, however, knows the exact location of *everything* amidst the grease, unsorted tools, beer cans and Americana souvenirs that can be found in any gift shop along Route 66.

'Good ole Pop. What an *asshole.*'

I scan through the chilly darkness and glance at the twelve-gauge. A Winchester 1200. Yeah, it can be taken apart for easy storage but I suppose it's found a home and a dramatic

25

presence mounted on the garage wall. I was seven when Dad bought it...

'Son, this gun ain't a toy. Never touch it. If I ever find out ya did I'll beat your ass.'

My father still uses that tone with me, just as he did ten years ago. But I feared him back then. He was bigger and sounded a lot meaner. Today it's not my fear of *him*, it's my fear of what might happen if him and I ever tangle. Serengeti death-battles on National Geographic Explorer would be nothing compared to the level of violence we could reach. Well, that gun he bought was never much to me but the 1971 Corvette Stingray certainly was and still is. Over the years my friends have come by just to *drool* over it, and hell, I didn't mind using it as a selling point. I'd even bullshit that I actually got to drive it around.

'Don't touch that gun and never touch that car. Well, someday this big mess will be a Corvette. It's gonna be beautiful! Just as long as ya don't come snoopin out here and messin with it. As a matter of fact just stay outta here all together, ya hear?'

Ain't nothin changed. Daddy just got a little greyer whilst I got a little taller...just like my interest in Daddy's twelve-gauge. I'd use it to murder him if I didn't want to kill *myself* so much. The problem is that I'd never killed anything more that a cockroach in my life.

'All I'd have to do is load it, stick the barrel in my mouth and...'

I raise my knee and cover a scuttling cockroach with the shadow of my tightly-laced, eight-eyed Doc Marten boot...and

26

smash its guts all over the concrete floor amidst the grease spots and sawdust. I gaze down as my heart sinks.

What is *life?*

One day…

The 'air-cushioned' sole of my boot wasn't cushioned enough as its crashes loudly against the floor. I freeze, cringing, holding my breath, praying I haven't woken my father.

Just my heartbeat…and the pitter-patter of the rain. Exhale.

With the lights out I move through the garage using a new level of caution, searching for that umbrella along the far wall, manoeuvring through the narrow paths between the clutter. Clumsily I kick a few bolts and screws, and freeze again…*shit!*

I wait for the ringing sound to cease…

Heartbeat.

Pitter-patter.

I gaze at the other window, *my father's window.* Perhaps this weather has him back to sleep. Or maybe he *knows*, just watching me through the crack in the drapes, just waiting for the right moment to attack. Nah, this rain is perfect for sleeping in and it's *really* coming down now. I've got to find that umbrella and get the hell out of here.

I move further back and notice the chrome sparkle. I can only salute. It's truly a beautiful beast. A muscle car through and through. A ghost of the American Highway. The perfect representation of speed and power sits in the depths of this garage, this *den,* like a black panther that I've just rudely woken. It glints its chrome fangs and snarls at me through the darkness.

But my salute scowls and I snarl right back. My swirling

emotions seize me as, from childhood's hour, this very machine has helped destroy my relationship with my father. I loath this car a lot more than I admire it, just as I have more hatred for my father than pride. But his voice still echoes through the garage like a ghost, from when I was just a little boy…

'Don't go near it. Don't touch it.'

Just like a ghost…

This 1971 Corvette Stingray represents a lot of pain.

But he built it with his own hands. The hands he gave to you, *Ethan…*

I open the refrigerator to find two cases of Bud, cold and ready to drink, with some t-bone steaks in the freezer above. I open the vegetable compartment and, yes, the shotgun's shells are still there. *Safekeeping.*

Some grey light sheds onto the bulletin board. Friends, family, cars and weekend barbecue moments through the years are on display here, with the help of a few thumbtacks. Some photos have faded more than others. I immediately notice the one of Charlie and me taken during a hot summer evening on the back porch. I was ten, wearing my Little League baseball jersey just after a game. Charlie was just a big puppy then, only a year old.

A very faded photo shows my father when *he* was a teenager. In it he's leaning against Grandma's '66 Chrysler, parked in the drive of the house that she sold the year I was born.

Dad had his whole life ahead of him back then…

'It's unreal, Ethan, just how much ya look like your father

in that photo!'

Further down the wall is another faded photo of a man sitting in a chair next to a white GTO. He wore a baseball cap and shades above a smug smirk. The same man is in one of the newer photos as well, sitting and sunglasses again, but underneath a black ten-gallon hat instead. Maybe he wore it to a Vegas casino? At his side was a horse with a sleek black shiny coat.

When I was little I asked who that man was…

'That's Tobias, son. He's a really good friend of your dad's. They were in the war together.'

'Have I met him before?'

'No, he lives in Mississippi. He's sittin because he's paralysed, which is why he's never come to visit.'

'How did he get paralysed?'

'When he was in the war he got hurt and the doctors told him he wouldn't walk again.'

Fuck! I've just kicked a metal toolbox over. The crashing disturbance echoes through the garage, much too loud that time.

'Hey, get the *fuck* outta there!' Dad yells from the backdoor. Wrapped in a bathrobe, his hair is greasy and messed.

'Where's the umbrella?' I ask, trying to save face. I want to disappear. I dread this confrontation.

'Your mother must have it. What've I told ya bout snoopin round out there?' My father watches me with the eyes of a junkyard dog until I exit his garage and shut his door. 'Ya pick that lock again, Son, and we're gonna have problems that you

29

could never imagine! Stay the fuck outta my garage! *Hear me?!*' The *neighbours* heard it, that's for sure. 'And stop hittin that snooze bar, ya hear? It's annoyin as *hell!* Easy, Ethan. Just breath. Control it...*

I throw my backpack over my shoulder and scamper off to school, tail still between my legs through the hard rain. Umbrella or not, I wouldn't stay home from school while he was in that mood if I was paid to! I turn up the collar of my jacket to help brave the downpour as my skin crawls from the soaking chill. Running, my Docs squeak and explode into puddles of rain while the legs of my jeans act as mud flaps. I wipe my long, dripping locks out of my eyes and shiver like a wet dog.

St. Charles Rock Road, the halfway point, is just ahead now.

Motivation: (*back to*) Zero.

But just as I believe the worst is over...

<SPLASH>

My jacket is brown with dripping earth. I've been fucked by the speeding tires of a tricked-out Cutlass driven by two assholes from my first-period PA class. I've got to tip my cap, though. They saw an opportunity and they delivered in the clutch. That front tire hit the mud puddle right as I crept alongside of it. Now I'm a muddy shit! 'Fuck school!' I cry out.

A book lies in the wet grass just ahead. Its beautiful crimson binding is getting ruined by the falling rain. I speed up to it and read the title in bold gothic print...

GHOSTS: MESSAGES FROM THE DEAD

30

I chuck it into my bag and brave forward.

the new girl

I'm late to first period. Photographic Arts.

I creep into my desk just inside the classroom door, *completely unnoticed*. Being unpopular does have its advantages, and it helps that old Lancashire doesn't see or hear so good anymore. But I've never felt so invisible. Like a ghost.

I look around at the automatic faces attached to numb bodies in the grid of desks. And time around here melts slowly, like an icicle dangling in the rays of a winter sun. If only there was a sun that shined through those fogged-up windowpanes, grey and wet with rain. Summer is over, that's for sure, and the dismal view intrudes our minds.

I shiver in the hallway draft as my clothes are still damp, but what a way to show off my concert T! *One For Sorrow* is scripted on the back and the front features a crow with *The Vampire Bats* printed over it. The rain didn't wash out its odour of last night's smoke and stale beer.

A white Camaro creeps alongside the school blaring that band's latest single through the murky moments. Ears perk up for a second, but the car drives away, taking the moody Goth-blues with it. But that Camaro can't take away last night's memories. I close my eyes and there I am inside that theatre. Amidst the

35

lights. The band. The crowd. Justin. That girl.

That girl…

I open my eyes and examine my camera as my still-wet hair annoyingly hangs down in my face. My ears are still ringing from the rock 'n roll so Ms. Lancashire's lesson is muffled, making me even sleepier. I need coffee or something sweet and energising to keep me going. I draw a sachet of pure cane sugar from the pocket of my jeans, the only part of my clothing that stayed dry. I rip off the corner and scoop some to my tongue with a salivated finger.

I gaze down upon the floor tile where a few granules fell. Suddenly, Photographic Arts class begins to fade out as the tile changes. A little bedroom appears down there, like of a dollhouse but on its own. It has only three walls and no roof, and it's begun to grow furniture and decor. A black spread and pillows appear on the bed, the red area rug grows from the hardwood floor and matching drapes now hang above both windows. A flat screen television hangs on the wall, Baseball bats dangle from a rack, an electric guitar leans against a shabby amp, several records and compact discs clutter the top of a pair of speakers, and dirty laundry is scattered all over the floor.

This is *my* room. It's got to be, devoid the fourth wall. It remains a three-walled bedroom surrounded by a little forest with a river rushing through it.

Strange voices echo between my ears…

FACE IN THE CROWD

      GONNA FALL IN LOVE

            FALL IN LOVE

IN THE CROWD

     FALL IN LOVE

36

That black horse races through the forest toward the bedroom...

<click-clack, click-clack, click-clack>

The sound of its galloping hooves changes into footsteps. The scent of roses is suddenly very strong.

With a hint *of cinnamon.*

She came to me in the middle of the night, and now she walks through the classroom door. I ignore the tiny bedroom on the floor and get a proper eyeful of this woman, looking more beautiful in this light of day, and even more horrifying...

She's tall and slinky, like a catwalk model. Her white gown drags the floor as she creepily struts toward me, very herky-jerky, like she's stepped right out of an old silent film. The stare she's fixed on me is deep, her huge green eyes piercing. How can they be so serene yet so ghastly? Her hair extends to the middle of her back, sparkling black. Her face is white and pristine. I just want to glide my fingers against it to be sure it's not actually porcelain! But I wouldn't dare get so close! Instead I sink into my desk in fear, as now she stands right before me, inebriating me with her cinnamon breath. But the rest of class is oblivious to her presence.

The woman sits down in the desk behind me. 'Hello, Ethan,' she says. Plainly. Calmly.

'Who are you?' I ask. But without reply she just continues to stare at me with that disturbing Mona Lisa smile.

'Your life is about to change. Amazing and horrible things are about to happen.' I wait for her to say more to enlighten me.

37

But she just stares at me in that subtle, yet dominating way. It's that little smile, the way her full, red, pouty lips curve up ever so slightly. And those eyes, the way they hold me spellbound. She knows things about me that I still don't.

Spellbound…

But I break free.

'Who *are* you?'

'Ethan Morgan!' Ms. Lancashire squawks. My head whips towards the whiteboard. Lancashire, with her back to me, writes in giant red letters…

$$SUICIDE$$

'You have one minute to explain you're outburst!' Lancashire shouts. The woman draped in white has vanished and suddenly I have everyone's full attention. 'Come on, Mr. Morgan. We're waiting.'

And upon my next glance at the whiteboard I see that it's clean.

<click-clack, click-clack, click-clack>

Emerald green Mary Janes trounce right through my three-walled room below, crunching the sugar granules beneath the

38

beautiful wearer's soles. A new girl walks past me to the front of the PA classroom. As I get my first glimpse of her I give my tired eyes a good rub.

It can't be! It's not my first glimpse of her at all!

The new girl speaks to Lancashire, moving her lips. I *know* those lips. And her hair, worn up this morning, burns red just as it did last night. A few tendrils fall into her eyes and she shoos them away with a smile.

Her *green eyes...*

They glance my way and lock onto mine.

Just like last night.

But this morning, in this depressing yet validating morning light, I'm taken aback by her perfectly chiselled face. Sharp jaw line, high cheek bones, edible neck, athletic shoulders, a tall frame supported by a long pair of legs rich with erotic muscle tone...*perfection*, walking in that pair of Mary Janes.

<click-clack, click-clack, click-clack>

In this downcast old classroom with brown water stains on the ceiling, menacing cracks in the masonry and a dirty floor that hasn't been mopped in weeks, there is vibrancy at last! I guess that the new girl is an athlete. Or her mother is a former pin-up girl and has passed on those genes. I just can't take my eyes off of her!

Just like last night.

Lancashire scans the grid of desks for a vacancy and shouts, 'Ethan Morgan! Move your books to your *own* desk. The desk behind you isn't for stacking all of your belongings! This is not where you *live*, remember.' *If I actually had to live here, Lancashire, I'd jump from the top of a tall building. Or put the barrel of that shotgun in my mouth.* Lancashire's voice flattens me like a hammer but I obey the ancient teacher. I'm delighted to do whatever necessary to accommodate this new girl in sitting right behind me. She follows Lancashire's direction toward the last desk in the row. Her pearly whites twinkle like diamonds and her warm smile is framed by quotation mark dimples. Her eyes squint charmingly as she struts down the aisle as if it *were* a catwalk. I take notice of the black knee-length pencil-skirt and green off-the-shoulder wool sweater that she wears. *Not a Goth at all. Thank God.*

She smiles (at me). Bumblebees buzz…

She winks (at me). Butterflies flutter…

She knows (it was me). The sun is shining…

Suddenly it feels like spring again. I'm warm with ready reproductive glands.

I return her smile, acknowledging that I remember her slipping away from me in the mosh pit.

The new girl pivots on that tile, where that tiny little bedroom has disappeared from, and sits behind me. All the boys have turned into wolves, setting their hungry eyes on the fresh fox, licking their chops.

'Is she always like that?' Felicity whispers. Her Southern accent melts into my ears. Her minty breath heats the back of my neck. I grip the edge of my desktop to keep from floating away. I close my eyes and imagine her lips moving as she whispers to me, 'She's so *ancient.*'

Gunshots of the Confederacy sound in the distance beyond The Promised Land. Magnolia trees eat the setting Dixie sun while blues twangs from shabby old guitars. Together we sip bourbon on the rocks while sitting on her daddy's porch.

But tea-stained visions crackle in my eyes of a culture

being born, created by bloody hands amidst flying time. Choctaw blood. Black hands picking cotton. Dead Confederate soldiers. Son House. Ghosts...

Warnings.

Felicity has disappeared from that porch. The vacant chair rocks back and forth as the late summer locusts buzz.

'My mama was in Lancashire's photography class when *she* went to this school. Lancashire's been around forever.'

The bell rings and I give a heaving sigh. Where did the time fly to? *I suppose I should ask those ghosts on her daddy's porch.* As I stand up to face the new girl my knees buckle and shyness mutes me. I barely muster the courage to glance into her eyes, but when I do I'm rewarded a feast of her brilliant shimmer of green!

'Ethan, right?' she asks.

'Yeah. Like Ms. Lancashire said,' I laugh.

'Ha, yeah! I think she *likes ya*.'

Laughing I ask, 'You are?'

'Felicity. Felicity Farmer.'

'Nice to meet ya.'

'Well, we sorta met last night. That's where ya got that shirt, right?'

'Yeah, last night,' I reply.

'I *thought* that was you,' she says.

'I *knew* it was you. I remember you. You must have slept a lot better than me.'

Felicity laughs and asks, 'What do ya mean?'

41

'You just...I mean...'

'Yeah?'

Jesus, I'm melting. And she knows *it. Shit!* 'You just look a lot better than I do this morning.' I recover and say.

'Yeah, I can see ya gotta a few scrapes and bruises,' she says as she gently glides her index finger against my forearm.

'Ya just...slipped away from me.' I nearly faint when I feel her touch.

'I know. I looked for ya but the pit was just too crazy!'

'They are...awesome. The Vampire Bats.'

'Awesome? No one says that back in Memphis. *Awesome!*'

Her smile liquefies me. Or did I just piss my pants? No, I'm still good, pshew! Somehow I'm able to *hold myself* together and stand just a couple inches taller than her, even though she's in those Mary Janes. 'Awesome.'

<Inevitable awkward moment>

'So, y'on Facebook?' Felicity asks.

'Um, no. I'm not.' I gotta get the internet in my room.

'Oh.'

'I'll see ya 'round, then.'

'Bye, Ethan.'

I turn away and weave towards my locker like a drunkard in search of a place to pass out, all the way down the main hall and around the corner to the North Wing. *That's a way to quit while you're ahead, Ethan old boy. That was pretty fucking intense.*

The various clubs and committees keep the hallways very

informative and colourful with the signs they've displayed, like the ones promoting the caravan to the varsity football game, the candy-striped blood drive signs featuring a bloody needle and the Student Council campaign signs plastered high and low. But the big black and orange signs that dominate are for the Homecoming Dance. It's only three weeks away and everybody's talking about it.

But the rainbow of talented artistry that brightens the otherwise drab corridors this morning just floats away into an ignored, cobwebbed corner of my mind. Felicity Farmer now dominates my imagination. Her silky southern drawl renders me spellbound and everything else might as well be in Japanese. *Just like that woman draped in white, but not horrifying at all. Just beautiful.*

<click-clack, click-clack, click-clack>

As I lunge for my locker, G-367, Felicity takes G-365!

'Small world it's turnin out to be,' Felicity says with that sexy smile.

'We're almost next-door neighbours,' I reply.

'Almost!' she laughs. 'Prolly would be a lot of fun if we were.'

Damn. I can't take my eyes off her as we share a good laugh. Felicity opens her locker and returns my long look.

the school bus

A car is the key to a social life in high school. In fact, the *keys* to a car are the keys to a social life in high school. Most of my classmates have access to a car without restriction, whether those cars are new, second hand or belong to their parents. I'm lucky and wise to be tight with Justin, who's in that majority because I certainly am not. I'll ride bitch or squeeze into the backseat when the alternative is sitting at home by myself. If I'm not in the car then I'm not with the gang. If I'm not with the gang then nothing exciting can happen.

Carloads of teens drive away from the safe cocoon of their bedrooms, beyond the reach of parents and teachers where The Real World is, and gradually become adults. Living life outside of authoritative boundaries and 'our own good' feels very natural, refreshing and compulsory. When I ride around with Justin in his electric blue '77 Firebird I watch the city scene pass. As it gets smaller and smaller in the rear view mirror I feel more and more like we're leaving it all behind.

And that just makes me want to go further...

'Where we goin, Ethan?'

'Just drive.'

'To where?'

47

'Until we run out of gas.'

'Then what?'

'Then we'll fill her up and keep drivin.'

'Ethan, yer crazy, dude.'

Yeah, I probably am crazy, or at least headed there. But I'm not stupid. Freedom is freedom. I would kill for a set of wheels.

Everybody knows my dad owns a Corvette, a car that would make me the hottest shit at Ritenour. But my father never lets me *sit* in it, let alone drive it. The mere thought of using it to stalk the roads of my peers makes me salivate. Instead, I only cringe. I'm trapped in what is just a sad and ironic story. Alas, I obey my father and never touch it.

'Ya wanna drive so bad, son? There! Take those keys the Corolla and get us some bread and milk. Directly to Schnucks and back. No where else! Bread, milk and eggs! Ya got twenty minutes.'

To Schnucks and back and no where else. I actually *work as a cashier* at that grocery store and not even when I'm scheduled am I allowed to drive the Corolla. It's strictly for Mom and errands.

My parents have an agreement. If I want my own wheels I'll have to save the dough myself, a tough task on just $9.25 per hour and twenty hours per week. Alas, my employment at Schnucks is just like being stuck in the mud, spinning my wheels in vain. Now that school has started my boss won't give me enough hours to save money for a car. Even if they did I'd probably flunk right out of school anyway. But my parents don't have much money either and are barely scraping middle class income. Even if we were rich they wouldn't buy me a car. They believe in my earning everything to build character, but I still wonder just what sort of character they have in mind. So, I can forget about a 'financial nudge'.

With no keys and no car, I've got to take the bus home. But the day I've had at school was one for the ages. With Felicity Farmer still fresh in my mind I climb the steps and am greeted by the stocky, forty-something lady that drives my route. She's very butch with a raspy voice from smoking, but pleasant enough. I imagine her out at Dive Bar, USA's Tuesday Night Happy Hour. North County. St. Charles. Cahokia, perhaps. But she's the type of woman that goes back on Wednesday, Thursday, Friday, Saturday and Sunday...and Monday, too.

'Another day another dollar, man,' she says as I climb the stairs. 'Well, not you, me!' she adds, laughing hysterically. I smirk in acknowledgement and look for a remote seat away from anymore annoyances. I choose the seat near the bespectacled kid with his face buried in a *Dungeons & Dragons* novel. It seems safe enough. He's just one of the cast of characters that board my bus.

Next to board: The invasion of little freshman jerks providing a lot of in pubescent noise and hysterics. The usual whining and squeaking. All of them are hotshots from the middle school and remind me of a pack of rabid Chihuahuas in the way they nip at your ankles and grit their tiny little fangs. Mighty as a group but individually, well, you know the saying about wet paper bags.

And now boarding, the slutty looking blonde sophomore who evidently has parents who don't care. Or, perhaps, she leaves *after* they do in the morning. Hell, there I go again, forgetting that she likely lives with just one parent and that I'm in the minority for having two. Anyway, there's no way a young teen girl gets out of an unbroken home dressed like that. She

49

shakes those young hips down the aisle in that tight short skirt with her only cares in the world stored on her iPod.

And straggling on board just before the bus pulls away: Donnie Applebaum and Tony Hollins. These two never ride the bus without looking for trouble. 'All these lil fuckin freshman!' Donnie shouts, thundering down the aisle as he imposingly hulks his shoulders to and fro.

Tony snatches the studious boy's D&D novel and asks, 'So, could a level five cleric score me a dime bag?'

'What?'

'Well, could he?' After receiving a scornful look, Tony throws the book and knocks the glasses right off the boy's head.

Donnie and Tony always sit in the very back unless trouble is somewhere else. When they don't find trouble they instead discuss drinking, smoking, violence and fucking in the most vulgar ways possible.

'I've been drivin ya now for four years.' the driver calls out to me. 'Ya must be graduatin this year.' I'm not back far enough as she can still make eye contact through her gigantic mirror, so big though that there's really no escape.

'Yeah, this'll be my last year.'

'Maybe Ya get that car for graduation, huh?'

'Yeah.' I cringe. *Ugh, that bites. You don't know the* half *of it, lady.*

There's one more student who rides this bus every now and then and this afternoon he's nearly missed it. Running alongside he smacks the closed door with his open palm. I don't know his name but I've seen him around school. He's a junior. Very effeminate with a sweet baby face. Meticulously-styled chocolate brown hair. He has a sassy hitch in his getty-up and countless other idiosyncrasies that lead someone even just half as observant to guess that he was gay. I've never spoken to him to

50

know for sure because the last thing I need while going to this school is to be caught speaking to a gay kid.

The driver reluctantly stops in the middle of the road and re-opens the door. 'Thank you,' the girlish boy huffs as he climbs the stairs. Donnie and Tony lick their chops for the opportunity to really raise some hell before going back to their broken homes to get drunk and stoned. You see, those bullies have already made this kid their whipping boy, just one month into the school year. If I were the girlish boy I'd take a detour from this sure-thing abuse and walk home everyday. But as he once again has boarded I dread what's coming.

Like me, the girlish boy looks for a seat away from the crowd. He glides down the aisle and coyly chooses the one across from me. He bends and slides across the brown vinyl seat, large enough for two students. He crams himself against the window and just stares out.

'Hey, look who's here!' shouts Donnie from the back of the bus. I quietly groan. I'm going to have a front row seat for this shit today.

'The queer's here!' shouts Tony.

My heart sinks when I hear the bullies trampling toward him. Donnie is a big wild-eyed boy, about 6'3' with equally wild shoulder length hair. He would be a linebacker but his poor grades keep him off the team. Tony, a junior, is a scrawny short stack who seems to only wear plain white T's. He has a mean mature face with crazy eyes smeared on a small, shaved head. Despite his size he's intimidating and probably tough to whip in a fight. Somehow he's already got a couple of tattoos on his arms and a muzzle of dark whiskers. The bullies leap into the seat right behind him. Donnie shouts, 'I saw ya at lunch starin at me, queer! With all yer fag hags cacklin away. Ya think I'm cute?'

I count the burger joints and car washes and taverns of St. Charles Rock Road hoping it will take my mind from the shenanigans. But the abuse on deck in the corner of my eye is

51

like a train about to crash into the ravine.

The girlish boy remains as still as a statue, gazing out the window in silence, probably counting burger joints and car washes and taverns. He never shows an ounce of attention for his hecklers. He's either tough or just used to it.

Tony slumps down and wraps around the side of the seat like a snake, slithering his tongue, hissing more abuse. 'Why do those girls love queers so much, queer? Why?' I can't help but turn my head and look. Tony's crazy eyes meet mine as he shines a wide, evil grin that flashes his gold tooth. 'What's up, Morgan.'

I swipe the locks of hair out of my eyes and say, 'Hey, Tony. What's up Donnie?'

'Shit.'

'Yeah,' I reply.

'Whatchya doin tonight, Morgan?' Donnie asks.

'Don't know yet. Prolly watchin baseball. Not much planned. What about you?'

Tony says, 'Gettin some beer. Gettin drunk.'

'Prolly smoke some too,' Donnie says, 'come on over, dude!'

And as the insect-thought of my wasting away with those delinquents lands and quivers its wings, I flick it away like the disease carrying mosquito that it is. Still, it's going to be a long school year, so to stay cool and save face I ask, 'Yer over there on Guthrie, right?'

'Yeah, right across from that church. Just come by. Prolly have some girls over.' *Nigga, please!* If I thought that girls would actually show I might have actually considered stopping by, despite all the guaranteed mischief and illegalities. 'Not that *this* queer would be interested in that!' Donnie shouts.

'Yeah, these girls aren't hags, queer!' Tony growls.

52

I'm saddened and ashamed, but I don't want to speak up. I'll have to ride the bus with these homophobic tormentors the rest of the year and I don't want to start a war when I know they're already cool with me. I mean, I've got enough problems, but their foul antics against this boy take a big toll on my conscience.

'Ya see that new girl today?' Donnie asks Tony. My ears perk up.

'That red-head, oh yeah!'

'Naw, she was strawberry-blonde, dude.' Donnie says.

'She's from the South. Pretty as hell!'

I listen closely to their description of the girl dominating my imagination.

'What's her name?'

'Fuck if I know.'

'That foxy strawberry-blonde, c'mon! What's her name?!'

'Naw, she's a red-head, asshole!'

Donnie punches the back of the girlish boy's seat good and hard, flinging his effeminacy forward. 'C'mon queer!' Donnie yells, slamming his knuckles into the back of the seat again. 'I'm *talkin* to ya!'

The bus finally enters my Woodson Terrace neighbourhood and I can't wait to get out. Tony chimes, 'Ya think *I'm* cute, queer? Oh, yer lucky I'm stayin home drinkin tonight, Pinky. Otherwise I'd be out fag-bashin! Lookin fer you!' The bullies lose control, like sharks at the sight of blood. They unload on the back of the girlish boy's seat with their fists and shout all the homophobic abuse they can muster until they're finally interrupted.

'Hey, enough back there!' the bus driver shouts as she glares the boys down in the mirror. The girlish boy maintains a

53

stone-faced calm demeanour. He's very good at ignoring them. And why not? He's had a lot of practice already.

Donnie shakes his finger at the driver and says, 'See, Morgan, these gays stick together.'

'Stupid lesbo,' Tony snarls. I just shrug my shoulders as I get up, barely able to conceal my disgusted cringe. We've arrived at my stop and not a moment to soon. 'Hey, dude, Guthrie, third house from the corner. The blue one with the boat in the driveway. BYOB! We're gonna play some *Red Dead Redemption*!'

'Yeah, and swipe yer daddy's wheels when ya do. We'll go joy ridin!'

I give an acknowledging wave to the cast and exit the bus stage right. Oh, the comedies and the tragedies.

I step onto the rain-soaked street, cluttered with fallen leaves and warming in the new sunshine. The girlish boy glares out the window, dead-eyed and expressionless. As the bus rolls away his face disappears in the glare of the sun, and then reappears as a skull, staring down upon me.

filthy magazines

I must be going insane. Tiny bedrooms, strange voices, women on horseback, students with skulls for heads…insanity or lack of sleep? And this hangover is killing me!

Home is right around the corner. I need a snack and a nap. Perhaps I'll fetch the boot box and see who tickles my fancy.

I squat on the wet curb to tie up my boots and notice my father and a couple guys in the garage, right when a squad car pulls up.

'Hey son,' blurts the cop from behind the wheel of a silver Crown Victoria, 'nice day it turned out to be.'

'Yeah.'

'Rainin cats n dogs this morning. Funny how fast things can change in a day. Downright miraculous!'

Everything about a cop and their squad car makes me nervous: The shiny badge, the gun, the nightstick, the handcuffs, the moustache, the haircut, the shoeshine, the siren lights, the steel screen between the seats, the technology wired up on the dash, and especially the dispatch noise coming from the radio. I just don't trust them.

This cop's stare has frozen me. I silently plead for mercy knowing he can see my eyes but I can't see his, just my helpless reflection in the lenses of his sunglasses.

But they're the police, right? Just conducting standard procedure? No apologies necessary for their reckless behaviour? Waste our time much playing the 'criminals-amongst-us numbers game'? Harass much? Intimidate much? Brutalise much? Does anyone really question the excessive amount of authority these regular people donning a badge have? Or is it that when they earned that badge they were no longer regular people?

They are cops, here among us because criminals will *always* be among us. The two forces are synonymous in their endless game of Cat and Mouse, taking from society whatever in Hell they want, whenever in Hell they want it. 'Just doin my job, m'am'.

I've got nothing to say to this cop, and I bet *he ain't got much to say* either. But you're damned right that I'll have to stop and listen to him talk when all I want to do is go home.

'Ya playin ball for the school this year?' The officer spits out below his quivering moustache. His name tag reads *STEPHENS*. Whenever I see him around town some Dick or Jane will be chatting with him, pretending to be enthralled. As my conversation with Officer Stephens lengthens it becomes evident that the badge provides him that fantasy.

'If I make it,' I say, 'still a long way off. Camp's not until February. *C'mon, let's have the punch line, Stephens.*

'Oh, *baseball? What the?* See, here I thought ya played football.'

'Nah, just baseball.' *Get to the point.*

'Nope, I remember, ya *did* play football. I heard about ya. You were good. But…you were *scared.*' 'Ya can't be scared, boy, playin a man's sport like football.' *Yeah, I remember. They fucked me up. And where were* you, *you fucking pig? What did* you *do about it?*

Voices echo…

IN WHITE SHEETS

IN WHITE SHEETS

I gently rub my temple as the voices remind me, and then fade away.

'What's the matter, son? Ya sick or somethin?'

Yeah, sick of you. 'No, just got a lil headache is all.'

I overheard my parents talking once…

'They're just gettin a little too close for comfort, now. Payin these little friendly visits to the garage almost everyday. Well, they ain't very friendly anymore.'

'What's an honorary deputy, anyway?'

'A load of bullshit. They're hawkin my auto-repair business to see what they can get out of it. They ain't gonna take advantage of me. I won't join their mafia.'

Dad also said…

'Fear plus authority equals submission. No questions asked. No repercussions. I was payin my dues for this country before half these cops were even born.'

I remember my parents waving to the police. But one day

59

the cops stopped waving back.

I stand back up, casting my shadow over the star on the squad car door. But I feel like I can't walk away until he gives me permission.

'Well, ya ain't big enough to play football anyway,' Stephens says, staring through his windshield towards the garage. There my father talks animatedly with his hands while waving a wrench, just entertaining his visitors. *Sad bastards.* 'Tell yer dad that he's gotta keep those antifreeze and oil puddles off the driveway, ya hear?'

'Yeah, he's been told before. I don't really keep up with his operation out there.'

'Good boy. Ya don't want to be doin that all yer life. I *wondered* if ya had any sense. But still, most the time the apple don't fall too far from the tree.' Stephens turns back to me and says, 'Tell em if he doesn't keep that stuff off the driveway he'll have to find a new career.' Despite the hatred I have for my dad I don't like the cops pushing him or anyone else around. 'Also, if that Vette ain't street legal when we come to inspect he's gonna have a big problem. We saw him takin it for a spin the other day.' Stephens replies to some radio jargon and grips the steering wheel. 'Have a nice day.' He drives away, past our house, giving the garage a death-glare.

I watch the squad car taillights pull away, until they stop right in front of the pin oak tree I planted in the front yard ten years ago. I was seven years old and it was Arbor Day. Like all the other 2nd grade students leaving St. Williams Catholic I was carrying what my mother thought was just a twig stuck in a plastic flower pot. But it would be my little effort in doing an ancient deed to help Mother Nature in the new green-aware times. My parents watched me dig into our zoysia front lawn on that last Friday in April, 2000. And on this last September day in 2010 that little 'twig in a plastic flower pot' stands over thirty

60

feet tall, fast-approaching the height of the other elderly oak trees that line Bataan Drive.

So, why is Officer Stephens standing in our yard looking at it? I stop at the foot of our driveway to observe. Stephens gawks up and down at my tree. Now he circles it like a dog looking for a place to piss then barks something into his radio clipped onto his shoulder. Why in Hell are you looking at my tree?

'Hey,' Stephens calls out, gesturing with his hand for me to come. As I approach him across the front lawn he says, 'This here tree's in violation. It's planted too close to the curb. See those branches there? They're hangin too far over into the road.'

'Can't I just cut them back?' I ask.

'Nah, fraid not boy. It ain't as easy as that. It's gotta come down, hate ta say it.' Stephens slides into his cruiser and shuts the door.

'Hey Stephens!' I shout. But he's already pulling away again, whether he heard me or not. Fuck you!

As I watch Stephens speed off I notice that the sun sinks a little faster on this last day of September. The obnoxious roar of another plane blasting out of Lambert Airport interrupts the last orchestra of locusts. Summer is over. Autumn is here. The season is changing just as my adolescent pin oak tree warns by slowly shedding its red and gold. I'm seventeen now, not seven when I planted it. But according to Law Enforcement I will be relieved of the first real responsibility in my life. I imagine it with anger as I whisper in sadness' 'They're gonna cut ya down.' Now I have a valid reason to hate cops.

Moping back across our front lawn I realise that seasons change. So does life. Treading through the fallen leaves I have this strange feeling that everything is about to change.

I march up our long driveway spotted like a Dalmatian with those various fluid stains Stephens mentioned. Inside the garage the Vette is on display. My dad and his mates gulp beer from their Busch cans and inhale Marlborough cigarettes underneath their moustaches. Together they worship the beautiful black machine in my father's smug shadow. It sits on 255 tires with 15x8 rally wheels. The fibre glass body is doused with twelve coats of ebony which gives it a wonderfully sharp contrast with the chrome. The hood is hoisted to showcase the 350 engine and the doors are opened to boast the black leather interior that's just been shined with a coat of Armor All. I wonder if my dad's selling tickets.

'I tell ya what,' preaches my father, 'this guy doesn't believe in American excellence. He wants to be President of the world, not the United States. There are too many hard-workin people in this country for that bastard to communise us. To bring us down a notch. This will all be so crystal clear one day!' *Swig of beer.*

'It already is to a lot of folks, Robert. Have ya seen the latest polls?' *Drag of nicotine.* 'But don't worry, his healthcare plan is unconstitutional.'

'He's got no chance in the next election no how. Immigration, the oil spill, the mosque at Ground Zero, the unemployment rate…' *Swig of beer.*

'Well, he'll always have the black vote in his back pocket.' *Drag of nicotine.*

Right on cue a patriotic spirit in the form of a gust of wind blows into the garage, waving each of the following flags hanging on the wall: Old Glory, POW/MIA, the Confederate, and *Don't Tread On Me.*

I try to sneak past the garage like I snuck into class this morning. With my head down I hold my breath and walk briskly. 'Hey, son!' my father shouts, 'Some dude named Justin called a minute ago!' I exhale and reply with a nod before hustling for the door.

'That *him*?' one of the mates asks as I duck inside.

As I stand in my room that tile in PA class flashes before my eyes, as does the woman draped in white. I remember her horseback gallivant to my window two nights ago and her creepy visit this morning. With my head spinning I fall into my bed and wonder if it's just fatigue. Maybe stress? Insanity perhaps? Fuck it. Now for that nap. I bury myself under the sheets and close my eyes.

Felicity...Felicity Farmer...I'm in my room, on my bed. Come and join me...

<click-clack, click-clack, click-clack, click-clack>

There you are, baby.

'Hey, boy!'

Those footsteps weren't Felicity's. They were *my father's*. It's a rude awakening and I've still got my Felicity-stiffy. I turn to face the rage on his face, hiding my impure act under the sheets. He continues, 'I get yer at that age and all but if I find anymore of those God-damned filthy magazines anywhere around this house again I'll toss y'out with em so fast it'll make yer head spin!' *My head's already spinning, you fucking dick!*

'What?'

'Ya heard me, boy! *GOD-DAMNED FILTHY MAGAZINES!*'

'Those ain't mine!'

'Well, who's are they then? Charlie's?'

'Dad, what in Hell are ya snoopin around here for anyway?'

'*What?! What* did ya say to me?! Son, I swear to God yer gonna realise immediately that this is not yer house, it's *mine!* And this ain't yer room, it's *my* room that I *let* ya sleep in because yer *mother* wants ya here. No matter *how* bad ya fuck up!'

Dad storms back outside. Naked, I jump on the chair and feel around on the top shelf of my closet. Nothing but dust and a pair of dress shoes that I haven't worn since...my First Communion! 'Hah-chooh!' I sneeze. I wipe my dust-covered hand on my bare ass. The boot box is gone. He sure as Hell *did* take the mags away. 'Well Jesus Christ!' I mutter. Angry, frustrated, embarrassed and sad, I collapse onto my unmade bed. *I'm going to start using that lock on my door. Hell, I'll lock my door right now!*

My cell phone buzzes. It displays Ritenour's radio station number as a MISSED CALL. I dial where Justin has an air shift three afternoons per week.

'KRHS!'

'What's up Justin?'

'Shit. Gettin outta here at five.'

'Ya called. Whatchya need?'

'Yeah. I'll pick y'up tomorrow morning, cool?'

'See ya then, dude.' I hang up and flick the stereo on. I tune it in to 90.1 FM and adjust the aerial to get the clearest reception possible of the little ten-watt station. Noise and crackle finally clears into Justin's voice...

'This is The Husky Howl. I'm Justin Ronan. Call in your requests to 423-KRHS. This one's a request by James Harrison, listening in Overland. Here's The Vampire Bats. It's *A Verse For The Broken'*.

I crank up the volume to the max and am levelled by the explosion of fuzz.

Underneath a stack of CD cases is my work schedule. I have a shift starting at 6pm tonight. I totally forgot about it. I know I need the money but this sucks. For the low pay and the monotony I'm not in the mood to deal with the customers of a grocery store built in the heart of social decline, especially while I'm hungover.

The Vampire Bats song drifts into a PSA, but I need more, *now*. I flip the receiver to CD and crank their album, *One For Sorrow*, loud enough to break the walls or even wake the dead.

After school is my time, when I stop worrying about my mom working too hard or fantasising about killing my dad. Suicide's not as great of an idea after school, either. I sprawl out on my bed and let my spinning head sink back into the same pillow that cradled it as my alarm went off this morning.

I think about Felicity again, remembering how she looked at me this morning, just like at the concert. There was nothing in that boot box better than even the *mere thought* of her anyway. Those magazines enticed a primal, cheap urgency that I'm actually ashamed of. Felicity lures something warmer and more meaningful that I don't want to hide at the top of my closet. My attraction to her has a purpose that makes me feel good about myself. It's as if, somehow, she's provided me hope. I want to know her in *every* way, not just physically. It's not just lust and it is so much more than a just crush. I've just never felt this way about a girl before, despite only speaking a few words to her. Is it love, baby, or is it confusion, Jimi Hendrix?

Or is it insanity?

I gaze up at the spinning ceiling fan, wondering how a girl could whirr my heart in so little time. I imagine Felicity lying on top of me, weightless but warm, as I caress her body underneath the soft wool of her sweater and the polyester glide of her skirt. My hands greet her every curve. Her whispers soothe and excite me. I embrace everything about her at once; her locked gaze, her soft lips, her silky skin and her sweet taste. Her strawberries, apples and cream flow all over me. I don't need those God-damned filthy magazines in the top of my closet after all.

<click-clack, click-clack, click-clack>

'I thought *that was you...'*

'I knew *it was you...'*

I climax remembering my conversation with her this morning, and how she looked and how she moved.

Yeah, home is where the humiliation is. But it's also where the heart is...and where the long after-school naps can be found. The spinning ceiling fan lulls me away, swirling the perfect amount of cool air against my body, whipping into a delightful, mind-numbing buzz. *Anything can happen in this room.* My eyelids are so very heavy. *Anything can happen in this room.* Ah, they finally give way. I...am...falling...so...good...sigh...

'Felicity. Felicity Farmer...'

in the wartorn sky

We're an inevitable target streaking through enemy territory, like bucks on a November morning, fleeing from the gunshots of Missouri hunters. But this ain't Missouri, Dad. This is the other side of the world; a place you didn't know existed until you got that letter from Uncle Sam. And now here we are; the lone American craft in the war torn sky.

Welcome to Viet *Nam!*

I sit close to my father upon a Huey chopper attempting to escape the battle zone. We're headed toward the setting sun, still roasting the Hell on Earth below. The whipping-sound of the blades clutches us between the bomb blasts. Blood-soaked jungles remain vivid in our minds, while rice patties laced with landmines will disturb our slumber forever. Our desperate prayers just flutter down to smoulder in the dancing fires.

Christmas Day at Grandma's. Road-trippin' afternoons. Drinking beer around the radio, just listening to the ballgame. Blue sky memories, oh so precious and wonderful suddenly, just float away like helium balloons escaping from a child's hand. Our blue skies have all been smeared into this grey gloom of war.

My dad nudges my shoulder. With a strapped-on helmet and vacant eyes he says, 'It plays back in my mind like an old movie, whenever it wants. The flashbacks control me, like they'll

69

control you someday. Life will haunt you, son. Time never stops.' He's just a teenager, like me, but the innocence has been burned from his face. He's my father. I'm his son. He looks just like me. He *is* me. I am *him*.

We're being bombarded. The blasts are everywhere. With every explosion our skulls glow red through our terrified faces.

Suddenly, thundering hooves throb between my ears in time with the fast beating of my heart. I straighten up and dare to look down at the violent pyre. The woman draped in white rides upon her galloping black horse across the sad, bloody stage of American History. As she weaves through it the wounds of the land the crumbled buildings magically ascend into the structures they once were. Fallen trees re-erect and blossom anew. Dead bodies rise to their feet and dance in celebration and are joined by the magically healed.

These miracles shift my mind to my mother. How I worry about her. How I love her. How all I want to do is get back to her safely. All I want to do is heal *her* wounds...

But another explosion pulls me back, and I notice the soldier across from me. *Farmer* is stitched over his heart. I pull from my pocket The Purple Heart medallion and hold it out to him. 'From yer daughter,' I say as the medallion throbs warm in my palm. His eyes and mouth gape open in astonishment. Together we watch the head of George Washington glisten and pulsate from it in the red rays of the sunset, while this Huey's blades whip above us...

an unkind commotion

'C'mon! Let's roll!' Justin says as he rips the sheets away from my warm, safe nest. Squinting through the sunlight I mutter vulgarities. 'It's 7:30, Ethan, c'mon!' The digits on my alarm clock confirm he is right.

'Yer shittin me,' I cry. How on *Earth*? Did I actually sleep for *sixteen hours*? Is my entire body made of rubber? My head spins and pulsates in pain. But despite my groggy daze I recall my vivid dream and my father's words. 'How in Hell did ya get in here?' I ask.

Justin rummages through the clothes on my floor and replies, 'Yer mom let me in, that's how. Whatchya need, dude? I'll help ya out. Ya got about five minutes. Ten if yer lucky, but *Hell*, ya don't look so lucky no how. Why do ya always do this to yerself?'

I run my hands through my stringy mussed hair and drop my feet to the red rug. 'Whatchya mean, *my mom*?' I haven't seen my mom all week.

'Yeah, I think I woke her up with my knockin.'

'Nah, dude, don't worry. Just, *why is she home*?'

'Beats me, man. Hey Charlie! Hey Boy!' Justin kneels down and Charlie licks his face. 'I gotta get me one of these.'

73

'Ya say that every time ya come over here.' Justin ignores me and continues to wrestle around with my suddenly-rambunctious-in-the-morning dog. 'Charlie's a good boy, though,' I admit, 'He's a nice distraction from all of the tension around this house.'

'Tension?' Justin enquires.

'That's a kind word to use, actually. I think my dad and I are gonna end up killin each other.'

'C'mon, Ethan, yer dad ain't that bad.' I glare at Justin for making such an ignorant comment. 'Is he?' he backtracks.

'It's a war around here, dude. A war.'

'I didn't realise…'

'You'll see. One day.'

'Ok, c'mon now, run this comb through that greasy mop and throw this shirt on.' Justin hits me in the face with my The Vampire Bats T. It's crusty and rancid as I still haven't washed it.

'This thing's *dirty*! I ain't wearin it.'

'Just throw it on, we gotsta go!'

'*Sniff* it, this thing's *filthy!*'

'Ethan, dude, what do I gotta do, hire a fuckin maid for ya?'

'Yeah, a drop dead gorgeous fuckin *slutty* maid. I need someone to take care of me.' I stand up and slide my jeans on. 'Damn, dude, got enough butch wax in that hair?'

Justin sneers at my comment as he inspects his sideburns in the mirror. He admires his pompadour ramp in front that wisps up and out before dangling down in his face. He licks a finger to paste that one strand of hair into place.

'Mom, y'alright?' I yell from the bathroom.

'I'm fine, Hun,' she calls from behind her closed bedroom

74

door, 'go on to school.' Justin sits on the edge of my unmade bed and chuckles.

'Whatchya laughin at, Justin? C'mon, *remember*? Let's go!'

'Ethan, dude, ya look like shit! By the way, how was work last night?'

'Oh fuck!' I exclaim. 'Work! I fuckin missed work!'

'Whatchya mean ya missed work?'

'I didn't go in!'

'Whatchya mean at didn't go in? What about all that stress about savin money for a car?'

'Dude, I know! I just…slept through it.'

'Slept through it? I thought yer shift started at 6pm?'

'It did.'

'Ethan, yer crazy, dude. Makin as much sense as a damn fool! What time ya go to bed then?'

'Uh, 3:30 yesterday afternoon.'

'So, yer tellin me ya slept for over sixteen hours?'

I say nothing.

'Fuckin Rip Van Winkle!'

We scat to Justin's Firebird. It's parked at the end of the driveway and leaves a long shadow in the morning sunlight. 'Ah, welcome to October!' Justin says, 'Look at the trees. The leaves are so beautiful as they die.'

I duck into the passenger side and say, 'Ya know, I wouldn't mind ownin an old dog like this.'

'Hey, call it what ya want but she can still move!' He turns the key and after a couple coughs it starts.

'And she still runs!' I say.

75

'Yeah, plus it's from the same year that Elvis died. That counts for somethin.'

'Are ya *finally admittin* he's dead? Hold on, man, say that again slowly while I record ya.' I whip out my cell phone and threaten to tape him.

We hear faint music and the subtle rumbling of bass. Justin says, 'Someone's still partyin. Can ya imagine?'

I slouch into the passenger seat and say, 'We gotsta go, remember? We gotsta be there in six minutes.' *Dad, you goddamned drunk!*

'Is that music comin from yer dad's garage? It *is*! What's he doin in there? It's not even eight yet!'

I just stare out the passenger window and mumble, 'Don't know.'

'Wait, has he been out there all night? He doesn't usually start work til late in the morning.'

'Yeah,'

Justin backs out of the driveway, shaking his head, and heads for Ritenour.

'Sometimes he just stays out there,' I say, 'all night.'

'Damn, if I had a car like the one he's got I'd prolly sleep out there, too!'

'It's just a car.'

Justin drives the Firebird around the bend of Bataan Drive. I look up through the windshield and see how the inferno shades of ginger, gold and crimson spawn out from the black branches. The trees seem to hold hands high above to form a bright tunnel. As we turn onto Edmundson Road an unkind commotion in the churchyard kills October's charm.

'What in *Hell*?' Another 'train' has just crashed into the ravine. Justin slows to a full stop on the shoulder and asks, 'What

76

should we do?'

'I don't know, but that's wrong, man.' I open the door and get out.

'Wait, whatchya doin?' blurts Justin, still gripping the wheel with both hands. 'We're gonna be late!'

'Those guys are crazy but they'll listen to me...*you* and me, anyway.' I stare back at Justin until he reluctantly follows. The evil this morning in the churchyard is a lot worse than anything I'd ever witnessed on the bus. But I feel brave enough to put a stop to it with Justin at my side. 'Donnie! Tony!' I interrupt. In the shadow of one of the oak trees Donnie holds the girlish boy down on the ground. Tony has a death grip on the back of his neck and rubs his head into the grass. They continue to heckle him as we approach. Their nasty smirks become more animated at the sight of us while their words became more colourful, as if we provide them a motivating audience.

'Hey, Morgan, this flamer popped off to us *again*, man. Can ya *believe it?!*'

'C'mon, break it up,' Justin says, 'We'll give ya a lift to school.'

'We ain't goin to no school, Ronan, not today. We're gonna make sure this little queer doesn't talk no more shit and then we're goin downtown.' The girlish boy whimpers and snarls and grits his teeth, but can't escape.

'Guys, c'mon, get off him. If the cops roll by they'll cuff ya.'

Justin looks at his watch and says, 'We're officially late, now. C'mon, get off that kid and go downtown or whatever.'

'Ronan, yer a party-pooper, dude.' Donnie says as he reluctantly follows Justin's instruction. 'Yer lucky I'm bored of beatin yer ass, faggot.'

'Don't be sayin that shit to us no more, queer,' Tony

77

chimes in, 'We'll kill ya!' Then he thrusts the girlish boy's face into the ground one last time, caking it with muddy turf. 'See ya, suckers!'

'Hey, guys,' Donnie yells, 'tonight, Guthrie, third house from the corner. The blue one with the boat in the driveway. BYOB!'

'The *fag* of Woodson Terrace!' Tony shouts as they trounce away. The bullies disappear around the corner as we help the victim to his feet.

'Y'alright, man?' I ask.

'Yes, fine.' the girlish boy answers.

'C'mon, we'll give ya a lift.'

'If you think I'm going to school looking like this you are fucking insane!' He struggles to his feet and stumbles off without saying another word, soiled and grass stained to match his muddy face.

Voices. Dreams. Hell, maybe the girlish boy's right. Maybe I *am* insane. I was a no-call-no-show to work last night because I was in the midst of a sixteen hour slumber. Hell, do I still *have* a job? And now I'm involved in this bullying saga. As I recall the past couple of days, home has a nice ring to it. I just want to go home and find out why my mom stayed home today, then just chill. I've had enough drama for one day and it's only 8am.

'They wouldn't really hurt em,' Justin says.

'Nah.' I concur.

'Hey, where ya goin?'

'Going home's a good idea, man.'

'What? Dude, I'm gonna be late now over all this!'

'Well, would ya rather some kid got his ass beat?

78

'Well, suit yerself. I gotta go in. I've got a monitored air shift today. C'mon, I'll give ya a lift home'.

fainting

I tip-toe across the worn carpeting in our house. Dad's promised Mom he'd replace it over and over again. It was a bright creamy white when it was installed just three years ago. But since then it's deteriorated to an elderly greyish, spotted with muck and grime. Many other parts of the house have also declined since brighter days. Dead leaves, cobwebs and dust decorate the foyers inside the entry doors. Nicotine yellows the walls where they meet the ceiling. Weeks of mail, newspapers and magazines are scattered around the coffee table and floor. The clutter on the dining table, where we haven't sat together as a family for a meal in years, could make us a small fortune if we put it all on the driveway and called for a garage sale. The state of our home has become a symbol for our family's decline to dysfunction.

A long time ago, before the Corvette project, the house was kept immaculately and friends and family would visit often. But eventually our house became just a place for us to crawl into to sleep, eat and bathe while we watched it fall apart around us as we do today. All the while, just across the back patio, the garage gobbled up every priority, where an auto repair business struggled, a classic muscle car was assembled and a man floated further away from fatherhood.

83

I step onto the kitchen floor and see his boots. Yeah, the music's over. The garage is shut and all is quiet. He's finally joined my mom in bed.

I like the change of being home in the morning when I should be at school. Daytime television is somehow enjoyable. The food in the fridge tastes so much better when I realise I could be eating Ritenour's cafeteria menu. Sitting in the safe confines doing absolutely nothing is not boring at all, but somehow pleasurable. I like the peace and quiet in the calm, dim blue of the house, while my father sleeps.

But in time my imagination explodes.

Why is Mom home?

What is Felicity doing right now?

What *will* happen to me, o woman draped in white?

I break the silence by emptying the rest of the Raisin Bran into a Tupperware bowl. I pour milk over the flakes and raisins and realise that it's best to just focus on good thoughts. Sweet thoughts. Hot thoughts. I think about Felicity, sweet as the sugar I sprinkle on my cereal. I will actually *miss* going to school today. The thought of not seeing her, hearing her or smelling her begins to process. My stomach rumbles like the spin-cycle of our washing machine. My knees weaken and I grip the edge of the countertop to keep my balance. Shit, why did I even bother pouring this cereal into a bowl! The last thing I want to do is eat, as the first is stumble into the bathroom a throw up. My head's spinning and everything's blurry.

Why I dab my finger into the sugar then put it to my tongue, just like yesterday, I don't know. Maybe Felicity will come walking through again and bring more beautiful clarity to my world. Instead a buzz sounds in my head and slowly intensifies, like an oncoming swarm of bees. And beyond that buzz, the thundering down of hooves.

84

I lose my balance and collapse. Just before I crash into the kitchen floor the wooden surface gives way. After falling through a dark chasm I land in my bedroom, my three-walled room, right onto my unmade bed that's covered in bright fallen leaves. Through the absence of the fourth wall a super-imposed forest glows bright. The autumnal hues of red and gold illuminate vibrantly. The darkness within lurks above the glowing woodland floor and slithers around the dim trunks. The scene calls to me under a blood-red sky, and a river flows somewhere beyond the trees.

From the highest branch to the crawling roots, I never could've dreamed of recreating this scene through photography. It's far beyond anything I could've comprehended.

If this is actually a *film* that I find myself in then there are breaks in it. It flickers, like the glitches in old home movies, as if I was rapidly blinking my eyes. I've learned that this can be attained when alternate processing is randomised. When half of the film is processed differently than the other half a charming flicker can be created. This can cause everything to look completely ordinary and natural for an instant before snapping right back into the dreamy state.

I've read about alternating processing, and I believe some of the steps of this 'forest film' were probably skipped after it was thrown into the chemical bath and the lights were dropped. Then, instead of spooling out the fail it was simply squished together. This film must have been pulled apart so delicately that the images came off pristine, hence, the alien glow.

If this *is* a film I find myself in then I must be the star. But I'm devoid a script, improvising for perhaps an invisible audience watching me from the other side of their television screens. Perhaps it's the world I live in, juxtaposed by my insanity, or another world on the other side. The flipside of life.

Or is it death?

Was I ever really alive?

85

What is it that makes me feel so alive for those rare golden moments, so few and so far between? Those peaks in life that I just somehow end up upon effortlessly. Almost like I woke up one morning and there I was, sniffing the clouds with a nosebleed and a smile, face to face with God. Those golden moments for me have been so few that they make the rest of my life look like just a breathing form of death.

I have no idea what this weird forest is, or means. I can only describe it as very alien, yet somehow very familiar. Somewhere that I somehow *belong*. Is there something here that I need to find? Or someone? I can feel their eyes on me. They're watching me. Who are *they*?

There's a whir that's orchestrated by movement. I wave my hand slowly in front of my face and the whirring heightens, then declines. I take another step toward my room and the whirring obeys my movement once more. I turn my head to the left and then to the right and I can't help but grin about this mysterious sound, much like Luke Skywalker's light sabre.

I get up off the bedroom floor and walk towards my records. I wonder how other sources will sound in this environment, like Rock 'n Roll. I put *One For Sorrow* on and the guitars and vocals enter foreign sonic territory that leaves me scraping my jaw off the floor! The whirring adds an unearthly dimension to the already vastly layered music. I never thought I would hear sounds like this in my life!

I want to do a hundred things at once. As the music plays I juggle a baseball around and it sounds like a hummingbird. I wind up and deliver a fastball into the dreamy distance. It makes an explosive noise as it leaves my hand, much like a rocket, before quieting down to a steady buzz, much like the swarm of bees I heard before. The ball hits a tree with a deep boom. It skips and skids and rolls until it disappears and becomes silent in the darkness, sounding like it rolled down a flight of stairs made of bass drums. I head into the woods after it and my treading on the dead neon leaves crackles in stereo. It's as if every noise has been digitally enhanced and run through a surround-sound system!

The deeper I trek into the woods the darker it gets. The blackness falls from the sky, oozes between the spider webs of branches, slithers between the trunks, and compromises the colourful radiance of the forest. The leaves and grass are becoming enshrouded by it and an eerie calm creates a magnified suspense. And right on cue, Track Two begins. These slow, wicked beats The Vampire Bats recorded provide a spooky overtone. Suddenly I don't care about finding my baseball. I just want to turn back.

Those watching eyes feel closer suddenly. They're live. They're *here*. They're taking tiny bites of me, consuming me slowly to preserve my taste. They enjoy it, knowing that they can have me anytime. Who are *they*?

Anytime they can reach right out and grab me.

Anytime they can stuff that shotgun into my hands.

Anytime they can watch me blow my brains out.

I stop. Panicked, short of breath with wide-open eyes, I can still hear the distant roar of the river rushing and a multitude of voices. Some chant while others sing...

FATAL GUNSHOT WOUND

GUNSHOT WOUND

GUNSHOT WOUND

I shake my head in an attempt to destroy the voices, wishing them to be nothing more than nuisance bugs buzzing inside my head. But they persist, carrying on in various lilts...

87

SHE HAD A HEART ATTACK

HAD A HEART ATTACK

HAD A HEART ATTACK

The beings that the voices come from are here, somewhere. But no matter how fast I twist and turn I cannot see them, just their faint trails of energy escaping the corners of my eyes. But I can feel them breeze past. They're flying all around! I'm afraid to take another step as I don't know what's waiting for me in the pitch black just ahead. My terror becomes unbearable and I'm so disoriented that I run right into a tree. I think I've broken my nose as I fall to my knees tasting blood. Shivering in fright, feeling blood ooze down my muzzle, I try to scream but can only gasp a pathetic little chirp.

Shadows…

They whip around me and steal my last ounce of bravery. They chant and croon and are so very close!

But the voices are muted by an awful screech, followed by a crash and the twisting of metal…

Now everything is silent…

Born from the short-lived silence to follow are silhouettes of men. As they march my way I press back up against a tree. They're clones in black uniforms. All wear moustaches underneath aviator glasses that mask their faces. They don silver badges over their hearts and are armed with guns and clubs. They brisk past me as I hold my breath, cowered down in a foxhole. The clones chant…

TO THE RIVER

TO THE RIVER

TO THE RIVER

88

spilled milk

'Honey, y'alright? Wake up, baby.' The familiar voice wakes and soothes me. 'Wake up, baby. What in the world are ya doin on the floor?' she whispers.

I feel the cool kitchen hardwood beneath me. I open my eyes to my mother's gaze. She doesn't look right. Oh yeah, why is she home? Why was my father still in the garage this morning? Does Justin hate me? Is the girlish boy alright? What's Felicity wearing today? Where in Hell was I just? Was it just a dream? What in the world *am* I doing on the floor?

'Ethan, you were talkin about a freight train.'

'Yeah, a freight train…'

'Baby, why is yer nose bleeding? What happened?' My face feels like someone cracked me with an uppercut! I cry out in pain as my mother holds a blood-soaked rag to my nose. 'I'm sorry, Ethan, I'm sorry. But we've gotta stop the bleeding.'

'Is it broken?' I ask.

'No. Just bleeding. What happened?'

My eyes regain full focus. My mother's left eye and cheek are black and blue. 'Forget about me, what happened to *you?*'

'Nothin.'

'He did this to ya?' I ask.

'No, just forget about *me!* I wanna know what in Hell happened to *you!* Are ya takin drugs?'

'He did this to ya, Mom?!'

'*No*, honey, it wasn't him. Ya know it wasn't *really* him.' Her face begins to crack. Her concern for my waking up in the kitchen floor quickly turns to the fear of my reaction to her appearance.

'How long are ya gonna let this go on for, Mom? How long?'

'Ethan, it wasn't really *him*. Ya know how he can get. The doctors told me that the guys who returned from Vietnam were havin the same experiences. They told me that long before you were ever born.'

'I'm so god-damned tired of hearin that excuse! What if he really hurts ya someday? Or kills ya? What's stoppin me from goin in that bedroom right now while he sleeps?!'

'Me, Ethan! Me! Please don't!' my mother weeps. A disarming tear rolls down her bruised cheek and extinguishes my angry fire. 'It's a sickness, son. Yer father's sick. All those guys came back sick. Some are just sicker than others.'

I stare at my father's boots parked three feet away. If the day ever comes, I'm bigger than, faster than and at least as strong as my old man. I have *real* anger to fuel my fight. Dad's emotions can't be as intense as mine. But the day still hasn't come. 'I can't let em do this to ya again, Mom. I can't.'

'Ya know that he can get like this when he drinks.'

'Mom, it's not the war. He's just an alcoholic.'

'No, Ethan, he has this reaction when he drinks, or is under high stress levels. When he gets the flu. High fever. Sometimes he'll have a nightmare and believe it's real for hours!'

'Mom, I just can't…' I tear up and my voice cracks.

92

'It hardly ever happens anymore.' Mom replies, 'Not for a long time. Please don't worry. He's never really hurt me. Please understand, and don't ever...'

'Don't ever what?' I ask.

'Don't ever...just don't fight him. If I were to lose either of ya over this I couldn't live on.' She knows how much I hate Dad.

I stand up and all the blood rushes to my head. I take a deep breath. Inhale. Exhale. My nose has stopped bleeding but not before it got all over my shirt. I notice that my Raisin Bran has gone soggy and I didn't put the milk away. 'Not like ya to let yer Raisin Bran get like that. Ya don't have to tell me what happened, Ethan. But if ya ever wanna talk-'

'I'm *not* on drugs, Mom. Put that outta yer mind. I was worried about ya so I told Justin that I was stayin home. Ya *never* miss work. Looks like my instincts never fail me.'

'I'll be fine, son.'

I take a bite of the cereal and grimace at the texture, and my sore face. Despite how soggy it is it still hurts to chew. I look at my mother's bruised face and, pointing at her with the spoon, say, 'I'm actually glad ya found a way to stay home for a change.' We share a relieving laugh.

'How did ya end up passed out on the floor?' she asks. 'I didn't smell any *booze* on yer breath.'

'I've often wondered what it would be like to have a catnap on the kitchen floor.'

'Very funny. And how would ya explain the blood?'

I say nothing. Instead I just eat another spoonful of milk-saturated bran flakes and raisins, trying not to wince.

'Yer boss called here last night wonderin where ya were. I tried to get ya but yer bedroom door was locked.' I don't reply and munch more cereal. Mom frowns and says, 'Alright, I don't need an explanation. I believe ya when ya say it's not drugs. I know that school and work can really suck sometimes. Are ya *ok?*'

'Yeah, just so damned tired lately. I'm not exactly sleeping well is all. When's the last time *you* played hooky, anyway?'

'Oh, it's been a long time,' she replies. 'I don't know what I'll do the rest of the day. Damn, maybe I should just put my make-up on and go on in.'

'No, Mom, of course not! 'Just stay home. I haven't seen ya in a while.'

'Prolly the best thing actually. I don't have a good excuse for the way I look, anyway.'

I lunge for the milk but knock the carton off the countertop. 'Shit!' Mom quickly rips the towel from the refrigerator door and kneels to wipe up the cold white splatter. I join her, armed with a spray-bottle of disinfectant. 'Sorry, Mom. I'll go get more.'

'This reminds me when ya were little and...do ya remember? Ya spilled the milk. It hit the floor. Ya looked up at me. Ya did just about everything ya could do to fight back the tears.'

'I remember that, yeah. That one time ya *didn't* scream at me for spillin somethin.'

'You were *seven*. You were *so upset*!'

'Yeah, only because ya screamed at me all the other times! I thought that spillin milk was one of the worst things I could do.'

'I should've never laid into ya like that. No wonder ya were so upset.' Mom washes the milky towel in the sink by hand and steps into the sunlight that pours in through the window. Her bruise's green and purple hues are brought out in the morning rays. 'I never forgave myself for screamin at ya like that. Never. I mean, we were pretty poor then, sure. Yer dad was laid off. He hadn't started workin for himself yet. We never had any money. I

94

remember thinkin, 'that's all the milk we'll have for the week!' When I realised how upset ya were I took a vow never to let my family live poor again. Not after that day.'

'Well, ya work too much now, Mom. Ya do man's work. I don't care what it pays. It's a factory. I mean, yer my *mom*! Ya work in that sweatbox, I work at the grocery but Dad doesn't give us any credit!'

Mom drops her head and sulks at my words and how true they are. 'It's not exactly a sweatbox.'

'Dad puts on a good show out there,' I say, 'but if he was really doin anything you'd be home more often.'

Mom brews coffee now while Dad snores away from the bedroom. The rich aroma fills the air as I wait for a cup at the cluttered table. Black. Two sugars. 'Mom, ya know that I believe a man hittin a women is wrong, right?'

'Son, yer gonna be fine.'

'Wrong…*evil*! I think *I'll* be fine…but will *you*?'

 She never spoke to me like I was an adult regarding Dad before. This morning was the first time. Our mother-to-son, adult-to-adult dialogue stays docile. She finally shows respect for my opinion of her relationship with Dad, and I finally acknowledge her comfort with him. She's been with him longer than I've been alive. We have a good debate. Discussion. Conversation.

She tells me what a wonderful man, father and husband he once was. She pleads to me that those wonderful qualities are still in him somewhere. She claims that his war experiences ultimately began to haunt him, which created the Corvette project.

I argue that the car has always been his excuse to rid himself of us. I remind her that Dad spent every spare moment in the garage during the Corvette project. He built it proudly from the ground up with his own hands. He truly believed the car would define him. After it was completed he spent even more time with his masterpiece. There were car shows which led to car clubs. Car clubs led to meetings. Meetings led to more competition and shows. Competition led to endless, relentless maintenance. Maintenance led to trophies, recognition and success that no one could ever take away from him. He deserved every ounce of success he gained from building that awesome machine, and more. But that success led to his obsession with the machine that he thought *defined* him. It was perhaps the *greatest* victory of his life.

From day one of its assembly though, as his masterpiece grew closer to completion, he drank more and more heavily. I have just as many hard feelings about the Vette as the Vette has man-hours. My mother and I have been on the outside of his life ever since. No dinners out, movie theatres, family vacations, parent-teacher conferences, fishing and camping trips, bowling nights, baseball games or rock concerts. There just wasn't enough time for us.

Will there ever be?

I want to murder my father as much as I want to admire him. He's humiliated me but there's still a sliver of my heart that will defend him, because one day I might be just like him. I might love him for his ways one day as much as I hate him for them now.

Hell, I hate myself, too. Sometimes I can't stand looking in the mirror, seeing how I'm beginning to look just like him. Just *like* him.

'It's unreal, Ethan, just how much ya look like yer father in that photo!'

When my mammalian instinct to survive and prosper kicks

in I'll try to understand all of his faults so that I can understand my own. Because I want to be better. Because I don't want to change into a monster. How can ill-fate in life destroy someone? My father's given up on becoming better. He's already changed into a monster. He was a teenager like me when he was drafted into the Army to fight a 'worthless' war. He was a victim. Then, like falling dominoes, so was my mother...and now so am I.

One day I'll have a son. I look forward to the days that I will be there for him. I'll cherish doing with him all that a loving father is supposed to do with his son. I don't ever want him to hate me.

So, I'll always remember my father's ways.

Because one day I'll have a son, too...

Life will haunt you.

Time never stops.

'Oh shit. Mom, ya think ya can give me a ride to school?'

'What? Ethan, why?'

'I forgot. I've got a huge Physics test today. No late takes.'

'No problem. Let's go.'

'Thanks, Mom.'

'Just, one thing.'

'What's that?' I ask.

'Despite yer feelings toward yer father being understood, and even justified, don't ya *ever believe* you'll ever understand what he went through.'

monkey in the zoo

Mom drops me off at the east wing of the school where there's a side entrance I can sneak into. My plan is to fetch my Physics book to study for that test while hidden in a bathroom stall. But in order to get it from my locker I must pass Lancashire's room, the class I should be in right now! I hold a fake hall pass in my right hand and secure my backpack with my left. Despite walking softly through the empty corridors the rubber tread on the soles of my Docs just wont stop squeaking against the tiles.

Lancashire's room is coming up on my right. I hold my breath and shift to the far side of the hall, hoping to slip past. I'm close enough now to hear Lancashire barking out the day's lesson. As I walk past her classroom door I can't help but peer in to spy on the students in the back rows. I wonder if they'll hawk out at me as I try to pass undetected. Will they rat me out? Will I see Felicity? Will she see me? Maybe she'll whisper something with her eyes.

And there she is! Sitting in that last desk in the first row she stares back at me with a surprised smile. Oh, her eyes, her green, green eyes! I crack a smile back as I keep storming ahead...but the strap on my backpack breaks. Ghosts: Messages from the Dead falls out and crashes against the floor! The disturbance echoes through the entire corridor! Felicity's smile turns into a grimace as my fumble has disrupted the class. 'There goes Ethan!' a female student cries. No matter how desperately I try to compose myself and pick it up I can't get my body to move correctly. My left leg goes left and right leg goes right. My arms flap about like a drunken pigeon and I end up on my knees like an injured giraffe trying to scoop the book into the bag.

'Mr. Morgan! Ah-ah-ah! Not today!' Lancashire gloats in the doorway, casting her shadow upon me from the sunny windows. I sigh deeply and slowly look up, hoping it's all another bad dream.

But were they actually dreams?

Behind her I can see twenty-pairs of eyes join Felicity's in watching me like I'm a monkey at the zoo. 'I know I'm getting long in the tooth, Mr. Morgan, but you can't expect to slip past me *two days in succession.* I've won this one, Ethan. Detention, after school today.' As she walks away Felicity gives me the *'oops'* look.

'You can't win them all, class. You can't win them all. Mr. Morgan, please come in and join us and put an end to your nuisance antics!'

'Ms. Lancashire, I have to go to my locker. To get my book and camera.'

'Very well, and hurry, Make haste not waste!'

I open my locker and just stand there. I hate this place. When does my life get better? I just want to go home but I can't. I should've just *stayed home with my mom*! I was only trying to be responsible and take my Physics test. But already I've been embarrassed, issued a detention and I'm still going to flunk that fucking Physics test!

Where's my God-damned camera? I rummage through my locker and footsteps approach.

<click-clack, click-clack, click-clack>

Still embarrassed and defeated I just keep my head buried in my locker as I wait for whomever it is to pass.

<click-clack, click-clack, click-clack>

But the footsteps stop right on the other side of my open locker door. I look down and can see her black, shiny Mary Janes. She smells amazing! A suggestion of fresh roses. A little dash of cinnamon…*holy shit!*

My curiosity forces me to peer around to see who the girl is, as she's just opened the vacant locker next to mine. She wears black stockings and a short black dress that flares out ever so slightly. The top of the dress is layered over by her black wool sweater. Her hair is a soft and silky black veil draping her white face and reaching down to the middle of her back. It's so shiny that it seems to sparkle. Her back is to me as she searches through the locker, but by her tall, slender, shapely figure I can tell that she is beautiful. And, hey, I happen to dig girls in retro.

The girl stops for a moment, then turns to face me. She flashes a gentle but stunning smile on a pale, glowing face that features a pair of enchanting emerald-green eyes! 'Felicity, but you were…I thought-'

The girl is Felicity but with black hair. She takes a very vintage-looking camera from the locker, shuts the door and gives an acknowledging smile that renders me speechless. Seriously. I cannot speak. Words won't come out of my mouth! As I watch her walk away down the empty hall I realise my tongue feels heavy and numb. As she turns the corner I finally get my legs to work. I sprint after her, but when *I* turn that corner she's disappeared!

103

detention with marilyn

It's been a long, bad day. When Justin woke me up this morning I didn't remember seeing a 'Top Ten To-do' list...

Friday, October 1

1) Oversleep

2) Get embarrassed by Dad

3) Police a couple of bullies

4) Piss Justin off

5) Faint

6) Have an insane dream (was it a dream?)

7) Bloody my nose

8) See Mom's bruises

9) Be shamed by Lancashire

10) Fail a very important Physics test

Number Eleven: Serve detention.

Lancashire decided to put me to work instead of just

having me sit and watch her grade papers for an hour. As Ritenour just received new computers and books this week nearly every classroom on the ground floor has boxes of old stuff sitting in the hall for removal. That's my job this afternoon. I struggle heaving these heavy boxes of old text books and computer hardware up two flights of stairs to the storage room. At least I don't have to look at Lancashire.

I'm sweating and out of breath as I drop another box into the storage area, a room that hasn't facilitated an actual class in years. I didn't bother flipping on the lights but I can still tell just how musty and dingy this room is. The tiles on the floor are all cracked, showing spots of the old cement floor underneath. There are no windows, either, nor do prison cells. A school district that builds a classroom without windows makes me question just how far we've actually come as a people.

I sit down on one of the boxes to catch my breath amongst the silhouettes of shelves of old books, computers, tables, chairs, sports equipment and other mysterious boxes. I wonder what's in them. My arms are aching and I'm thirsty, but before I get up to go to the drinking fountain footsteps approach from down the hall.

<click-clack, click-clack, click-clack>

Hopefully it's help. I mean, I can't believe Lancashire would expect me to move all of those boxes *all by myself!* But I can't leave until I get the entire ground hall cleared, *at least* an hour of work!

<click-clack, click-clack, click-clack>

108

The footsteps grow louder and closer and finally enter the storage room. I can't tell who it is as the only light is what pours in from the hallway. I feel creepy sitting in the dark now that someone else has come in. She's wearing black and seems to be searching for something, opening the lids of different boxes and peering inside. 'Hi there,' I say. 'Whatchya need?'

'I'm lookin for my photos,' the girl says.

'I would've turned the light on but I-'

'Have ya seen any photos? They're in one of these boxes. I wanna take em home.'

'Um, no. It's really dark in here. Try turnin on the light.'

She ignores my suggestion. 'They gotta be here somewhere,' she says.

'Which period do ya have Lancashire then?' I ask.

'First.'

'First? *I* have her first period! Who are you?' Her face is obscured by the darkness. Wondering who it is, the girls in PA class rotate in my head. 'Turn on that light so we can see what we're doin in here.' I stand up and move towards her while she hunts through another box. I flip the light switch, but nothing happens. 'Damn, it's burned out,' I say. But as the girl frantically turns to search another box the light from the hallway illuminates her face. It's Felicity with black hair again! 'Felicity! It's you! It's-'

'Why do ya keep callin me Felicity?' she asks.

'What?'

'Pretty name n'all, but my name's Marilyn.'

'But, if yer not Felicity then ya can't be in Lancashire's first period.'

'What? Boy, of course I am!' she laughs. 'I've got the

photos here to prove it, if I can just find em.' I'm astonished that she's of the same height, size, demeanour and Southern drawl. If she's not Felicity with black hair, then…

'So, are ya gonna help me or just stand there like a statue?' she asks.

'I've just…never seen ya before. I know now that yer *not* who I thought ya were. I mean, I've been goin to this school for four years now and this is the first time I've ever seen ya.'

'So? I've been goin to this school since 1972!'

'*What?*'

'Ah, never mind, boy. Here they are.' She takes a thick portfolio from the box and exits the room. I try to dart out into the hallway but I trip over another box in the dark! My knee bashes against the floor and I wince in pain. I strain to get to my feet and out to the hallway but she's disappeared, just like this morning! Completely spooked I re-enter the storage room and try turning the lights on again…and this time they come on! I kneel before the box that the girl found her photos in and find a ragged notebook with lots of doodles and graffiti sketched on the cover. At the top, written in very pretty, feminine handwriting is…

Marilyn Treadwell

Class of 1976

…and at the bottom, beneath all of the weird doodling and graffiti is…

I Love Tobias

I open the notebook to see that all the pages have been ripped out, but there is a black and white photo of a very handsome young man wearing an army uniform, displaying many medals upon his chest. He's got deep set eyes and a chiselled face: sharp jaw line, Roman nose, high cheek bones and thick lips. I notice on the back someone has written in blue ink...

December 6, 1974

Dearest Marilyn,

You'll always be in my heart while I'm away. I want to always be in yours. I know we only met this past spring but by summertime, by the time I was drafted into this hell hole, I had fallen in love with you. It's the thought of you and all of our wonderful times that gets me through each day. When I come back I'm going to marry you and we're going to move back to Memphis to start a life together. As soon as you graduate high school. I'll always love you,

Love, Tobias

The smell of roses and cinnamon is strong again. 'I need that, too.' Marilyn stands right above me. She swipes the photo and notebook from my hands and disappears into thin air!

'Mr. Morgan!' Ms. Lancashire squawks. She stands big and tall in the doorway and blocks out all the light. 'This is a *detention*, young man! Get the lead out and move these boxes! You've hardly moved anything!'

sleep is for the daytime

<BOOM-BOO-BO-BOOM-BO-BOOM>

Saturday morning's thunder wakes me. Just after 3am, it's still dark outside...

<FLASH>

...until the lightning strikes. The bolt from the heavens brightens my room, the same way Felicity did just two days ago. Boy, she was like a strike of lightning!

The chance of meeting a girl like that at a concert...

The chances of having her sit right behind me...

How shitty my life was before her ...

No, she *was* a strike of lightning, right through my heart. I have an electrified crush on a girl I've spent less than an hour with. I guess I've got a big problem. I wonder if I'm just being silly. What if Felicity is just a friendly, hospitable Southern girl who charms the pants off of every boy she meets? I wonder if I can get the nerve up to call her, that is, if I can find her in the listings as I don't have her cell number. That is, if she'd want me to call her or even come within a *mile* of me outside of class. To distract my mind from her and any more stalker-thoughts I count between thunder strikes. One…two…three…

<FLASH>

One…two…three…

<BOOM-BOOM-BO-BO-BOOM>

It's no use. She's driving me crazy! And I need something good to carry into that dead-end job tonight at the grocery store. It's my senior year, god damn it! I need to sprinkle a little spice on my dull, fucked-up life. What do I have to lose? I'll just have to stop worrying about her rejecting me and dust off all those high school fairy tales. As stupid as they are there must be at least one with my name on it.

<FLASH>

One…two…

<BOOM-BO-BOOM-BOO-BOOM>

The storm is getting closer as rain blitzes the windowpanes. How am I going to fall back to sleep with all this racket outside my window? Inside my head?

If I had her number I'd call her right now. *Fuck off, Ethan.*

116

Calling her at this hour would ruin everything! *Wait a minute,* everything? *At this moment you've got absolutely* nothing *with Felicity! Fuck it. Now, just relax and slowly fall back…*

Shit! What would I even *say* to her? Calling her could be an absolute disaster, no matter what time of day!

<FLASH>

The lightning bolts entertain as they slash across the sky and illuminate my room.

And illuminate *her*.

The woman draped in white sits upright and calmly on the end of my bed, right by my feet. Her white face. Her red lips. Her green eyes…

And it's dark again. But she's still there. I can smell her. Roses…cinnamon…

<BOOM-BOOM-BO-BO-BOOM>

The thunder crashes but my heart pounds harder. She just sits there, staring at me with those green eyes glowing from her feminine silhouette. Her posture is perfect and her hands rest on her thighs. Like a statue, she doesn't move a muscle.

Neither do I. She has startled me into paralysis. I can't breath and my hearts pounds against my chest. My room is spinning. She is the centre of the kaleidoscope.

<FLASH>

The lightning strike is longer this time, and so is my view of her. She is gorgeous. Stunning. Wicked. Petrifying.

But I think I'm going to die.

<BOO-BO-BO-BOOM-BOOM>

In the dark, she asks, 'Ya don't smoke, do ya Ethan?'

I can't reply. Have my lips been sewn shut? My tongue is numb, yet my teeth chatter.

'Of course ya don't. Such a good boy, ya are. You're perfect for her. You'll never burn down *your* mama's house.'

The woman draped in white stands up but not one bedspring moves! Toward the wall she elegantly walks…right *through it!* She's disappeared!

* * *

118

After a noon breakfast I'm still suffering from the horrors of a restless night. I lie on my back across my bed, staring at the ceiling and waiting for the seven Eggo waffles smothered in butter and maple syrup to settle in my stomach. All those calories have my mind racing.

No, I don't smoke and, no, I'd never burn my 'mama's' house down. I have no idea what that woman means or who she is or if I'm even sane anymore. This *obsession* I have with finding Felicity before Monday morning, despite being dead-ass tired from the very little shuteye I managed to get, *must* be insanity.

But news does travel fast in high school and I fear there are hungrier wolves. Pretty girls (especially new ones with charming differences from the other bores, bitches and skanks) can be gobbled up by any front man of Ritenour popularity with a little game of his own. I ain't got game, but I was in the right place at the right time when Felicity first strolled into class. She met me first and her locker is very close. I guess it's better to be lucky than good.

But I could've been luckier if I would've not worried so damn much about being a dork. I was much too shy talking to Felicity and I didn't strike while the iron was hot, if it even got hot at all. I suppose I *did* have a lot on my mind yesterday morning.

As much as I look forward to this weekend, to catch up on rest, relaxation and fun, I honestly just want Monday to arrive. Crazy but true…I'm crazy about Felicity. But between now and then I've got another dreadfully mundane Saturday night shift at Schnucks and I'm still so tired!

I haven't had enough sleep. I better take a nap. *Sigh, sleep is for the daytime.* I pull the drapes closed and lock my door. I climb into bed underneath the blankets and pretend that the warmth they provide is Felicity's body pressed against mine. I close my eyes and imagine her scent. Sweet strawberries, fresh mint and delicious apples in the form of sexy, toned legs that just will not stop. In this fantasy, she has been waiting in my bed for me all day. Oh, the way her hair dangles in her face (and into mine)! I'm about to explode, so I remember her strutting down the row in PA class. Her ankles…her thighs…her hips…her slender waist and round breasts…that perfect athletic ass…those green, penetrating eyes! Lord have mercy, all those buttered-down waffles and syrup have turned right into baby batter! It feels so damn good…I'm going to lose my…mind…my…

Sigh…so tired now…time…to…sleep…

* * *

'It   hardly   ever   happens   anymore...happens anymore...happens anymore...'

'Mom-'

'It wasn't really him...really him...really him...'

'He *hit* you!'

'Yer father is sick...father is sick...father is sick...'

'I'm gonna kill em!'

'Ethan,' Felicity says, lying naked at my side, 'go out to that garage, get that gun and make everything better.'

I exit my room as it dissolves into blackness behind me, as does the hallway, and the kitchen, and my entire house as I exit, following Felicity's orders. I march towards the garage, where my father's twelve-gauge is. The voices demand...

GET HIS GUN

GET HIS GUN

GET HIS GUN

I open the garage door, take the shotgun off the wall and turn back towards the house. But it's Grandma's old house, where my father grew up, not ours. I recognise it from old photographs. Her old Chrysler is parked in the driveway. But she's been dead for seven years now!

I carry the gun up the back porch steps, past a rickety wooden rocking chair, through the backdoor. Grandma's son; the man that fathered me, is inside somewhere. He hurt my mom again. He's got Hell to pay.

'Hey Joe' crackles from the radio in one of the bedrooms. I

121

tip-toe, quiet as a mouse, through the kitchen and down the hall decorated with old photos in fancy frames. All of them portray the family, but are from many years ago. Most are in black and white and one of those includes a young boy sitting in a wooden rocking chair. He's seven years old, and he's stroking a black cat that sits calmly in his lap. As I look even closer, I notice that the photo was taken on the back porch of *this very house*. I walk back to the kitchen, just to compare the photo to the back porch, and discover that my guess is correct. I'll be damned if that same black cat now sits upon it out there, watching my every move, and the chair rocks to and fro in the sudden wind.

I turn back to the hallway believing that my insanity has been confirmed! The chair in the photograph moves just like the one on the porch! The young boy rocks in it, forward and back. He turns his head to the left and then to the right before staring at me with a big grin. He strokes the cat delicately as it purrs and flops its tail around.

'Wanna play catch?' the boy asks me, with the utmost enthusiasm. 'I gotta a brand new baseball. You gotta glove?'

'Robert, come in for supper!' a woman calls from inside the photo. Robert, my father aged seven, springs up while the cat darts away. The photo is now just of that old chair rocking on the back porch, slowing down...coming to a full stop. And now, a screeching of tires...

I'll bet that cat's alright. Cats have nine lives, after all. But I've only got one...

Cigarette smoke seeps from the room at the end of the hall. As I march toward it I cock the gun and point it at the door. I'm going to kick it open, step inside and blow his head off. But, as Jimi Hendrix boasts about shooting *his lady* down to the ground, a boy cries. His sad whimpering forces me to lower the gun to my side. I peer into the room through the half-opened door to find a young man with a flowing dark mane of hair. He

122

kneels at the foot of his unmade bed, reading a letter. I just watch him from the doorway with my gun pointed at the ground. The sight of him turns my heart inside out.

'Dad,' I call out. The weeping teenager squashes the cigarette butt into the ashtray and turns to me, displaying the saddest face I've ever seen. He's the spitting image of me, as if I'm looking in the mirror! He hands me the letter and says, 'Go on, do what ya came here to do.' I take the letter from his hand. His *draft* letter. Dad's going to Vietnam. He says, 'Go on, son, I don't wanna become the man ya hate.'

'Hello boys,' Grandma says. She stands behind me and asks, 'Ethan, are you and yer father stayin for supper?'

whiskey

10:45pm.

I'll clock out in fifteen minutes.

The end of the night has arrived. Finally.

It was a tough night at Schnucks. I've really had to earn my $9.25-an-hour tonight as my line of customers never broke. Milk, bread and eggs attacked me on the conveyor belt relentlessly throughout my shift. I had change from the previous order dropping out of my left hand while scanning the next order with my right. Just the way Schnucks likes it.

I've turned off my OPEN light. One last customer. I can't wait to get rid of her and count my till down but I still just barely manage to crack one last smile and say, 'Hello, m'am.' There. My smile muscles are shot. *C'mon, just find the barcodes and make sure they scan. Concentrate, Ethan. It's almost over.*

Funny, she didn't say 'Hello' back. No matter. I press the TOTAL key and say, '$8.88, please.'

'Ya forgot the apples,' she snarls, 'for the horse.' I look up and take notice of the unique customer that assails me with a cold stare. She wears her thin salt and pepper hair pulled back tightly in a ponytail. Lines and wrinkles crawl all about her face that features a pair of thick eyebrows and a witch's nose. Her skin is pale, even grey, especially as it contrasts with the black

127

woollen coat that she's bundled in. She seems so frail but she's only middle-aged.

Still, her eyes are big, green, vibrant and locked on me. You'd never expect beautiful orbs such as those to be staring from such a haggard face. Perhaps it's just been a long night, but her presence is very unsettling.

'For the *horse*?' I lazily enquire. I scan the apples and say, '$11.47.'

'You.'

'M'am?' I ask. I just can't look at her.

'*Yer* that boy.' I don't know what to do. I've scanned her groceries but she just stands there, still owing $11.47. '*Yer* that boy!'

'What? M'am, what's wrong?'

'She's *told* me about you! Yer the *one*!'

'M'am, I'm sorry but I don't know what yer talkin about. That's $11.47, please.'

'But *yer the one*, boy. Don't ya understand?'

'No, I don't understand, M'am. Now, please, I need yer payment so that I can count my till down.'

'Is there a *problem*, M'am?' My manager George has come over to intervene. The woman stares at *him* the same way, then right back at me. The wicked look on her face lessens and she says, 'No. no problem at all, sir. Please. Here, take it,' she says, dropping bills and coins on the conveyer belt from her long, trembling fingers. With my manager present I quickly pick up the twelve dollars and sort it into my till. I finger the fifty-three cents change but when I look up she's on her way out the exit doors.

'M'am, yer change!' I yell, but she's gone.

'Put it in yer pocket' George says. 'Don't worry bout her, son, she's just one of the weirdoes livin round here. Go on. Count down and get the Hell outta here.'

Justin and James blow in with the cold wind and the dead leaves. Justin sports those well-groomed pork chop sideburns and black-rimmed specs while James is draped in a black Misfits hoodie and a level-two buzz cut dyed cherry. Yeah, they're on a mission and they'll want me to join them. After the long shift I feel like a kitten, not sure whether to take a cosy nap or to be frisky and salvage the night. Drained but curiously excited, I count my till down as fast as I can knowing that my boys are waiting.

'Damn, yer still not off?' James barks.

The three of us dash out of the store into the parking lot where Justin's Firebird waits. Visible breath and fogged-up windows. It's a cold night.

'Shit, it's freezing out here!' I say.

'We're hittin Donnie Applebaum's tonight,' James says, 'There's a big party.'

'Yer shittin me.' I reply.

'I'm not shittin ya, dude.'

'That's gonna be a real fuck-up,' I say.

'So, what?' Justin barks. 'If it gets messed up or whatever we'll just leave.'

Justin revs the engine and blasts off like a bat out of hell through the back roads of Woodson Terrace. Tires screeching, engine growling.

'Ya *do know* about the cops around here, right?'

'Whatchya talkin bout Ethan?'

'Donnie's over on Guthrie. Guthrie's in Woodson Terrace. Woodson Terrace is a fuckin police state.'

'Hell, all of *North County* is a police state!' Justin divulges. 'Nothin's gonna happen like that though, Ethan. We'll just go over there, have a few beers and creepy-crawl back to yer place for the night.'

'Yeah, ya mind?' James asks.

The windows are down and the cold night air against my face is refreshing and inspiring. Even though Donnie's house is a guaranteed danger-dungeon I suddenly want to go. I think about sprinkling that little spice in my life and dusting off those high school fairy tales. This kitten wants to play now. But suddenly I've grown big fangs and claws. I've grown into a tiger.

'Fuck it,' I say, 'Let's do this!'

'That's my boy!'

Guthrie Avenue.

Justin flips down the headlights and skulks the car quietly through the moonlight. He parks about three houses down from Donnie's, in front of a dark residence with a black cat on the front porch. It spies on us with marble-eyes as bright as lanterns. I stare back at it and remember the rocking chair. The boy in the photograph. The shotgun I carried. My father.

Donnie's house doesn't look so festive from where we're sitting. It looks just like any other calm, quiet house with a few lights spilling through cracked drapes. I fear we've arrived at another lame sausage fest with loads of Bud Light and hockey.

'Are ya sure there's a party here, guys?' I ask.

'As soon as I park this thing somewhere we'll find out,'

'Grab that bottle back there, Ethan.' Justin demands.

130

'What bottle?' I ask as I kick something made of glass in the floor board.

'*That* bottle,' Justin says, turning around.

Jack Daniels is scripted in white on that famous black label, on a bottle full of whiskey. I unscrew the top and smell the strong, sweet aroma spread through the car. I take a swig of it and gasp like a puking dog. Justin and James chuckle, then follow suit.

'Where did ya get *this* shit from?' I ask.

'A *ghost* gave it to me,' Justin cracks.

'Very funny. PX?' I ask

'Yeah, from the X-man,' James says, 'and we better play a little catch up. Donnie might have this party way ahead of us.'

We sit there in the dark with *The Point* on at a reasonable volume. '*A Verse For The Broken*', a bluesy, Animals-esque track from The Vampire Bats' album, fills the Firebird's now whiskey-scented interior…

'I forgot…to make the bed

Because…of what…you said

And I…still smell your…sweet perfume

Everywhere…O everywhere…it looms

So, where's the real you?

Where's the real you?

That old…familiar scent

I'll never…smell again…I lament

Is on my doorstep! She's on my doorstep

For the last time…walk on through

131

I'm gonna cry tonight!

You're gonna die tonight!'

We pass the bottle around while keeping our eyes on the quiet neighbourhood that surrounds us, wary of cops. The wind rustles fallen leaves across the lawns and onto the moonlit street.

'The Vampire Bats!' James exclaims. 'Those crazy fucks!'

'Whadya make of em? I ask

Justin says, 'Remind me of The Cure-'

'Like *Hell* they do!' James retorts.

'Hey,' I snort, 'I saw their video the other day!'

'Which one?' Justin asks.

I sing out, 'Monday I will fall apart, Tuesday, Wednesday, break my heart…'

Justin chimes in, crooning like Sinatra, 'Thursday never even starts cuz Friday I'm in love.'

'Ya drunken queens,' James scoffs.

I take another gulp of Jack and grumble, 'Anyway, in that video, there's a guy that had the name of the song tattooed on his arm.'

James takes the bottle from me. 'Fuckin idiot!'

'Yeah, right? So, like, he was probably this saddo roadie of theirs. Robert Smith prolly promised him that if he actually went through with the tattoo then the band would film him getting it as *Friday I'm In Love's* official MTV video release.'

'Go on,' James says, 'yer on to something here.'

'Well, this asshole sits down, the tattoo artist has already inked *Friday* before it dawns on em, 'where in fuckin Dodge is

132

the film crew?' Justin and James laugh hysterically, with help from Jack. 'Wait, wait, I'm not done. Ok, so, he gets this horrible tattoo and Robert feels totally guilty about the empty promise he's made. So he tells the guy not to worry, and that he'll still be in the actual video…'

'Ok,' Justin says, 'So then what?'

'Well, he's in the video, alright…for like a *second!* They didn't even show his face! Just his little wussy arm tattooed, 'Friday I'm In Love,' over a heart!'

'It's official! He's a dork forever!'

'Not The Cure, though, Justin.' I say. 'The Vampire Bats are more like Bauhaus really.'

'Nah,' James argues, 'their too heavy. They're more like Ministry.'

Justin says, 'Nine Inch Nails, but somehow with a bluesy-tinge, which reminds me of The Doors, or The Animals.'

'That's just because of the vocals,' I say.

'Not entirely,' James says, 'there *is* a lot of blues in their sound, but they somehow mash it up with Goth. And the front man sounds exactly like Peter Murphy.

I take the bottle from Justin. 'All I got to say is that their concert reminded me *a lot* of The Dead Weather, but way better.'

'Ooh,' Justin replies, 'that's…kinda cuttin it.'

'This is officially a bullshit conversation!' James blasts. 'They sound like fuckin Joy Division, ok? There, I said it. They sound like Joy Division.'

'Chhhilll, doood,' Justin slurs.

'But as much as I love all this dark shit,' I retort, 'I just can't stand some of the other fans.'

133

'I know what ya mean,' James replies.

'Ya know, these ugly Goth girls who dress slutty just to take the attention away from their unfortunate looks.'

'They look ridiculous,' Justin says.

'And they act just downright *weird!*' I say.

'Dude...'

'I know,' I say, 'WE ARE A BUNCH OF-'

'*HYPOCRITES!*' we all say in unison before bursting into laughter.

'They are some ugly ass bitches though...'

The last drop of whiskey disappears with our sober clarity of the suburban distance. We are indeed outside of those authoritative boundaries wearing the clothing of men, but the clothes don't fit us just yet. We've just thrown back illegally-purchased whiskey in a parked car watching for cops, after all. We didn't exactly sip it from glass tumblers while puffing stogies in the den while reminiscing our youthful days gone by.

We stagger out of the car leaving the empty bottle in the floorboard. 'Dude, get rid of that thing,' Justin demands. 'I don't want evidence in my car.' James crouches to fetch the bottle. He winds up and chucks it down the street. The bottle hit's the tarmac and shatters into a hundred pieces. 'Are ya fucking *crazy?!*' Justin gasps.

'Holy shit!' I screech. 'The cops will come for sure now. We are drunk as shit!'

'We're not drunk, ok, *juschill.*' James slurs. '*Chill...out.*'

'Easy for you say, Cheese Whiz! *You threw* the fuckin thing!'

'Alright, alright,' I say, 'Let's just get to the party before the cops come.'

Justin opens the trunk to unveil a case of Budweiser, another bottle of Jack and a bottle of red wine.

'Who's drinkin wine?' I ask, completely perplexed.

'There was this girl with Donnie when we ran into em at the library,' Justin says.

'Hot, dude. Fuckin hot!' James confirms. 'I couldn't believe a girl like that was even *with* Donnie!' James tucks the case of Bud underneath his arm and shuts the trunk.

'Wait a minute,' I say, 'Donnie was with a *hot girl* at the *library?*' Neither of my friends reply while they swivel their heads for cops. 'What the hell was he doin at the *library?*'

'I guess that was his angle,' Justin says, 'Anyway, she said she drank wine.'

'Hold on a second,' I say, 'what were *you* two doin at the library?'

the party

Donnie's flimsy storm door sways in the wind, crashing shut and creaking open again. Crashing shut and creaking open, I notice that the screen is torn out at the bottom. It squeals as James pulls it open to knock on the main door which is chipped up and shredded around the edges. His knuckles push it open, giving way to a living room even shabbier than mine.

'Hello!' James calls out. We cautiously enter and I smell stale nicotine and fresh hash laced through the musty odour of the neglected premises. We stand in the middle of the living room wondering what to do. *'I Was Killed On CNN'* is muffled, coming from the basement. The bass pulsates beneath our feet. *Yeah, the* bass-*ment, alright.* 'Sounds like The Vampire Bats are everywhere.'

'Party's down stairs, boys!' a girl calls out.

We jerk our heads toward a tall brunette standing in the bathroom doorway. She has bright red streaks dyed through her dark locks. She wears short denim cut-offs and a bikini top with black soccer socks pulled up to her knees. With big dead eyes she smiles, then takes a long hit from a glass bong. A giant of a black guy walks out of the bathroom and throws his grizzly arms around her as he sprinkles her neck with his lips. He also takes a hit as she holds the bong for him. He gazes out at us, holding the smoke in his lungs. He tilts his head up, slides his hands down her long, white legs, and exhales against the low ceiling. 'Wuss up, y'all,' he gurgles.

We nod at them and file down the stairs to the basement. Two more guys we'd never seen sit on the steps while they talk to a husky but very cute blonde wearing a softball uniform from another school. She sucks on a longneck with the label peeled off and flashes us a friendly smile.

'Wuss up,' Justin says.

The two guys stare us down ignorantly until they see we've brought more alcohol. 'Nice!' says the Italian-looking one, still wearing his Raiders jacket in the drafty stairwell, 'Juss takidown day, Dog. Day shooby an open coolah some place!'

'Ya know Donnie?' I ask.

'Hey, you know Donnie!' the Raiders fan replies.

The rock 'n roll explodes from the speakers. This party is live and loud. There's fifty people down here and the three of us are about to take the last bit of space. Some stare at us newcomers while others are too far gone to even take notice. Everyone is drinking, whether it's beer or spirits. And everyone smokes, whether or not they've got a cigarette, stogie or a joint between their fingers, as a thick second-hand plume hangs from the rafters.

We walk across the very dim-lit basement, swerving around the kids and furniture, glad-handing the guys and hugging the girls that we know. Some of these people I've seen around school but have never met. And some of them I've never seen in my life.

Enjoying a good, hard Tennessee buzz, I take it all in. The party feels very lunchtime-in-the-school-cafeteria-and-I'm-looking-for-a-place-to-sit-and-eat-my-burrito-and-fries. But I've never drank a third of a bottle of Jack Daniels before lunchtime at school. Maybe I should sometime, if it's contributing to my

140

extremely rare sense of belonging. Just like at The Vampire Bats. Perhaps alcohol would solve all my problems at school. Right now I feel like I can go up to anyone. Say anything. I feel so *in control. Confident.* I have *courage.* Everything just feels so *right.* It feels so good to be social and *everything* at school is social. Class, tests, lunch, clubs, sports...the time between classes...I want to feel like I do *now* during all of that. Everything would be *different.* Everything would be *better.*

I spot Donnie behind the bar on the far wall that's covered with bottles of assorted liquors and weed. 'Morgan!' he howls, holding his arms over his head like he's just scored. But he's sleepy-eyed, buzzed and blown.

'Bartendin tonight?' I ask.

'When I have to! People wanna get fucked up so I can't serve em fast enough. This is where the *real* party's at anyways so it's all good!'

Justin and James crack open the case of Bud amidst the dope smoking and line snorting. Merely drinking beer suddenly looks very humdrum but we have to start *somewhere*, the night is still so young.

'Lisa! Lisa!' Donnie shouts. I'll be damned if he's not calling that slutty-looking sophomore that rides our bus! She prances toward him letting her short, wavy blonde tresses bounce around that 'fuck-me' face, featuring sharp, thin eyebrows above bright blue, eager eyes, a perfect little nose and full, edible lips. She wants attention and is getting it as she's wearing another one of her trademark hooker-skirts. Who would've thought that the bus slut was also Donnie's wine drinker?

And she shouts, 'There's my mother-fuckin wine! Gimme that shit!' She has a raspy voice that sounds like she's been screaming all day. The combination of her beauty and vulgarity is shockingly entertaining. 'Aw, fuck!' she cries, 'Donnie, where's a corkscrew?'

James says in my ear, 'Well, at least she's *hot*.'

Watching her struggle to pop the cork makes me snicker. Donnie takes the bottle away from her, as if she's a small child, and finishes the job.

'I don't know,' Justin says, 'I kinda like the potty-mouth thing, comin from a pretty face like that.'

Lisa takes the bottle back from Donnie and swigs the wine straight from it, no glass required. The third or fourth swig runs down her chin and neck before she quickly thrusts forward laughing.

'Class. Pure class,' James remarks.

'Who's gonna pay the cleaning bill for that hooker-skirt?' Justin adds.

'So, let me get this straight!' I say, 'Of all the people that came tonight *we* were the only ones that brought wine?'

'Yup!' Donnie replies.

'Couldn't ya have asked someone else to bring wine for yer girl?'

'Nope!'

'Oh! Right!' I say.

Lisa's wine drinking is a sideshow that we can't take our eyes from. Donnie says, 'Thanks for the wine!'

'Don't mention it,' I reply as Donnie throws back a shot of whiskey. 'So, Donnie…'

'Yup?'

'Ya know a girl named Felicity?'

'Yup!'

'She here tonight?' I ask.

'Yup!'

'No shit! Really?'

Donnie replies, 'Nope! Prolly not! Hot blonde though!'

'Red-head,' I say.

'Wanna shot?' Donnie asks.

'Sure.'

The party is in top gear now. Tony jigs down the steps waving a forty-ounce in one hand while balancing a pizza in the other. He gives us a wink and whispers something in a random girl's ear to make her laugh.

'That guy's been a total pussy-mother fucker tonight!' Donnie growls. He explains to me that Tony has let too many people in that didn't belong.

'There *is* a shit load of people here!' I say.

The couple that greeted us up in the living room comes down, still sucking on that bong. Tony takes it from them and takes a deep hit of his own.

'Like that nigger right there!' Donnie says, 'The only reason why he's here is because he brought two things Tony wanted! Weed and pussy!'

'I wouldn't wanna try turning that guy away from *my* party!' I say. 'He's huge!'

'Yer just as much a pussy as Tony is, then!'

'Well, what would ya suggest, then?' I ask.

'Ever heard of a .38?' Donnie lifts his t-shirt to flash the butt of the black pistol sticking up from inside his belt. I've seen guns in display cases. I've seen them being cleaned by hunters. I've seen them on television. I've seen them in magazines. I've seen one mounted on the wall. The *garage* wall. But never have I seen one sticking out of someone's pants at a party.

'Is it loaded?' I ask.

Donnie just laughs at my question and then replies, 'Ya can't *shoot* it if it's not *loaded*. Yer gettun dumb on me, man!'

This game of Show and Tell makes me nervous. Crazy-eyed Donnie's loaded gun plus this party's illegal ingredients are a recipe for disaster.

'C'mon, Ethan, do another shot with me!' Donnie pours two overflowing double-shots of whiskey. 'To school…and that shitty bus!' Donnie toasts, and then knocks it back. 'And to that lesbo carpet-muncher that drives it. Hey, who do ya hate more, man? Gays or niggers?'

'*What*?' I gasp, still with a bottle of beer in hand and a double-shot of whiskey in waiting.

'Well, if I were you I'd hate niggers more.'

'Donnie, why in Hell do ya ask?'

'Shit, those niggers almost killed ya yer freshman year. Remember?' I just sip my beer and ignore him. 'Then again, dude, I'd hate having that fag who rides our bus lookin at me the way I see em lookin at you.'

I can't ignore that. 'What the fuck do ya mean?'

'I'm sayin that faggot prolly *wants* yer ass. Don't worry, Ethan, I know ya ain't like that.' Donnie swipes the shot glass he poured for me and throws *it* back. 'The question is, do *other* people know yer not?' He slams the shot glass down on the bar and walks away saying, 'I beat his ass again yesterday, though. Ya shoulda seen it!'

'Hey, guys!' I yell at Justin and James as they shoot rum on the other end of the bar. I join them and covertly mention the gun. 'We need to get the fuck outta here.'

144

'What?!' Justin replies.

'Where is it?' James asks.

'In his belt.'

'Dude, nothins gonna happen!' Justin replies.

'Yeah,' James says, 'He's crazy enough to have it in his belt but he's not crazy enough to actually use it!'

'Use what?' Lisa asks, very drunk.

'Lisa, gorgeous!' Justin says, 'How are ya, honey! I hear ya ride the bus with Ethan. That makes him a lucky boy.'

'A *very* lucky boy. Hey, Tony's got *pizza!*' she squeals. She struts over to Tony, plopped onto one of the couches with the pizza box closed and in his lap. We watch him and the others smirking with boisterous laughter cocked and ready.

'What do you assholes think this is, *The Wild West?* I say. 'Like havin a gun, a *loaded* fucking gun, is just business as usual?'

'Ethan, don't worry-'

'Hey, guys, Justin alerts, 'Check this out. Over there, Lisa and Tony.'

'Gimme a fuckin piece, dude!' Lisa begs Tony who wears a sly smile. Lisa opens that pizza box to find nothing in it but Tony's penis…sticking out through the hole he'd cut in the bottom!

After the explosion of laughter dissipates Justin turns to me and says, 'Don't worry about the gun.'

I douse my worries of guns, freshman year beat-downs and homophobia with more booze. I drink anything I can get my hands on. Beer, whiskey, rum, Mad Dog, Schnapps, even gin…as my nerves melt away…

145

I…am…so…dumb…so…*numb*…

'Yer life's about to change,' says the woman draped in white, standing behind the bar, alone.

'Who the *fuck* are you?' I scream at her. But she replies with just an intense stare. And ever so slowly her face changes into Ms. Lancashire's…

'Ethan Morgan!' Lancashire squawks, from behind the bar and in front of that whiteboard. And written on that whiteboard, in big, red letters…

SUICIDE

'We're waiting, Mr. Morgan…'

What time is it?

I am *so* drunk. *Too* drunk. The room is spinning. Shadows crawl and demons spit laughter at my obliterated state. The Vampire Bats still croon down from the heavens. Their song *'Murders Of My Heart'* swirls into *'Youth Into Death'*, and there I am, a wasted joke, alone in the hot swinging lamp light. I was a fool to think these people were my true friends. None of these kids would ever save a seat for me in the lunch room. This is just how I feel at Ritenour High School. Everyday. Who *are* these people? I need more to drink...

Donnie shouts with an angry face. His hand caresses his belly and his fingers caress the handle of the gun in his belt. I imagine his loose-fitting white t-shirt stained with his own blood and become nauseas.

Tony looks at me with nervous eyes and a crinkled nose. His mouth drops open before he falls back into the same laughter as the other demons holding hands in the shadows. Together, they devour me, laughing madly all the while. I'm just a sad, loser of a bastard.

Darkness.

Voices...

THROUGH THE WINDSHIELD

                                        ON THE RIVERBANK

                    THE WINDSHIELD

                                          THE RIVERBANK

                    THE WINDSHIELD

THE RIVERBANK

    'Soon, Ethan, amazing and horrible things are going to happen.'

Muddy water sloshes into my ears and nose and burns my eyes.

River water.

Every time I try to breathe I swallow more. I'm being pulled down into it. I'm submerged, floating upside down. I'm waving my arms to no avail, grabbing for anything to save myself. But my hands clutch nothing but pockets of rushing sludge. I can't shift my body or gain any sort of control. The pull strengthens. I'm drowning.

Something's hit the back of my head. It feels like a giant wet marshmallow. Arms attached to a half-dressed female torso floats about. Red hair levitates in the water and dead eyes stare into mine. She's just a floating bag of bones. The girl's face is half gone and her lifeless body is tangled with mine. I feel like I'm holding her there, and she is holding me. She's dead in the water but I believe she will speak, in the new silence, to my new numbness, while I drown with her in my arms.

The hooves thunder down again. Perhaps the woman draped in white storms through the dark woods to show me a sign. To show me something. Anything.

I feel a blow to my head and to my knees and ribs.

My hands are locked into someone else's and I'm lifted from the muddy river.

'He probably got drugged, and he had too much to drink.' Justin tells the police, 'We promise to get him home safe.'

The demons fly away beyond the flashing police lights and the shadows crawl back into the black of the night. The party kids have fled back to their bedroom's safe cocoons, just as I'm now safe in mine. In the peaceful arms of sleep, a hangover from hell and stories I won't remember await in the coming morning.

148

a new school day

'Damn, what in Hell happened to you, man?' the bus driver asks.

The cut on my forehead is still healing and I have a severe limp. James told me everything over the phone yesterday during his sympathy call. Officer Stevens and his gang of deputies gave me a beating when they mistakenly thought a bag of coke and weed were mine. I was in such a drunken and obliterated state that I don't even remember police *raiding* the party, let alone getting beat down. Donnie and some others were arrested and spent the night in jail on misdemeanour drug possession and disturbing the peace. I guess they didn't find the gun.

'Ya'll right?'

'Yeah. Just got hurt playing a little football.'

'I thought ya quit playing football,' she said, 'after what happened.' Three years later the most unlikely of people still remind me.

'Yeah, it was just a pickup game with some friends.'

'Still don't have that car, huh?'

'Um, no. Not yet,' I reply before trying to escape down the aisle.

Cruising through the sunshine she says, 'I hardly ever see

151

ya in the mornin, though. Whatchya do, walk to school?'

I take the seat ten rows back on the left and reply, 'I get a ride from a friend.'

'Good friend!' she laughs jollily and stops at the church. The girlish boy boards. '*Damn*, what in Hell happened to *you*?'

The girlish boy ignores her and shuffles past. He sees me staring at his dilapidated state, just as the rest of the students do. He looks ten times worse than me!

'Shit, *everybody* got their ass kicked *this* weekend!' grunts the driver.

The girlish boy returns my glare as he comes down the aisle. When he gets close to me he whispers, 'Could you-' He's received a severe beating. His right eye is nearly swollen shut and is much more bruised than his banged up *left* eye. He has a fat lip and cat scratches on his chin, jaw line and neck. 'Um, could you, ugh-' he tries to say as the moments stretch out long. As the bus driver peers back at us through the mirror I'm uncertain what to think. He seems incoherent. A little nervous. He still winces in pain.

'What happened, man?' I ask, not knowing what else to say.

'I just, um…yeah.' He stops trying to speak and moves to a seat further back, leaving me in suspense. Then, perhaps the last thing I remember from Donnie's party comes back to me.

'I beat his ass yesterday, though. Ya shoulda seen it!'

I sit up in my seat and scan the back of the bus. I don't see Donnie or Tony and wonder if they're still in jail.

As we get off the bus the other students make loud, rash

152

comments about the girlish boy's appearance, magnifying his every bruise and cut. Despite my condition, his being much worse saves me from any unwanted attention. My slow limp into school allows the girlish boy to catch up with me. As he passes me I ask, 'Hey, are y'alright?' But the girlish boy continues to march toward the school with his head down. 'Don't let Donnie-'

'Just leave me alone! Alright? Just leave me the fuck alone!' He disappears into the rushing crowd of students.

'Hey Morgan,' the asshole from PA who splashed me with his car calls out, 'what happened, did you and yer boyfriend have a lover's spat?' He and his group laugh out loud as they stroll past me.

As much as I just want to carry on with the game plan of keeping my head down, minding my own business and graduating from this place in the spring, I still have the overwhelming urge to *do* something. I'm scared for that kid. Annoyed. Saddened. But what am I going to do about it alone? Nobody cares about kids like him. Kids like me…

I'm early. Taking the bus to school always means killing a little time, alternative to catching a ride with Justin and barely slipping into class before the opening bell. I go to the place that puts the ingredients of Ritenour Society on display as clearly as the shop windows in the Delmar Loop: the Senior Class Parking Lot, one hundred spaces on the west side of the school.

Some cars that fill those spaces are new. Mechanically and environmentally sound. They're of a red shiny hue and Japanese, complete with that new car-smell and most importantly, look cool. These cars are driven by the cutest and most popular girls and boys. Daddy makes sure that daddy's little girl has a top-notch ride that enhances her appearance even more and, most importantly, won't break down in bad neighbourhoods or desolate stretches of interstate. Mama makes sure that mama's big boy has the wheels to pick up those girls and open the gates

153

of debauchery. If they only knew, I enviously say, about the goings on in Ritenour's exclusive Mama's Boy's club. Rooma-zooma-zoom-zoom-and a-boom-boom...

Then there are the projects of junior-mechanics that appear to have survived thermo-nuclear wars. They might look even cooler than that Mama's Boy's car one day, or they might just be Point A to Point B until they keel over and die on the side of the road. These are driven by guys who brag about their rides in metal shop with the latest Car & Driver mag open for reference. Most of these cars are absolute shit and they sound even worse. Let's just say that Ritenour's Facilities Department has Jerry's Towing on speed dial for a reason, the same reason why I don't want to bother with cars until I get enough money saved to buy something dependable.

My story's ironic in that I don't have a car to drive while my father owns a completely restored '71 Corvette Stingray which is faster and meaner than anything on wheels in the county let alone this little parking lot. Oh, what I'd give to be a Mama's Boy this year. Hell, I'd even consider being a Daddy's Girl if it meant getting to drive my father's Vette.

The parking lot is like a tailgate party everyday before and after school. The students just pull up, hang out and exercise their liberties to smoke or go into the gym to shoot baskets. Seniors run this area and underclassmen must know their place. The car-less aren't welcome so I just stand in the doorway of the gymnasium. The students pull into their spaces with manic smiles below ecstatic eyes. Each one is a delicately wrapped soul tied with a pretty bow to blend in with their clique.

And I just watch them all through a faceless head of long, shaggy hair, like a wallflower wondering where I fit in. I don't know how to talk to them while they jump and scream and perform for the audience they either truly have or just pretend to have. So the gymnasium doorway is the safest place for me, just out of the warm sunlight.

154

I'm afraid of my own shadow after the Freshman Year Incident, as reminded by the bus driver this morning. In this doorway my shadow doesn't follow me like it would if I were to step into that sun those car-kids are in. But that sunlight creeps closer to my feet as the opening bell nears. I cringe knowing that it's all I'm doing with this stupid game plan of mine: Keep my head down, mind my own business, ignore the distractions…and just wait for that bell to ring. Al the while I'm loathing popularity. I'm loathing participation. I'm loathing them. I'm loathing *myself.*

Behind me the kids play basketball in the gym. I get the same feeling watching them as I do reading about the football team in the paper. Knowing I'm as good as them makes me want to play again, but not yet. I'm through with sports for now. I'm still getting over the incident. I still have nightmares about what happened three years ago.

Trash-talk raps over the bass of the dribbling basketballs. The squeaky treble of sneakers against the hardwood sounds like a DJ's record-scratching. I compare this Hip Hop track to the Pop song in the senior parking lot overdubbed with motors revving, car doors slamming and abrupt laughter. Out there the kids take their cigarette drags and exhale. The smoke from their lips rises and disappears, just like these moments of my youth. And the ghost that has haunted me since I've attended this high school echoes in my head again…

IN WHITE SHEETS

IN WHITE SHEETS

IN WHITE SHEETS

'How's that head?'

155

'Justin, hey.'

'Whoa! Did I scare ya, dude? Looks like ya just saw a ghost! Did it give you another pair of concert tickets?'

'Very funny. I think my hangover's finally going away. So, tell me again what ya said to the cops to get me the hell out of that party?'

'I just said, 'That shit ain't his, now let us go.' That's all.

'Yeah, I doubt it was that easy.'

'Damn, those cops really kicked yer ass, Ethan.'

'It feels like it. Funny thing is I don't remember any cops laying a finger on me.'

'Oh, they did alright.'

'Hear anything more about Donnie?'

'He got pretty lucky,' Justin replies. 'He was bailed out of jail Sunday morning. All they did was confiscate some very small amounts of pot and give him a court date.'

'And what about the coke?'

'I think it was all snorted.'

'Think he'll do time?'

'Nah, because all he'll say is that his party was crashed and none of it was his,' Justin points out. I think about Donnie's bullying and part of me hopes he *will* do time.

We watch basketball players fly up and down the hardwood. 'Go on, man. Ya know can run with those guys.' Justin says.

'Naw, man, I'm done with all that shit. And even if I wasn't this headache wouldn't let me.'

'How long ya gonna stay scared? Yer as good as they are. So what if they're black.'

I change the subject, 'When did ya get here? I didn't see ya pull up?'

Squinting his eyes through the bright sun he replies, 'Nowhere here to park. No spaces left. Had to park on the God-damned street.'

I say, 'At least you've got a car to park.'

'Oh hell, here we go!' Justin says, rolling his eyes.

'Ya know I hate to rant-'

Justin roars a laugh and says, 'Nah, ya don't hate to rant about it, do ya?' Then he disarms me with a stern look and says, 'Ethan, yer gonna figure the car thing out.'

I mumble about how frustrated I am and I start to describe how things would be so much better for me if I had a car. Justin cuts in, 'Ethan, dude, the best days are yet to come. I get how ya feel. Yer a senior now and the situation yer in leaves ya, well, lamenting and frustrated.'

'*Lamenting*?' I snicker.

'You can get smart if ya want but I'm just tellin ya that there's gonna be better things. I see ya lookin at that court and seethin. I see ya lookin out to that lot and wantin what they have.' Justin steps closer to me and says, 'I see that ya want what *I* have, what ya *think* ya need. Ya don't have what ya *know you want* and *think ya deserve*. Because of all that shit yer not confident. Yer lettin yer fears and frustrations get the better of ya. Yer goin about this thing all wrong, bro!'

'Ya know what man?' I snap, 'I know this place is shit. I think I'm just pissed that…'

Justin steals the pause with, 'Pissed that we have to come to this *prison* every day. That's it! We ain't *prisoners*, man! Yet we gotta come here every day and abide by these rules and conform to these standards.'

157

'It's a prison alright,' I say.

'I mean, these teachers don't care about *us*, man,' Justin adds. 'These counsellors are just gettin paid to go through the motions.' It's good to know Justin feels this way. Deep down he's as frustrated as me. 'I mean, there are things that *I* still want. Things *I* crave. There are things that I'm worried may never happen for *me*.'

'Ya know those movies?' I ask. Ya know those class reunions? Those stories that people tell about their glory days, I get that it's all bullshit. *All* of it.'

'*All* of it!' Justin agrees. 'Our best days are ahead, man. But they ain't gonna happen if ya let this place get to ya.'

The warning bell sounds and the students in the senior parking lot slowly disperse and head for the doors.

I look out toward St. Charles Rock Road and watch the rush hour traffic. All those people eventually got their cars and lives, some good and some bad. Men in suits march toward St. John's Bank. Police scout the Overland neighbourhoods in their cruisers. The gas station attendant sweeps cigarette butts off the blacktop and a bum asks that man with the broom for spare change.

And I enter Ritenour High with the other students. Our whole lives are ahead of us.

The present holds the messages about the future.

The past is just full of ghosts.

Life will haunt you…if you let it.

'I just wish I'd had more fun while I had to be here,' I say.

'Then take this year and change. Let loose. Enjoy it. Save the worryin for *after* we graduate! We're all gonna laugh about high school…someday.'

158

The senior parking lot is empty and the rays of sun flash against the cars. A new school day has begun while the waiting world continues to hustle and bustle around us.

in white sheets

Felicity has dominated my imagination since I first saw her. Anxious to see her again, I waste no time in getting to PA class. I've waited all weekend and my craving for her has a hallucinogenic effect. I navigate through the hallway traffic woozily, past the distorted caricatures of fellow students. Their long, rubbery voices stretch my ears and tickle my drums deep inside. My heart thumps hard and fast through my slow-motion head-trip. The new hallway signs flash in neon…

HOMECOMING 2010

HUYUTAYKIN???

BUY TICKETS NOW!!!

The Homecoming Dance is advertised everywhere.

I take a preparatory deep breath and run my hands through my hair. Saliva is now being produced. My hands have stopped shaking. I turn into the sun-drenched PA classroom and find Felicity sitting in the desk behind mine. She's got her legs crossed, wearing orange soccer shorts and adjusting the lens on her camera. 'Hey, Felicity,' I say coolly.

'Ethan, hey, good weekend?'

'Worked.'

'Damn, yeah, *I* need to get a job. I don't know what, though.'

'Did ya work in Memphis?'

'Yeah, just on weekends at my neighbour's shop.'

'What sort of shop was it?'

'Well, it was really mom-n-poppy. It *was* an electronics store though, with a wide range of supplies. But when I started there two years ago it mainly carried just cameras and film equipment.'

'Which is why yer here?'

'I've always had an interest in photography and cameras, but not like boring photo albums and stuff.'

'Yeah, I realized that there was so much, much more to taking pictures than -'

'Other people's boring photos?' Felicity finishes my sentence.

'Yes, *exactly*!' I smile.

'Photography, photo-journalism, that field I guess, has taken over my imagination for the last few years.'

You've taken over my imagination…

'Are y'alright? She asks.

'Oh, yeah. I was just listenin. Please go on.'

'Right. Well, I became a real geek working at that shop.' She stops and studies my face.

'Yeah?' I watch her eyes slant and her nose crinkle.

164

'What?' I ask.

'Don't take this the wrong way, Ethan, but, well, what *happened* to ya?

'What do ya mean?'

She leans in and whispers, 'Ya look like ya got yer ass kicked.'

'Oh, haha, yeah. It was just...an altercation. At a party I went to.'

'Does it hurt?'

'Yeah, a little.'

'Hey, what's that book?' Felicity points to the one I rescued from the rain. It has somehow crawled into view from the bottom of my bag.

'Oh, it's just a book that I...'

'Ghosts?'

I blush and say nothing as I bend down to zip up the bag.

She adds, '*You* are interested in ghosts?'

'No, not really. I-'

'Why are ya so shy about it? Do ya *believe* in ghosts or not?'

'*There are no such things as ghosts, boowoohoo-hoo-hoo!*' blurts the boy from the next row who victimised me in the drive-by mud-splashing.

His accomplice, his little *sidekick*, chuckles and chimes in, 'Ethan, tell her about the ghosts. C'mon. *You* remember.'

'Yeah, looks like those ghosts got to ya again! What happened to yer face *this* time, Ethan?'

Despite these two being fucking losers they are

165

succeeding in rubbing salt in my wounds. I *do* remember what they're referring to…

IN WHITE SHEETS

IN WHITE SHEETS

IN WHITE SHEETS

Some people still find it hilarious. *Some* people.

And still no one's been blamed. *No* one.

But *everyone* remembers the night I got roughed up. *Everyone*.

Three years ago, on the night of my first school day at Ritenour I was a freshman enjoying the great news I'd received. I'd won one of the starting wide receiver positions on the Varsity Football team. I was scheduled to start the first game the following Friday.

When I walked into camp that summer I was a scrawny fourteen-year-old that had some height and a lot of speed, 'for a white boy'. That 'white boy' shit never used to bother me, despite being one of the few trying out. Hell, maybe being white *did* curse me with an athletic disadvantage. But regardless, when I put the pads and the jersey on I felt like I was just as big, fast, strong and agile as any one else trying out.

Still, the coaches wanted to see how I could throw and kick. And maybe that *was* because I was white. But I just kept running my 4.5 - 40s and sometimes I'd run it in 4.4. I didn't drop a damn thing and when I got hit going across the middle I just popped back up with the pigskin cradled underneath my arm like it was my baby. I never showed them that I felt the pain. I made the quarterback, a senior who signed a letter of intent to Kansas University named Rickey Ramsey, look really pretty by running my routes with perfect precision. He didn't have to throw perfect passes. He knew he could lead me. He could just float it into the open field and just knew I'd get underneath it.

My performance during tryouts should have spoken louder than the colour of my skin. But in St. Louis, in Missouri, in America, at a desegregated-by-law high school in *this town*, it did not.

'That's what it's about, young blood! Y.A.C.! Yards after the catch! We're gonna have some fun *this year, baby!*

'A senior quarterback leading a freshman receiver, a white boy, I'll be damned!'

Once that rare passing chemistry of senior to freshman got instant notoriety, the coaching staff couldn't afford to ignore me as a wide receiver candidate anymore. They had to make an exception that year. I was going to be the first white starting wide-out for Ritenour Varsity since 1981 and the first freshman starter at that position since the seventies.

The day I was named a starter I was worked over like never before. It was 102°F that afternoon and we smouldered on the field. I was riding on the pride of being named a Varsity starter and it got me though the hot day. But even though I'd survived all the cuts I was still getting my helmet cracked. Nobody was going to let me enjoy winning the starting position and everybody craved the taste of my blood. I quickly realised that I was *the* target and it was as if the extreme heat made the linebackers and cornerbacks even more ferocious. They were hitting me harder than ever.

Rickey had a gun for an arm and fired the ball into my chest so hard that he knocked the wind right out of me on a couple of his short-yardage strikes. Coach Osborne barked at me...

'C'mon, Morgan! Ya better toughen up! Ya think this is tough? Wait til game time! This is the Suburban North Conference! Those guys will literally eat *y'up and shit y'out!*

They did anything and everything to shake me up out there. Some players even told me that I was *given* the starting position. At the end of that practice my fourteen-year-old heart had been sunk a bit. Black or white, upper-classman or freshman, cornerback or wide receiver, we all sweat, bruised and bled the same...and I kept telling myself that I hadn't been *given* a damn thing.

But it would be my last football practice. After that day I lost my interest in scholastic sports participation, and I still haven't found it back. Here's why...

All but us wide receivers had been dismissed from the practice field that evening. We were made to do suicides; uphill sprints repeated several times, until the sun dropped below the horizon. The rest of the team had already showered and were thinking about dinner. When our marathon session finally ended that evening I felt that the six of us had developed a solid sense of camaraderie. As we headed into the locker room the rest of the team rumbled past us, headed home reeking of Right Guard and salivating for a meal.

I hit the showers and was surprised to find my naked self the only one standing underneath a nozzle. As the lukewarm water rushed down my aching muscles and splashed against the dingy tiled-floor it occurred to me that the splashing was the only sound, echoing eerily through the empty locker room. Bewildered, and a bit concerned, I hurried to rinse the lather off my body. I just wanted to get towelled and dressed and out the door. Where had the other receivers gone? Where were the coaches? Was I the only one that wanted a shower?

I stepped carefully barefoot across the cold cement floor to my locker. I buried my head in the towel and briskly dried my hair. It was then that a fist cracked me on the head. I fell backwards over the bench and the back of my head crashed against the steel lockers. Stars and purple flashing lights danced around three people. Like trick-or-treating ghosts on Halloween Night, white sheets were draped over their heads and flowed past their knees. Violent, crazy eyes peered from each of their six eyeholes and black skin surrounded their eyes. I lost track of how many times they punched and kicked me, and still they didn't relent. They spit 'Whiteboy', 'Cracker' and 'Honky', laughing maniacally as my blood splattered their sheets. They beat the hell out of me right there on the floor of the boy's locker room until everything faded to black. Before I lost consciousness they told me to quit football and never come back.

I thought I was going to die that night. I'd never been so scared. I woke up in the hospital with three broken ribs, a broken arm and nose. They blackened my eyes and heart and gave me the disposition of a scared rabbit in the cold woods.

I failed to identify anyone and, therefore, couldn't press any charges. I have my suspicions who they were but I've never had he guts to blame anyone. No one was ever arrested despite my being interviewed by police. Coaches knew nothing. Players knew nothing. Life went on at Ritenour but not before I was shamed and humiliated. I quit football and never played again.

And now these two rat bastards sitting in the next row are

169

trying to embarrass me in front of Felicity. But she looks disgusted, even without knowing the story. *Or does she?* It's the first time I've seen her without her million-dollar smile. 'Excuse me, what's yer name?' she asks the boy.

The podgy driver of the mud-slinging Cutlass answers, 'I'm Mike. Mike *Biggio*.'

'Do ya'll believe in ghosts?' Felicity asks them. She has them. The rat bastards are mesmerised.

'I've never seen one so, no, I guess not.'

'Well ya probably ain't lookin hard enough.'

The bell rings and Ms. Lancashire opens class with, 'Good morning. I read your papers over the weekend and I'm afraid that there might be a bit of confusion. I gathered that many of you are just not paying much attention to me or the text book.'

Felicity leans forward and whispers, 'Are we *ever* gonna use any film in this class? She goes on and on!'

'You need to ask for ISO/ASA 125 film,' Ms. Lancashire waffles on. 'It can be used in ninety percent of situations and is ideal for beginners.'

'I'm not a beginner.' Felicity whispers on.

I just smile a victorious smile. Something has happened this morning. She's defended me from those assholes' commentary and now she can't keep her voice, laced with a Southern-drawl and perfumed with mint, out of my ear. 'Lancashire is ridiculous,' she giggles.

Lancashire continues, 'Many of you don't understand that black and white film also needs coloured filters to bring out the best in it.'

'Duh.' Felicity sighs, warming my ear again, just as the bell rings. The students rush the door for the busy hallways between classes.

'Remember, class, your film projects are due Friday! It is an open project! Partner up or go solo! Think of it as a trial run for your later, and hopefully more astute, projects!'

'Oh I get it,' Felicity says, 'she won't care if we turn in a load of shit for this first project. Perfect!'

I can't take it anymore. I stand up, turn to Felicity and ask, 'Will ya be my partner?'

delmar boulevard

St. Louis Metro Bus - To Delmar Boulevard

Felicity and I draw stares and smirks from other passengers. Understood. They see a couple of lilywhite county kids lugging bags of photo equipment on board and wonder why our parents didn't give us a lift. Or they just think we're nuts. We sit together right behind the driver feeling odd and unwelcome.

The bus sucks in the wind through its cracked-open windows. It blows through Felicity's hair and into my face. The cold apple-scented blast gives me goose bumps, then calms me. Ah, it's been her shampoo all this time, never ceasing to smell delicious.

Outside, the sights of St. Charles Rock Road pass behind her and a little daydream flies across my mind...

I'm driving through the desert, eighty miles-an-hour with the top down. There's not a soul in sight for as far as our eyes can see. Nothing but cactus-spotted burnt orange for miles and miles. Plateaus create long shadows in the sun that sets behind purple mountains. The road is wide open and ours.

Felicity is on my passenger side sunk comfortably into the bucket seat. She absorbs that wind with the red sun setting faster behind her. But this is *my car*, not a bus.

'Pull over, Ethan.'

'Is everything alright?'

'Everything is perfect. This is where I want us to be. To live. To stay. Forever and ever.'

I pull over. Two tires on western scrubland and two on tarmac. 'Forever and ever,' I sigh.

She slides over and tangles her legs with mine. She runs her fingers through my hair and looks into my eyes. 'Kiss me.' Our lips connect, passionately, eyes closed, trading sweat and saliva. 'Kiss me in the shadow.'

We make love in the front seat, on the side of the highway, in the middle of the desert. 'Shadow?' I enquire, drunk with fervour.

'Yes, Ethan, kiss me. Kiss me…in the shadow…of a doubt.'

As Sonic Youth's lyrics fall from Felicity's tongue a boy's shadow covers our love, while cold steel presses against the back of my head. I break away from Felicity and look behind me, to the backseat, past the barrel of his shotgun and into his eyes.

My eyes.

I flinch so hard that I kick the back of the driver's seat, who then scolds me through his mirror. *Just another dream.*

'Ethan!' Are ya ok?'

'Sorry.' I apologise to the driver who sneers and hits the gas as the light turns green. 'Yeah, I'm fine.' *Just a little dream.*

As we pull into the Delmar Loop, the buzz of the place reminds me of what I want to capture. Keeping our eyes peeled for photo opportunities we rush off the bus at Kingsland Avenue and walk against the heavy traffic. Under a cream soda sky the perfect amount of sunset pours into the scores of cafes, shops and restaurants that serve food from all over the world.

At Vintage Vinyl an eccentric strums an acoustic and sings about his dead dog. At Fitz's, a group of kids rap and flow freestyle. Incense burns and decants from Sunshine Daydream while tie-dyed people jangle from there to Iron Age to contemplate their next tattoos. Saxophones and bongo drums inspire dancers in front of Blueberry Hill, where Chuck Berry can still be seen one night a month. Flyleaf with Story Of The Year will rock The Pageant *tonight*. Steamy jazz and blues will rise from The Red Carpet Lounge at Brandt's Cafe. Reggae lovers get their positive vibe fix by sinking into the basement of The Red Sea, where Felicity and I will stop for a drink. Unlike most parts of St. Louis, The Loop conforms to no one theme and marches to no one beat. Here, no one style is illegal, but *having no style* is.

Orthodox Jews and Muslims dress to custom on this street of America and receive no glares. Gays and lesbians hold hands on this peculiar branch of a Midwestern tree and blend into the hetero-affectionate majority between the rainbow banners. Police are relaxed in this nook of St. Louis County and accept the festive, hassle-free atmosphere. People of all creeds, colours and cultures converge, and speak in languages other than English.

The Loop is where you go to see, smell, hear, taste and feel something, *anything*, different. It's such a unique shining light for St. Louis that it's misconstrued as just a novelty that seems too good to be true. I hope it stays like this always, as this place is cherished dearly by so many. We're lucky to have it in our backyard, but our backyard should gain more inspiration from it. If more of St. Louis matched the festivity of The Loop, its present day could rival its heyday of 1904. Back then it was America's fourth largest city and hosted The World's Fair. As the ghosts of that time mourn the slow death of the city they built, they still smile upon this strip of Delmar that Felicity and I walk.

We're seated at a sidewalk table outside The Red Sea under a flickering streetlight, just illuminated for the evening. As the headlights of the bustling traffic sparkle in the dusk I'm moved by Felicity being here for the first time, elated to capture this fascination street with her tonight. Instead of ordering from the Ethiopian menu we ask for lattes and listen to the street musicians across the way. We trade flirtatious glances as she calmly smiles and bats her lashes. I grin back and flash a little incisor of my own. In the presence of Felicity The Loop fades behind her, despite all of its glory. She's all I can focus on now The thought crosses my mind that she'll be too distracting for me to actually shoot tonight and put anything worthwhile on Lancashire's desk.

A young African woman serves our lattes on a large silver tray in white porcelain cups and saucers. Felicity unwraps one of the two chocolate mints immediately, giggling while she peels the green foil away. The steam rises between us and floats toward a cook that's stepped out to light a cigarette. He glances our way and then back out to the goings on in The Loop. He purses his lips and inhales, then exhales rings that dissipate into the night. 'You smoke,' I ask.

'No, I, I quit…over the summer. Do you?'

'Of course ya don't. Such a good boy, ya are. You're perfect for her. You'll never burn down your *mama's house.'*

'N-n-no. I…never have.'

'Are ya *sure* yer alright, Ethan?'

Shake it off *man!* 'Don't be silly! Of course I'm alright. I couldn't be better!'

Felicity smiles and raises her cup to her lips, then asks,

178

'Know what yer gonna do?'

I stir some brown sugar into mine and say, 'All of it. And look at this place! I'm bound to get a masterpiece.'

Felicity takes her first sip and says, 'It's a much younger vibe than Beale. It feels more like a circus…a circus without Elvis. Beale doesn't have these cute lil vintage clothing boutiques, though. We gotta come back here and do some shoppin sometime! Whadya say?'

My inspiration is growing fast. I grab a pen and jot on the napkin:

I bought a Neil Young record for ten dollars

And sold it back to Vintage Vinyl for three,

Went to Delmar Lounge for a bottle of beer

And never have I felt so good and so free

It's such a foolish thing to fuck rock 'n roll

But there and then it was such a perfect crime

Just another teen living for here and now

Just another victim of the modern time

We finish our lattes and continue eastbound toward The Tivoli Theater. Along the way we traipse over the bronzed stars of the St. Louis Walk of Fame that honour the likes of Ike Turner, Vincent Price, Miles Davis and Bob Costas. From here the photographic possibilities seem endless from Big Bend's multi-million dollar mansions to the ghettos beyond Goodfellow Boulevard, all within a mile of street.

The streetlights are burning bright against the darkening

179

dusk. 'Felicity, I think we're runnin outta light.'

'Don't worry. I know some ways we can shoot with even less light than we have even now. After all, *I'll* be shootin in the dark.' Felicity finds the filter and says, 'Here, yer gonna need this.'

'Yes, this'll make *all* the difference!' I set my old mechanically driven camera to the slowest shutter speed of one second which I believe is necessary in the fading light. I think I can overcome the lack of shutter speed with the bulb setting. I adjust the shutter dial to *B* and take a final hard look at the bustling boulevard before shooting. It looks gorgeous underneath the crimson glow of the sunset, speckled with early stars. 'Felicity, say cheese!' Felicity poses, flashing a coy smile. Her green eyes sparkle right on cue, just before the camera flashes.

We continue our hike toward the cemetery through The Loop's east end, between Eastgate and Skinker. 'So, all this talk about cemeteries reminds me of that question I asked ya.'

'Question?'

'Yeah. *Do you* believe in ghosts?' Felicity asks.

'Oh, yeah. *Of course* I do.'

'Good. I'm glad,' she grins.

'I mean, I've never really seen one. I've never had anyone close to me die. I imagine that's why.'

'Yeah, that's *one* reason why,' she says.

'Wow!'

'What?'

'I just can't believe just how confident ya seem about ghosts.'

The Vampire Bats' *'Marilyn'* blares from a Range Rover that speeds past us, and then abruptly slows. A cop hiding in

Shell's parking lot flicks on his cruiser's whoopee lights. The rainbow of colours decorates the service station like a disco as the officer tears away in hot pursuit of the speeder.

'Does that happen a lot?' Felicity asks.

'Not so much here in The Loop, but I see shit like that happen every day in North County.'

'Speed traps?'

'That's how little suburbs can make their money.' I say, 'Although ya don't have to be speedin. You can also have yer speakers up too loud like him, Vampire Bats or not.'

'Shit like that happens *all over* Memphis. A lot of bored cops where I used to live, too.'

'Ever get pulled over?' I ask.

'Yeah, once.'

'Just *once*.'

'I was fourteen. Never drove since.'

'*What*? *Fourteen?*'

Felicity smirks, 'The cops weren't the only bored ones. Damn, I must have been *so bored* that night, goodness gracious! I did a stupid thing, man! My mama went to bed early and then my friends called me about a party on the other side of town. The only way to get there, ya see, was to just take my mama's keys and go.'

'Just take yer mom's keys and...*just go?*'

'Yep. And I just went.'

'Weren't ya aware that ya couldn't legally drive until you were sixteen?'

'Yep, I was aware of that.'

'Weren't ya scared?'

'Damn right I was! I knew if Mama found out she'd skin my hide! Cuz they were drinkin over there and that.'

'No, I mean about drivin at fourteen.'

'Nah, my daddy used to let me drive round his place in Mississippi all the time. Nothin to it. But I was stopped that unfortunate night and there was a lot of trouble. I don't know the first thing about gettin my licence now. Lots of legal repercussions. The penalties and all that prevented me from gettin it when I turned sixteen.'

'Damn, not many seniors at Ritenour without their licence.'

'I don't have a car anyway so it doesn't really matter.'

'I don't either. Yet.' Our pace slows as we walk past the cop writing a ticket. The 'disco inferno' draws an audience and passing drivers slow up to get a good look, subsequently backing up traffic even more. I sneer, 'I *never* would've done anything like taking a car without permission. My dad would *kill* me.' *Unless I kill him or* myself *first.*

Felicity replies, 'That wasn't the worst thing I ever did.'

182

the cemetery

Felicity and I lug our equipment through the forest, hiking along a paved pathway branching from the boulevard. By day this is a popular route for a leisurely stroll, especially to participate in a very popular seasonal activity: Admiring Fall Colours. And this serene woodland that surrounds the cemetery is one of the most underrated places in all of St. Louis to do so. But at night the cold, dark spirit of the season is strong and palpable and reminds me that this path leads us to the dead.

The cemetery, a grid of gravestones behind an old church, is on the other side of these woods. The sun is down and it's very dark under these tall oak trees. I gulp and ask, 'Am I getting too personal by asking what that might have been?'

'What *what* might've been?'

'The worst thing ya ever did.'

Felicity does not smile or frown. Silence follows and the moment passes before she replies, 'We must be getting pretty close.'

'Yeah, there's the steeple' I say, just going with it, trying to deflect the awkward moment. 'Not too far now.'

'Thanks for comin here with me, Ethan. It's prolly not smart for a girl to come round here at night alone.'

'It's prolly not smart for *anyone* to come round here at night alone. But, we'll be fine, together.' I remember the cemetery well and am very surprised Felicity chose it. 'I think yer right about shootin here,' I say. 'It's a great idea for a project.'

'Thanks.'

'By the way, how did ya know it was here?'

'Know *who* was here?'

'Haha, not *who*,' I say, '*but what*. Ya know. The *cemetery*.'

'Well, ain't there cemeteries everywhere?'

'I guess. Just funny that ya chose this one.'

Felicity's face goes white. 'Why do ya say *that*?'

'Well, I've been here before.'

'Ya *have*?' Felicity's natural colour has returned, but still she seems overly concerned. 'Was it a funeral?'

'No. Nothin like that,' I reply. 'But I guess that would've been the most appropriate reason. Some old friends and I, three summers ago, sort of introduced ourselves to *adolescence* here.' Felicity stops biting her lip, and I continue, 'It was a group of us. We were tight growing up, through Elementary and Middle school. I've lost track of them all but I'll always remember what we got up to.'

'Which was?' Felicity looks enthused and what a trooper! Gleaming with curiosity, she's not letting the weight of her equipment bag drag her down.

'We'd hang out around the gravestones. I never inhaled, but I drank.'

'There were girls there weren't there?'

'Yes, there were girls.'

'Wow! You and Bill Clinton have so much in common!'

186

This ignites my explosive laughter. I drop my bag and walk off the path, letting every last giggle out. I return to Felicity, pressing my thumb into the side of my index finger, saying, 'I...never...inhaled!' in my best acid-refluxed former president's voice.

'Hey, that's pretty good!' she laughs. 'Or, how about, 'I did not...have...sexual...relations...with...*that woman!*''

'Awesome!' I laugh.

'And...did *you*, like Mr. Clinton, get lucky?' she asks.

'What?'

'Honest question. A good-lookin guy like you. How old were ya?'

I laugh, '*Fourteen!* Bucky Beaver with acne setting in! So, yeah, I guess I *did* get lucky! I made out with a few girls before they realised how ugly and revolting I was. Before I got *sick* behind one of these trees!' *Wow,* she *thinks* I'm *good-looking!*

'Oh, I bet that tasted good!' Felicity laughs.

'I was still learning to *drink* as well as kiss.'

'And how was the makin out?'

Definitely not as good as it would be with you, Felicity. 'At the time it was great. But lookin back, it kinda sucked. I wasn't very good and they weren't much better. Lotsa confused tongues.'

Felicity laughs and says, 'Well, I bet yer pretty good at it by now.' Her words make me shiver, horny. Unexpected and therefore hot as Hell. *Wanna try me, baby?* 'Yeah, fourteen's young.' she proclaims. 'Fourteen's tough.'

'Yeah, which is why I had to lie to my Mom about spending the night at Justin's. We'd only come here at night and I had a curfew.'

187

'Didn't we all.'

'The graveyard inspired our fourteen-year-old imaginations to get the better of us, too. *Especially* at night. We heard bizarre sounds and saw shadows of the dead. Spooked the shit out of us! The last time I ever came these undertakers chased us out with shovels.'

'*Yer kidding!*'

'Nope. I never came back.

'Til tonight,' she says.

'Til tonight. Good times. Good friends. Ha, so good I don't even know em anymore.'

'See, ya gotta get on Facebook, Ethan.'

'Yeah. I guess. But ya know, in a way I regret it all,' I say.

'Why do ya say that?'

'Well, ya might think I'm crazy, but I think we disrespected the dead back then. Those sounds. Those shadows. Sometimes I believe that the dead were-'

'Of course yer not crazy! Ethan, yer right. I realise you were just fourteen and, trust me; I did something that makes your graveyard adventures look *angelic*. But, a graveyard...a cemetery is hallowed ground. What's buried six feet underneath it should be-'

'*Respected.*' We say in unison. 'Seems we agree on all that.' I say. 'So, about what ya did that made our graveyarding look angelic? Were ya fourteen, like me? Like when ya stole yer mom's car?'

'Um, no. Seventeen.'

'Wow, pretty recent, then.' I point out.

'Yeah. It happened over the summer.'

188

I stop and ask, 'Was this *the worst thing ya ever did*?'

Felicity drops her bag underneath a huge oak tree. She looks like an angel underneath the bright fire of leaves about to fall to the cemetery ground. She looks me in the eyes and with genuine sincerity says, 'I want ya to know, but this isn't a good time.'

'Felicity, it's no problem. I'm sorry to-'

'Don't apologise. Let's just get this project done, shall we?'

'Felicity, I don't look at this night like a-'

'Project, no, I don't either. I like ya, Ethan. I'm enjoying it.' *But Felicity, I* really more than *like you.*

The church, Gothic and made of stone, makes me shiver *and* smile. I'm even more excited to bring Felicity *here* than The Loop and nervous to be with her here alone. Being here with her has made all of those other cemetery memories seem dumb.

Despite the romantic ingredient of this night, the University City police are still wise to teenagers being here at night, lax or not. They have an agenda to prevent sex, underage drinking and other forms of witchcraft at such a place. School project or not, trespassing here isn't taken lightly.

The further into the forest we hike the darker the realm becomes. Felicity's mouth has flattened again and her eyes shift instead of shine. She's even more stone-faced and silent now than before my recalling my graveyard days. As we move into even a darker darkness I sense that something's truly wrong. Maybe she's just nervous or scared about being in such a strange dark place, but I believe my stupid prying into her personal life has sparked something. 'It's not too dark for ya, is it?' I ask to re-break the ice.

Felicity chuckles, 'No, not quite.' It's good to hear her

189

laugh again, even if it's not genuine.

'No locusts. Do ya hear any?'

'No. I guess they're gone now.'

'Til next summer.'

'Yeah, next summer.' she sighs.

'So, tell me some of the steps you'll take in getting these shots in the dark.'

'Well, there are several but they're all pretty simple. I'm gonna use some special effects.'

'Special effects?'

'Yeah, you'll see.'

Behold the gravestones that mark the burial places of hundreds of the departed. Some are tall and rounded while others are short and square. Some are grand and made of smooth marble while others are just shabby stone slabs as tall as the grass. Some are new, set at perfect ninety-degree angles to the ground while others are crooked from setting here for over a century.

'I guess there will be much longer exposure times,' I say. Felicity's voice quivers, 'Yeah, since its dark we don't have to worry about the sky washin out.' She stops and heaves her bag to hang more comfortably from her shoulder. 'So, this is it,' she sighs.

'Yep, this is it.'

'Just not how I remember-' Felicity is interrupted by the hoot of an owl. We look up to see its radiant white feathers against the night sky. It dives and perches a lower branch of a towering oak skeleton.

'Felicity, c'mon! Are ya alright? You can tell me.'

'Ethan, please. I'm fine. Really.'

But Felicity's actions speak louder than her words. My thrill of being here with her has been compromised by her strange behaviour.

I drop my bag and turn in place, taking in a 360 degree-view. I can still hear those *other* sounds even after all this time I've stayed away. Just as bizarre as always, they still raise the hair on the back of my neck. And the shadows still dance in the corners of my eyes, so I rub them hard and just focus on Felicity. She's such a vixen-in-the-wild in this place, calming my overactive imagination. I watch her scan the gravestones and detect her fascination with the names and dates engraved. I look upon them myself and become just as engrossed. Who *were* the ones buried here? What did they accomplish during their time on Earth? Some lived for over one hundred years and others died when they were just teenagers.

*

IN LOVING MEMORY

JULIET LINDLEY

BORN MARCH 26, 1893

DIED APRIL 24, 1993

*

*

REST IN PEACE

JEREMIAH JACOBS

BORN SEPTEMBER 30, 1940

DIED OCTOBER 12, 1957

*

Why did some live so long and others die so young?

'*So, are ya gonna help me or just stand there like a statue?*'

'Yes, Felicity, I'm here to help.' I reply. But she looks at me like I've got three heads.

'Ok?' she replies, 'Why did ya just say that?'

'*Why do ya keep callin me Felicity?*'

Marilyn. She's not Marilyn, Ethan, she's Felicity. Now screw that head on straight and get real before you ruin this! 'Just sayin, let me know what ya need me to do…and I'll do it.'

'Ok,' Felicity says, 'then I need ya to get the flashgun out of my bag, please. I'm gonna take a look around.' She breaks away from me and continues stalking the gravestones. With her fox-eyes open wide in the darkness her pace quickens. She stops and spins to her left. She darts to her right. She slows up. She dashes further away.

I shake the cobwebs, and Marilyn's voice, from my head and grab the flashgun. 'Felicity, here ya…'

As I look up I see that she's fallen to her knees. Across the darkness she sits on her heels with her arms limp to her sides. Her back is hunched and her head hangs down. Her red hair dances in the breeze. She looks so sombre as she kneels before a short, broad headstone. As I hurry to her she stands up and turns my way, seeping the most melancholy face I've ever seen.

'Felicity!' She rushes toward me, head down. 'Felicity!' I

192

cry out again, but she whisks right past me. 'Felicity, what's the matter?'

She heaves her bag over her shoulder and says, 'I'm sorry. I gotta go, man.'

'Felicity, come back! Don't walk away from me! Ya can't go home alone! Not around here!' But she can. And she does, as she retreats through the dark forest toward Delmar Blvd.

I lunge after her but I trip and fall hard. My hands and knees drive into the moist ground. My chin follows and my teeth chomp together. I smell the mud smeared all over my shirt and face. I grunt and look up but Felicity has vanished, leaving me behind on the cold ground.

And with every passing moment I see and hear more and more of when I was fourteen. Now I can swear, on any of these graves or my grandmother's, that someone is right behind me, above me. And as my shadow in the bright fire light has been joined by another I know that I am right. It's someone, or something…perhaps a demon floating just over my head, looking down upon me.

Smoke suddenly begins to rise from the church and fill the graveyard before giving way to violent flames. The church is burning before my eyes! But as the flames consume the grand old cathedral I whip my head around to find that no one else is here. And as the sky is being smudged with smoke, the shadow, the presence, the man, the beast…the *demon*…slinks around my body and holds me in its huge claws. Now I'm certain that the flames scorching this church are from the pyres of Hell.

The short, broad headstone that brought Felicity to her knees glows a vivid emerald green. Incandescent rays shine from it through the smoke and flames infesting the graveyard.

Scattered voices ricochet around…

193

SHE WANTED A CIGARETTE

WANTED A CIGARETTE

WANTED A CIGARETTE

The voices swerve in from the left and swirl around from the right, ranging from soprano to baritone. Cryptically, they croon on…

SHE DIED IN A FIRE

IN A FIRE

IN A FIRE

I freeze as a ghost passes right through me! It screams through my neck and out of my mouth, in its own voice…

PLEASE HELP ME!

HELP ME!

HELP ME!

It's such a shrilling voice of sudden death, as if it belongs to the soul of someone being murdered.

The flames from the church shed flickering light on my three-walled room that stands just on my other side. Felicity sits on my bed wearing a gorgeous emerald green dress that shines in the same tinge and radiance as her eyes. The dress contours around her shape snugly. The spaghetti straps hang on her sculpted shoulders while the length drapes the floor. In the flickering fire light her skin looks snow white. She reclines and

194

takes a long drag of a cigarette, watching the church burn down behind me. Donning a Mona Lisa smile, she's calm and numb to it all. And her lips move…

'Like shards of fire burnin ya slowly inside, all the way to yer heart.'

From afar, Felicity's words are somehow whispered from her lips to my ears.

A horse cries out and blasts through the flaming church…and driven by the woman draped in white. *This can't be happening!*

But it is, Ethan. Just like that presence. That man. That beast. That demon…behind you…poking the back of your head with the barrel of his shotgun. You can see his shadow, Ethan, cast in the firelight.

Just like that boy…

'Why, Dad?' the boy asks, *'Why?'*

'Ethan, wake up.' I wake to a familiar and loving voice. 'Ethan, wake up. Are ya ok?' Gone are the sights of glowing gravestones, burning churches and flying horses. So is the boy and his shotgun. My eyes rest upon Felicity's beautiful face and wishful eyes. 'Ethan, what in God's name are ya doin'!'

Night birds sing as I lay on a bed of fallen leaves. The breeze is soothing; Octobers in St. Louis are beautiful.

patio showdown

'I woke up in the graveyard and there she was! I thought she left me behind!' I grip my cell phone tighter. 'No horse, no woman draped in white, no glowin headstones and the church was perfectly fine.'

'Some dream *that* was, dude,' Justin replies.

'If it *was* a dream.'

'Huh?'

'Not so sure that it was,' I say, 'It was just fucked up, the way it all seemed so real. The way it was happenin all around me. I want answers, Justin. Answers.'

'If you've been blackin out then ya need to see a doctor.' Justin says. 'What else happened?'

'I'll tell ya all about it when ya get here with that case of Bud.'

'Cool, but I don't need a case of Bud to tell ya that ya just fainted and had a bad dream. A burnin church would've made the local news.'

'Gee, thanks.'

'Seriously, dude.'

'I guess yer right, man.'

'That's what friends are for. I'm out.'

'Wait. Make sure ya bring the new stylus cuz mine's shot. I ain't gonna be blamed for yer records gettin screwed up.'

'No problem. I was at Vintage Vinyl last week. Picked up a stylus along with some new LPs. I'll bring em over.'

'Come in through the back door. I don't want ya to wake my mom.'

'What about yer dad?'

'Don't worry bout that bastard. He's doin the garage-thing again tonight.'

'Ha, yeah I remember.'

'Yeah, he won't know what *year* it is, let alone hear ya arrive.'

'Cool. Oh, and by the way, dude, why didn't ya tell me that ya met Felicity at The Vampire Bats show?'

'I didn't tell ya that?'

'No. Why not?'

'Well, I didn't actually *meet* her there. I just-'

'Look, spare me the details, Ethan. The fact is that she's in my trig class…and she really likes ya.' Justin hangs up.

I think he just said that Felicity likes me and that she's in his trig class. Or did he say Felicity likes me *because* she's in his trig class? Maybe he meant that because she's in his trig class she *admitted* that she likes me? What if she did say that she likes me but only to be *nice* in knowing that Justin is my best friend? What if she meant that she liked me as just a *friend*? What if she didn't say it at all and Justin's just blowing smoke up my ass so that I'll get the balls up to ask her to Homecoming? *What if she…*

The *landline* rings in my room. My obsessing has been

interrupted by Justin calling back. *Shit! It's after ten o'clock!* Why didn't he just call my cell at this hour? My dad's going to be pissed for sure! I quickly answer it before Dad can pick up the garage extension. I flip down the speakers and bark, 'Justin, are ya *crazy?*'

'Um, *Ethan*?' a girl's voice replies. 'Hello, *Ethan...*?'

'Yeah, who's this?'

'Ethan, it's *Felicity. Felicity Farmer,* from-'

From the concert. From PA class. From my dreams. '*Felicity,* yeah, hey!' I cry.

'I hope ya don't mind, I looked ya up in the phone book.'

And you *looked* me *up in the phone book!* 'Really? I mean, no, of course I don't mind. Wow, what's up?' I ask.

'Well, funny thing, I'm usually in bed by this time. I know, I know, I'm *so* boring.'

'No, don't say *that*!'

'Well, what time do *you* fall asleep usually?' she asks.

'I'd worry ya if I answered that!'

Girls of my past would look down upon from a mountain top. They wanted to know what I was selling. I'd put on a character fuelled by my nerves until I had to throw up. Just being *me* never felt good enough, until Felicity. Maybe it's because of last night in the graveyard. Perhaps it's because of what Justin told me just minutes ago. Possibly it's because she picked up the phone tonight and called *me*. Felicity makes me feel...just awesome, while I devour her sweet brogue through telephone wires.

Our conversation is effortless small talk, but it's anything but small to me. For the first time in my life I'm at ease and speak confidently to a girl that I really like, instead of feeling nauseas. Except, I don't merely *really like* Felicity. I'm afraid it's far beyond that. She lives in a two-story house inside me. Sometimes she's upstairs in my head. Other times she's downstairs in my heart. I don't want her to leave and I hope she never does. Why do I feel this way so soon?

'So, ya gotta turntable?' she asks.

'Yeah, my grandma left it to me when she passed. I only got it because when I was a little kid she used to play her old records and I would dance for the whole family. I guess she got a kick out of it.'

Felicity laughs and says, 'I used to have a turntable.'

'Not anymore?' I ask.

'Nah. But, anyhow, we had a *truckload* of vinyl. My daddy was very particular about his collection! We had this walk-in closet and it was exclusively for record storage. He built shelves and alphabetised em. I'd say he had a couple thousand! Anyway, when he split and bought that farm he left em all behind.'

'Left em behind? What, he never came back for em?'

'Well, he prolly would've but-'

'Where are those records now?' I ask, but Felicity remains silent. Only her steady breathing in reply. 'Felicity, are ya there?'

'Yeah, I'm here.'

'Oh, good. Are ya ok?' I ask.

'Yeah, fine. I just saw something strange in one of my photos.'

'Photos? Ya mean the cemetery photos?'

'Yeah. I bathed them after school.'

'Oh, I don't remember ya shootin.'

'Yeah, of course I did.'

'Oh. Awesome. I can't wait to see them.' *And they just might contain the answers I want.* 'Hey, hold on a minute. Something's goin on outside.' I put the phone down and walk to the rear window. Through the panes I watch two shadows move on the patio. My father yells. Justin replies.

'Felicity, I'm sorry, but I gotta go. I'll see ya tomorrow, ok?'

'Ethan, is everything alright?'

'Don't worry. I'll call ya.' I reluctantly hang up on her and dash through the house to the back door. I fling it open and shout, 'Dad, stop!'

Neighbourhood dogs bark along with Charlie and Jim Morrison howls, *'It's all over for the unknown soldier,'* from the Corvette's speakers in the garage. Justin is standing against the back wall of the house, hands up, mouth wide open, a case of Bud and a couple of vinyl records rest at his feet. My dad's got that twelve-gauge pointed at his chest.

'Call the police, son!' my father shouts. He has that crazy look in his eyes and a wobbly stance. He's drunk again and fired up. I'm mortified! *Is the gun loaded?* As my father's finger twitches against that trigger I watch a tragedy about spill all over the back of the house.

'Dad, put the gun down, man!' The macabre possibility flashes in my mind and jerk tears from my eyes. 'Charlie, stay *in* here!' I shout. Maintaining my death-grip on his collar, Charlie's barking has been reduced to desperate gasps.

'Call the God-damned cops, now!' my father cries again. Suddenly he calms down and eerily staggers a bit. He jabbers, 'Nah, to Hell with the police, I've got this under control!'

'Dad, that's *Justin*!' I cry out, 'My *friend*, Justin, from

203

school!'

'Please, Mr. Morgan,' Justin judders, 'I'm just visiting. Just wanted to listen to some records with yer son.' I've never seen someone *that* scared before, but perhaps I should've looked in the mirror. My entire body shakes and all I can do is *watch and pray*.

My worst fear keeps playing out during these waning, helpless moments. Somewhere in the distance, as if projected onto the darkness of our backyard, there's a split screen of what's *actually happening* and what I *pray will not:* Justin's guts spraying all over the white siding of our house while the vinyl records and case of Bud float away in the pool of his blood. And from beyond that split screen the woman draped in white approaches me. Her gown drags the grass as she walks right through those gruesome images:

My father holding a smoking shotgun.

Justin's slug-sprayed dead body in a pool of blood on our patio.

The white siding on the back of our house dripping red.

My mother's death-shriek.

My father's vacant eyes.

My knees crashing against the back porch as shock melts my face.

She stops where the lawn meets the cement. No one else can see her nor hears her say, 'Are ya ready, Ethan? Are ya ready for all of this?'

'Please make him stop!' I scream, but not to my mom, or to God. I was pleading to this mysterious woman who speaks in riddles. And she replies to me with another.

'Life will haunt you, so never stop believing…as she will give you hope.'

'Please, stop him!' I cry out, but the woman draped in white has disappeared.

'No one's gonna stop *me*, boy!' Dad proclaims.

Trouncing from behind me, my mother wears just her dressing gown and shouts, 'Robert, put that gun down now, ya sick fucking maniac!'

'Melinda, do ya know who in Hell this is? This *intruder?*'

'Mr. Morgan, I'm sorry!' Justin cries. 'Yer son told me to come in through the back so I wouldn't wake Mrs. Morgan.'

'Dad, it's alright,' I try to say more calmly. 'We were just gonna listen to some records in my room.' But my emotion gets the best of me and I join Justin in snivelling. The possibility of my drunken father pulling the trigger seems so real!

'We went over this, Robert! Mom shouts at Dad. 'We went over this!' Mom went over this with me, too. The war, the booze, the car…and right here, right now there's a patio showdown between The Man Dad Used To Be and The Man I Hate.

The Man I Hate is holding the shotgun…

But dad slowly lowers it to his side and stumbles back a step. 'Doesn't a man have the right to protect his home and his family? It's after ten o'clock on a weeknight! I got some fuckin punk trespassin on my premises!

I want to claim again that Justin is my best friend. I want to tell my dad just how drunk and pathetic he is. But he's still got that gun in his hand, albeit lowered. So I just bite my tongue and keep praying. *Please, God. Please…*

'I've maybe met ya, what, twice, ever?' Dad retorts. 'It's dark out here and I can't see who y'are. What if I would've shot ya, boy? Then what?'

'Boys, come on in and listen to yer records.' Mom says. 'And don't worry about me. I sleep like a rock.'

205

But Justin doesn't move. He just keeps his eyes on the man with the gun.

'Justin, come on in, man, it's fine,' I tell him.

Justin snivels, 'No. I'm leaving. I'm sorry, Mr. Morgan. I shouldn't have come over so late. I'll see my way out.' Justin breaks free from his paralysis and darts through the open gate. He disappears down the dark driveway to his Firebird and speeds off into the suburban night.

'To Hell with him,' Dad growls and slams the garage door behind him, muffling Jim's voice. *'Music is your only friend...until the end...'*

'Y'all right, son?' Mom asks.

'Yeah. You?'

'I'm fine. It's late, though. Maybe ya should just get some sleep.'

'Sure, Mom. Sure.' Mom turns to retreat to bed and upon doing so slouches over and falls into the kitchen counter. She grabs the edge as her knees buckle. 'Mom! What's wrong?!'

'Ha, I'm fine, Ethan. Just lost my balance is all.'

'Here, take my arm. I'll walk ya to bed.'

I walk her across the kitchen and down the hall to her room. 'I'm just really tired,' she says. 'I'll be fine.'

'Ya work too hard, Mom.'

The October wind blows fallen leaves across the patio that, for five minutes, had all the makings of a crime scene. Charlie rushes out to inspect and the other dogs are silent. The nights are getting so cold.

206

special effects

Friday, October 8

<click-clack, click-clack, click-clack>

Black Mary Janes sashay into PA class. They're attached to a sexy pair of gams encased in black tights, extending from a short black tennis skirt. Felicity removes her jacket to unveil her blazing little red v-neck sweater. She looks more fantastic today than ever, but also eerily familiar.

'Pretty name n'all, but my name's Marilyn.'

'Ethan, ya don't look very happy to see me,' Felicity says. *These blasted voices in my head. C'mon Ethan, get it together!*

I press my SMILE button and hope it looks real. 'Do I finally get to see?' I ask. She looks so much like Marilyn.

'Hmm, well, only if ya can keep a secret.'

The eyes of the other students ogle in our direction. I glance back at Felicity who smiles and says, 'Now do ya understand why I'm bein so discreet?'

'I think they're starin at yer legs.' I reply.

'The girls, too?'

209

I've been waiting for this moment all week. The folder protecting her cemetery photos rests between us. Inside are the answers I want, at last. Her smile disappears and she burns her gaze right into my eyes, 'Promise me that you'll stay quiet about these.'

'I don't understand,' I reply. 'They'll be displayed anyway. Everyone will see them eventually.'

'Sorry, Ethan, ya *don't* understand.' She scans the room carefully before opening the portfolio. 'Let me show ya.' she sighs, 'and please don't say a word.'

'Not a word,' I promise. She carefully pulls the photos from the sleeves. 'Ya have so many,' I say as I reach for the top of the stack.

'No, not that one!' Felicity cries, grabbing my hand.

I cast my eyes upon it and gasp, 'What *is* that?'

'Uh, those are special effects,' she claims, letting my hand go. *Those are some pretty wild special effects, Felicity. What planet did you develop this on?* 'Ya weren't supposed to...'

'I wasn't supposed to what?'

'Nothin, Ethan. Nothin, it's just-'

'Felicity, I'm sorry. I didn't mean to-'

'Ethan don't worry,' she insists. She smiles and caresses my hand.

'I've got the photos here to prove it.'

I'm a novice photographer with intermediate knowledge of what special effects can be accomplished with the equipment we used. I consider that Felicity is more advanced than I am. But

210

still I'm taken aback by how closely the images in the photograph match the unbelievable visions I experienced in the graveyard.

I rub my eyes.

'Do ya see what I'm sayin now?' she asks. It's a very dark shot, dominated by the shadows, but all the visible objects glow in a variety of colours. The church blushes orange and red, like it was on fire, but the flames and smoke are smeared.

What I think is the glowing headstone is just a neon smudge, as if someone smashed a firefly and wiped it. Even though someone else would never think it was a headstone, it's exactly where the headstone that brought Felicity to her knees was located.

There's a white and orange surge that at first glance looks like the tail of a comet. But from another angle I believe that this 'light' is actually coming from the church. My eyes adjust and I'm shocked to see how much this 'comet' looks like the woman draped in white riding upon her horse! Perhaps they *are* blasting majestically through the burning church, just as I 'dreamed'. *Justin, you've got to see this, man.* The brightest light marks the horse's eyes and hooves and outlines its magnificent ebony frame against the darkness, just as it does the rider's wispy shape. It's as if I never 'blacked out' at all and 'my dream' actually took place! I just can't believe what I'm looking at! How can it be?

'So what do ya think?' she asks.

I run my hands through my hair and stare down at this unbelievable photo through eyes that feel larger than saucers! I want to speak my mind and tell Felicity what I saw Monday night at the cemetery. I want to find out what she actually saw or knows. I want her to know my secret and I want to know hers. But I can't eliminate the possibility that this photo is truly a product of special effects and, most importantly, her talent. I can't risk offending her or sounding insane. *But am I?* Still, I'm freaked out.

211

'Ethan. Hey, boy! Well?'

I'm not prepared to answer and stutter and mumble a bunch of gibberish.

'Sorry, *what*?' Felicity pries as her smile fades.

I save face and exclaim, 'They're awesome! Fucking awesome! *Way* better than mine!'

She giggles at my reaction. Luckily I sounded authentic. 'No, Ethan, don't say that.' She snatches my folder right out of my hand and sets her eyes on my Loop shots. 'Not bad. Not bad at all, boy. Very nice! I knew these would turn out well!'

'Well, I didn't mess with any alternate techniques in the processing. I played it by the book. Boring but solid. No special effects.' That was just nervous chatter as I'm too shaken up to genuinely acknowledge her praise. I gulp and ask, 'So, how did ya get all those crazy glowin effects? Did ya do anything funky in the dark room?'

'I think I can show ya a lot easier than describin it. I mean, I don't know, perhaps maybe one day if ya feel like it I could show ya how it's done.' She gazes even deeper into my eyes and whispers, 'Think we could sometime?'

Felicity again has put me at ease and jolted my heart again. I focus on her hand holding mine and absorb her warm touch. An electric current runs through our interlocking fingers. I know that we both feel that there's something here, between us. It's something that we share. It's something that dwarfs my worry about the night in the cemetery. I return her gaze and say, 'Definitely. I'd love to.' I look back at her photo and say, 'I can't wait to see the reaction of the other students when they see this!'

'Oh, no, I'm not submittin *this* one, just the others. See, these here.' She flips through the other sleeves, showing me some other shots that were very well done to her credit but contain nothing that seems supernatural. I'm still shocked by it

212

all, and express it by repeating, 'I just don't remember ya shooting that night.'

'I've got the photos here to prove it.'

With my eyes feeling as big as saucers again I whisper, 'Say that again.'

'What! Ok…I've got the photos here to prove it.'

'I've got the photos here to prove it, if I can just find em.'

'Yer crazy, boy! So, where's that one ya took of me? Did ya frame it above yer bed or something?' She flips through my portfolio unable to find her beautiful portrait that I distinctively remember placing in the very back sleeve. It's gone!

'Uh, yeah, it's right there, up on my wall.' I pray that it just fell out in my room or something. I fear that it slipped out on the bus or on the side of the road for some pervert to pick up.

Ms. Lancashire stands at the front of the room as a signal that class has begun. 'Class, it's time to pass your portfolios forward. Will the students at the front of the rows please place them in the basket on my desk?' Felicity gives me hers, minus the one depicting 'my dream', and I pass it forward with mine.

'Now prepare your project reports to be read,' Lancashire announces. 'You'll be reading them aloud to the class. We will start at the front of row six.'

'So why aren't ya submittin *that* photo?' I ask.

'It's just…special. It reminds me of things.'

'Things?' I pry.

'Yes, Ethan. It reminds me of…look, I know ya believe in…'

213

'Felicity, what? Tell me.'

'Ethan Morgan!' Ms. Lancashire cries, 'Do you plan on disrupting my class *all year* with such consistency?' I turn around and face the old goat. My face is burning with embarrassment. 'Do I have to treat the two you like kindergartners and move one of you? Miss Farmer? What do you have to say?'

'Ms. Lancashire,' I say, 'it's *my* fault.'

'Mr. Morgan, silence! I am addressing Miss Farmer.'

'Ms. Lancashire, I'm terribly sorry,' Felicity cries. 'It won't happen again.'

'Alright, fine. Now then, Mr. Lawless, you're the first seat in row six. We'll start with you. Please read your report.'

Felicity whispers in my ear, 'That photo reminds me of *you*. I'm not turnin it in.'

Despite Felicity's warmth, my cemetery fear just won't go away. Felicity has somehow captured it. I must study that photo some more. So, I turn around to Felicity and ask, 'About that lesson on special effects, are ya free tonight?'

'Ethan Morgan!' Lancashire screams, 'What am I to *do* with you?!'

a to b

The sun is low and my shadow following me home from school is long. I don't have the heart to take the bus and I've got a lot on my mind. The long walk might just sort me out, and the sun on my face feels good.

Coach Garrison, while pitching batting practice for Little League, told us that girls would be the cause of at least half of our problems in life…

'…problems in life are much bigger than hittin a nasty curveball. What will matter most is how ya handle those problems. That's how ya'll will become men. So, while you're still boys becoming men, I want you to play baseball hard, respect the game, respect your teammates, listen to your coaches…and most importantly, have fun while ya play. While ya can. While you're still young…'

Life was a lot easier then. But now I'm disillusioned by my hometown. I hate my dad and worry about my mom. I can barely stand school. I don't own a car, am haunted by my past, and might be insane. I'm seeing things, hearing things…and I just can't focus on these problems with Felicity in my life. She looms everywhere and has become everything to me. She dwarfs *all* my

217

problems, not just the cemetery episode. What if she makes my problems worse? I'm falling for her and she could break my heart. I'm too young to feel like this. It's just too soon. *But I want her*, more than anything else, and just maybe she's the perfect distraction from my fucked up life. My feelings are bittersweet, and remind me of what Coach Garrison said.

Felicity...

I'm going out with her tonight. Yeah, it started out as a 'crash course on special effects' but now it seems more like a *date*. Just to *suspect* that she feels the same way about me makes me float. It's more difficult now to remain cool and not assume. I've been catching myself in deeper thought and more complex analysis, when I should've been studying, or paying attention in class, or focusing on my cash till at work.

...you've blown my mind.

And just how long will a catch like Felicity remain interested in a guy without car? I worked very hard at Schnucks over the summer and thought that I'd have my own wheels by now. However, I didn't know that my employer would sign a regulation to limit the amount of hours for high school students. Unless I find another job that will give me enough hours I might have to wait until graduation in the spring.

Justin was lucky. He bought a '77 Camaro that never fails to start for him. It's a second hand car that just happens to *rock*! Its age and the few minor rust spots enabled him to get it cheap. It looks good otherwise and it can really move. I know I won't get that lucky and the amount of money I've got saved now might buy me an old scooter or a nice mountain bike. Guys who are too thrifty in buying a used car almost always end up with a pile of junk anyway. Inevitably, their purchases become money pits of maintenance and never-ending headaches. I'm not one of the boys in Shop class flipping through Car & Driver and I've worked too hard already to make a poor investment in a lemon.

This walk home has been good for me. During it I've made the decision to hang on to the money I've got and wait to buy a car, unless this crazy discussion that I hope to have with my mom goes well tonight. Otherwise I'll just keep saving anyway I can and roll the dice *without* a car for now. I just hope that Felicity won't think I'm a loser.

Mom's car is parked at the end of our driveway and snaps me out of one set of worries and into another. *It's great to see you home before me, Mom, but I'm not used to it.*

Metal clangs and a ratchet twists. I walk up the driveway and notice that the garage is open. There's no music coming from the speakers. I don't hear any beer-lubricated voices. My dad seems to be working hard on something else besides his Vette. I walk up the driveway and peek into the garage. He's slaving away underneath a disabled blue sedan. Pleasantly surprised, I tip-toe away. My father and I still play the ignoring-one-another game very well. I remember when I would come home from school and say hello to him before going inside. That was a long time ago and those days are long gone. Dad occasionally beating Mom and every now and then pulling shotguns on my friends doesn't make things any better. Mom has become the central source of communication in our home and without her I think Dad would've killed me, or I would've killed him.

'Mom, ya home?' I shout as I enter the house.

'In the kitchen!' she answers.

I join her at the dining table, cluttered with old mail and laundry again. 'When's the last time ya beat me home from school?'

'God, I can't remember!' she laughs. She chops vegetables and seasons slabs of raw pork steak. She feeds Charlie, who was sitting and waiting patiently, a slice of carrot. 'Stayin for dinner tonight?' she asks.

219

'Nah, got plans.'

'Hear that, Charlie? Ethan won't be here. You'll get some leftovers!' Charlie wags his tail and gives a happy bark in reply to my mom's excited tone.

'Well, don't give it *all* to Charlie. Try to save me some, will ya?'

'Where ya off to, anyway?'

'Movies.'

'Who with?'

'Ya don't know her.'

Mom puts down the knife and smiles at me. She asks, 'Ya gotta date?'

'Damn, Mom, don't go callin it that, now.' I slouch a bit in the chair.

'School girl?' Mom pries.

'No, I mean, yeah. Sorta. A *girl at school.*' Mom keeps her stare fixed on me, trying like Hell to read my mind. 'Yeah, yeah, Mom I'll tell ya *all* about it, ok?'

'That would be a first!' she cries, back to peeling carrots again. 'Son, I'm afraid that we ain't gonna know yer in love til we get a wedding invitation! Or she ends up pregnant.'

'No girl is ever gonna marry me unless I get a car. And, without a car, well, there's no backseat to...' Mom glares back at me over her glasses that sit low on her nose. 'I mean, I might as well not even try.'

Mom sips her glass of iced Diet Coke and asks, 'How much ya saved?'

I look up to the ceiling in thought and sigh, 'Not enough.'

'Not enough *exactly*?' she says.

'I've worked hard. I passed on that Cardinals season ticket and some other stuff to focus on workin and savin. Now that school's back in session I can't save a dime! Due to this stupid *regulation*. Or whatever it is.'

'It's a good rule. High-schoolers should be studyin, not workin full time.' *And not saving enough money for a car, Mom?* 'Ya workin this weekend?' she asks.

'Sunday from four til ten. Then not again til Wednesday. Over the summer I worked a lot of forty-hour weeks! I get that there's this regulation now that says I can only work up to twenty per week. But lately I'm not even getting *that*! How am I supposed to save any money for a car with this stupid regulation?'

'I think ya can get a nice, dependable ride with a couple hundred more. Hell, ya might be able to find somethin right now with what ya got.'

'Oh, no! I'm not settlin for some cheap heap, no matter how long it takes. Or...'

'*Or...?*'

At last my chance has come to the surface. Let this *discussion* begin. 'Or I can talk to my boss, explain a few things and get you and Dad to co-sign for a newer car. A newer *used* car, like somethin less than five years old. Somethin that won't break down on the side of the highway.'

'Ethan, yer dad just ain't gonna go for it-'

'Well what about *you*, Mom? What about *you*?'

'Lemme get somethin straight here, son. This isn't just about ya gettin from A to B, is it?'

I get the Pepsi out of the fridge and remain silent. I fill a tall glass with ice and avoid eye contact.

'What's this girl's name?' she asks.

221

I pour the Pepsi over the ice and say, 'Felicity. But, she's got nothin to do with my wantin a car,' I lie.

'She must be a cute lil thing.'

I take a long sip from my fizzing glass and nod before saying, 'Ya got that right.' I can't control my ear-to-ear smile. Mom and I both chuckle before I add, 'She ain't no dog, that's for sure!'

'Give me some time, son. I'll see what I can do about a car.'

holding hands

The gusty wind blows my locks into my face as I walk to Felicity's house. The air has cooled dramatically, giving the evening a chill that excites the butterflies in my stomach. I walk fast under the streetlights.

I have a little budget of cash for the evening in my wallet. I've had a clean shave and my jeans are my newest pair. The black dress shirt underneath my jacket looks sharp but I'm not used to wearing it. Despite the itchy neck the collar gives me, I'm confident. I look good.

From the top of Marvin Avenue I spot the huge oak tree in Felicity's front yard, just as she said there'd be. Neatly trimmed hedges line the huge front porch with a wide wooden staircase. It's an older wood-framed home with newly-installed bay windows on either side of the front door. On the left of the door there's a wooden bench swing that hangs from chains attached to the awning. When I passed this house on my bike hundreds of times throughout my youth it just blended in with rest of the homes. But now it's a very significant house.

I hike up the steep lawn and walk up the stairs to the porch. Lights peer gloriously from the stained-glass above the wooden front door. The wooden beams of the porch creak under my feet as I approach to ring the bell.

Felicity's about to answer. This is it...

225

Suddenly, doubt crashes into my confidence.

My cologne is a bit too strong. My hair's still a little damp. I'm quite thirsty, nervous, excited, and still a little worried. I take a deep breath.

I'm cool. Still confident. Fuck the doubts.

Felicity opens the door just enough to slip outside. She's got a file folder in her hand that I assume contains the 'dream photo'. 'Is that *him*? Is that *Ethan*?' A woman says with a cracked voice from inside. '*Tell* him! Felicity, *tell* him!' the woman cries.

'Hello, Ethan!' Felicity says as she quickly shuts the door behind her.

'Tell me what?' I ask

'Oh, don't mind her.'

'Is she alright?'

'Yeah, just…she's just my crazy old aunt.'

And I really don't care, to be honest, as Felicity looks stunning as always, aglow in the moonlight. Should I hug her? Kiss her? Just peck her cheek? Felicity saves me from an awkward moment by taking my hand in hers and escorting me down the steps. 'What are we seein?' she asks.

'How about we go see *Winter's Bone*.'

'Oh yeah!' Felicity exclaims. 'I thought I was the only one who wanted to see that!'

'Are ya *kidding!*' I shout. 'Awesome book!. It was written by-'

'Daniel Woodrell,' we say simultaneously.

'Wow,' I cry, 'I thought *I* was the only one I knew who'd read that!

'Well, it took place right here in Missouri!' Felicity

exclaims. 'I hope the flick's as good as the book.' But no matter how entertaining the movie is it won't be the main feature, as the girl of my dreams will be sitting next to me in a dark theatre.

* * *

Felicity and I exit the theatre with the masses. We are greeted by the chilly night. After two hours of having her right at my side, holding her hand, getting high on her scent of apples and strawberries...and just feeling her *breathe*...I'm finally able to get an eyeful of her. How beautiful she looks under the streetlight! She still wears the same cute outfit that she wore to school today, except she's traded the Mary Janes for a sleek pair of black indoor soccer shoes. I mentally undress her until she takes notice and blushes. 'C'mon. What are we doin, boy? Shall we talk special effects?'

'Special effects?'

'Yeah,' she replies, 'like we *said* we were gonna?'

The wind is gusting harder now and makes a chilly night feel bitterly cold! Does Felicity really like me or is she just cold? She clings to me, shivering like a leaf while I'm nippy even *with* my jacket cinched up. Tonight I look down upon her as she's lost three inches of height in trading heels for Samba Classics. She presses her cheek against my shoulder, probably able to hear my rapid heartbeat. Her small, turned-up nose is bright red as she looks up at me and smiles.

'I'll call a cab for us,' I say.

'What? Boy, don't be silly!' she squawks.

'C'mon, yer cold. It's freezin out here!'

'It's really not that bad. Once we start walkin we'll be fine.'

'I insist. I'll call us one.'

'No, Ethan, *I* insist. I think it would be nicer if we walked. After all,' she adds, 'I did change into my kickers.' Felicity stops and thrusts her leg high into the air to show off her footwear. 'We might as well put em to good use.' I gladly take the extra opportunity to acknowledge her shoes and gawk up her legs. She takes my hand and gently squeezes it. My heart thumps even

228

harder and a warm sensation melts over my entire body.

'Here, Felicity, take my jacket.'

'Thanks, but what about you?'

'I'll be fine, just keep holding my hand.'

We walk across the vast parking lot of Northwest Plaza to the busy St. Charles Rock Road. Braving this weather without my jacket isn't going to be easy, but I've walked further in colder temperatures alone. And during those lonesome walks I've wished for someone like Felicity to walk with me. I hold her left hand with my right and stuff my other hand in the pocket of my jeans. Despite only the cotton/polyester blend of my shirt protecting me from the cold wind of a deeper autumn, I've never felt so warm.

Holding hands down the three-mile stretch of road we pass the same burger joints, car washes and taverns that I've gawped at during lonely bus rides to and from school. Felicity makes this boring, rough-around-the-edges bit of North County feel like heaven. But too many times in my life things that seemed heavenly were actually too good to be true. Black clouds swirled into my mind's blue sky and vultures circled. I'd look up with a sceptical smile, holding hope in my hands and there them crooked vultures would be, waiting to storm down and feed on my dead dreams.

But tonight feels different. New. Brilliant, like the stars twinkling high above on this clear night. No black clouds. I squeeze Felicity's hand and she squeezes back, looking up at me.

But there are still vultures…dead…*the graveyard.*

I know what I saw there…

< Inevitable rush of negativity >

229

'I've been thinking about those photos ya took.' I say.

'Yeah?'

'Yeah, and, ya don't have to tell me or anything it's just that-'

'Just that...?'

Is this the right moment to explain everything? The words conjure in my mind and then flow onto my tongue, but I just can't spit them out. The night's been too wonderful and I don't want to put it all at risk. I swallow those words and instead say, 'Well, it's just that I really think Photography might be a career option for me and I just can't believe that someone could make those images possible. Yer photos were unbelievable!'

Felicity wears a dubious smile. She pauses in thought, and then says, 'So, ya think they were unbelievable-*awesome* or unbelievable-*fake*.'

My heart jumps into my throat. I gulp it back down into my chest and respond, '*Awesome*! Felicity, they were unbelievably-*awesome*! I mean, that's why I'm askin ya. I mean-'

'Relax, man, I wasn't implyin...what I'm sayin is that *somethin happened* out there and the next thing I knew ya were unconscious. And then I developed them and-'

'And *what*?' I blurt out. 'What *happened*, exactly?'

'Nothin.' she says.

More silence ensues. *Awkward* silence. My hand is sweating now and suddenly a steel wall has erected between us.

'I passed out or fainted or somethin. I just think that somethin might be wrong with me, or, I don't know. I saw some stuff and I think I might be going nuts.'

'Ethan,' she says, 'yer not nuts. Ya just fainted is all. I'll tell ya how I took those photos.'

230

I almost said too much. Felicity didn't say enough. Still, as she explains her technique to attain those crazy glowing effects I think I should feel satisfied. I *want* to be satisfied. I just want everything between us to be right, not haunted by my insanity or whatever it is that I've been experiencing.

'Special effects are easy when ya shoot at night.' Felicity carries on, 'I used white flashlight and a couple different filters. The woods surroundin us made it dark enough. Special effects like the ones I got are best to get at night with little or no light at all.'

'I thought the flashguns were in the bag.'

'Ya gave one to me. Don't ya remember?'

'Yeah, see, I guess maybe I forgot a few things,' I say, 'So you had the flashgun, then?' *I never gave you a flashgun, Felicity.*

Felicity starts again, 'Yeah, and because it was so dark out there I had much longer exposure times. I didn't have to worry bout the sky washin out. I was gonna explain all this on Friday but Lancashire didn't get to us.' I remain attentive and continue to grip her hand. Her *sweaty* hand. Sweatier than mine!

We turn north down a very dark stretch of Edmundson Road where there are no street lights. She continues, 'See, my camera has a multiple exposure mode so I fired the shutter separately for each exposure. I blasted the church with two flashes. I also flashed a row of headstones.'

I sort all of that in my mind and ask, 'So how did the church end up with the fiery glow?'

'I flashed it with an orange filter and I used a green one for the headstone.'

'Ok, then how did ya get the figure that looked a bit like a horseman? The horse and rider looked like they were on fire,

231

blitzin through the church!'

'Horse and rider?'

'Yeah.'

'Ethan, honey, ya don't remember me askin ya to stand on top of that one particular giant headstone?'

'No, ya didn't ask me anything, did ya?' *You never asked me a thing. You ran off and left me there. I would've remembered standing on a gravestone. I didn't even try that stunt over that summer when I was fourteen!*

'Ethan, I sure as Hell did. I told ya that ya needed to get up there so we could make the ghost.'

'*Ghost?* Felicity, I'm sorry. I just don't remember.'

Felicity puts her arm around me and rests her head against my shoulder. 'Oh, Ethan, you'll be alright!'

'So, yer saying *I'm* the horseman in the photos?'

'I don't know about any horseman, but yeah, I shot ya with the orange filter to give ya that fiery glow that the church had. The exposures were three seconds and I moved the gun from right to left as I shot. That's how I got the glow to come out blurry. I'll show ya the photo again tonight if we have time.'

Blurry is the operative word, with bullshit *waiting on deck.* 'Maybe my fainting caused some memory loss?'

'Ethan, maybe ya were blinded by the flash and ya fell off. The next thing I knew ya were on the ground, out cold.'

'I remember ya walking away from me towards the forest,' I say. 'I mean, ya seemed disturbed by somethin. I went after ya but I slipped. Then I-' *here's my chance,* 'then I came to and you...'

'Yeah?'

232

'…were right there above me.' *Chance gone.*

'Baby, don't worry bout it. Everything came off fine and ya got yer photos. I got mine. I bet we get high grades. Just wait til Monday!' *She called me Baby.*

'But of all those other shots, the one we're still talkin bout is the one in yer hand, and ya didn't submit it. It's a winner, Felicity. Why didn't ya turn it in?'

I told ya, this one is *special* to me. I…it shouldn't be graded or be submitted for critique. It's *mine*. I'm keepin it. It's *you* inside here, Ethan. I want to remember the wonderful night we had together.' *Her words are priceless. I'll never forget what she just said. So, who cares what actually happened out there anyway?*

'So, ya weren't upset about anything?' I ask.

'Ethan, gollie, why would I have been upset? I mean, I was a little frustrated at first about how to get started, but I certainly wasn't upset. Ya bein there with me meant everything!' *Priceless.*

We've come to the top of Marvin Avenue and I hope she's about to invite me into her home, where I've imagined her watching television, eating meals and dreaming while she sleeps. I've wondered so many times already what it would be like to do all of those things together. Felicity says, 'I was kind of jealous the other night when ya told me ya had a turntable.'

'Yeah?'

'Yeah!'

'And Justin left one of his styluses behind on my back patio so I've been breakin in some of my new vinyl.' *And a case of Bud, thanks to my psychopath, gun-toting father.*

'Back patio? Why in Hell would he do that?'

'Long story…' *I hope I never have to tell it to you.*

'Well…?'

'Oh, ya wanna come over and spin some?'

Her eyes light up and she replies, 'I thought you'd never ask!'

she's in my room

'Just wait here a minute,' I say to Felicity, standing on my front porch. She nods as I go inside to make sure the coast is clear. My mom snores behind her bedroom door and the lights are on in the garage.

'Yeah, c'mon in,' I whisper, gesturing her inside. She follows me to my room.

'Does yer dad live with ya?' she asks.

'Uh, yeah.' I lead her down the hall to where I sleep, holding my finger up to my lips for quiet. Felicity tip-toes behind me into my bedroom and shuts the door. 'Sorry bout the mess,' I say as I refer to a pile of laundry that's been ready for the wash for over a week.

'Oh, Lord, it's after eleven!' she gasps.

'Well, ya can stay, right?'

'Oh, yeah!' she laughs. 'Just can't believe how fast time flies with ya!'

'Does it?' I ask.

'I'm eighteen. I can stay out as late as I like.'

'Yer a big girl now, huh?' I cringe. *How perverted I sound!*

I catch her studying the confines strange to her. I'm

uneasy knowing that it's *her* first look at where *I* watch television, eat and sleep. I bet she didn't think I did all three in the same room, however. There's a glass half full of watered-down soda on the nightstand, growing mould. Records are clumsily stacked in no particular order and a baseball glove and bat sticks out from underneath my bed. I've left the closet door open, displaying how I just chuck anything and everything in there to clear it out of the way. If I just would've done more of that at least this shambles of a bedroom would look better. But I didn't think she would actually be in here tonight, or ever.

Felicity sits on the edge of my bed and lets her strawberry locks dangle down in her face. She takes her shoes off to display white cotton ankle socks worn over her tights. She rubs her feet against the rug at the foot of my bed and says, 'So this is where ya sleep.'

'And eat. And watch TV.' I sit down next to her, 'Yep, this is my room, where the magic happens.' *Stop it, pervert! You are playing with fire talking like that! She's in your room, for Christ-sake! Just relax and say nothing else at all! She wouldn't be in here if she didn't want to be.*

She leans across my lap and picks up a CD instead of a vinyl record. 'Hey, The Vampire Bats! Go on, spin it!' I put on their album, *'One For Sorrow'*. *'Tragedy'* is the first track and I immediately reminisce the night I saw her at the concert, the *first time* I ever saw her. Ok, we're not spinning vinyl, we're playing CDs. We're not looking at her cemetery photo and I'm not getting that crash course on special effects, either. Who cares? She smells *so* good! 'Hey remember, Ethan? This was the song they were playin when I first saw ya.'

The heavy, dark song fuses with the mood and I can't resist falling towards her as I reply, 'Yeah. I remember.' Our lips connect in slow motion, but not slow enough. I want that moment back, over and over again. For the first time in my life I notice a moment leave the present tense for the past, *Our First*

238

Kiss. The taste and the feeling drive me crazy with passion. My lips break from hers to explore her silky peaks and smooth valleys. Her aroused exhalation spurs on my relentless drive to feed her my love. Our tangled bodies slither and sweat. As our first time together spills onto my bed I want the world to stop. But time never stops…and all I can do is enjoy this while it lasts, savour her physical decisions, and relish the maddening effect of her touch. With every push further we get hotter. Our breathing has been reduced to desperate gasps. Am I going to suffocate? I don't care. I press my lips back to hers and suck her breath into my lungs, and it's better than biting into a fresh, juicy peach on a summer day.

Or an apple.

Or a strawberry.

'Ethan, open one of the windows just a bit,' Felicity gasps, 'and turn off the lights.'

'Yeah. It's a little stuffy in here.' I can barely speak.

'No,' she says, 'it ain't stuffy. It's just the way ya kiss me.' She whispers in my ear, 'Like shards of fire burnin ya slowly inside…all the way to yer heart.'

My heart skips as her words freak me out. Did she really just say those words? Those very words she said at the cemetery? From my 'three-walled room' in the light of the burning church? Déjà vu? Dreams? Reality? Insanity? Fire? All of it is *her* sitting right before me in my room, my *four-walled room*, not three. She gazes upon me with that same Mona Lisa smile that she wore while the church burned in the graveyard. I can't tell the difference. Perhaps there *is no difference.* Felicity has spoken those very words before. What really happened in the cemetery on Monday night?

But my appetite for sex trumps my fears. I flip the light switch to OFF, but as I go to close the rear window I kick the

239

bedpost and fall to the floor. I shriek in surprise but I'm not hurt, just very embarrassed.

'Ethan, she laughs, 'ya shoulda cracked the window first, baby! Ya obviously can't see in the dark.'

'*Now* ya tell me!' I giggle. *Ethan! You horny bumbling fool!* I get back to my feet and move cautiously through my dark room. I unlock the rear window and raise it six inches. I twist to look back at her silhouette reclining comfortably on my bed. She rests on her elbows, her head is perked up and I can feel her eyes piercing me through the darkness. One of her long legs rests off the bed while her foot grinds my rug. She's removed her tights. A strip of patio light has entered between the blinds. It crosses her lips so I can see them move when she says, 'That'll do, now come back to me, I'm gettin lonely over here.' I cautiously approach her.

'*Walkin' Blues'* by Son House pours into the open window from the garage, behind loud alcohol-laden voices of men. Ghosts of the Mississippi Delta twang and cackle through the speakers over drunken curses. 'Hell, I shit *daily*!' one of the men bellows. My father and his friends are at it again. The noise neutralises The Vampire Bats and threatens to ruin the mood. I take a discreet glance out that window but can only see their shadows.

'Ethan, baby, what's wrong?'

'Nothin,' I sigh.

'Who *is* that out there?'

I pause before I answer. I'm not sure if I want to admit to Felicity that my father is one of the rowdy men. But I say, 'Oh, it's my dad and some of his friends. Must be havin a late night. Wow, he hasn't been out this late in a long time.' *Liar. I better shut this window.*

'Keep the window open just a bit,' Felicity demands, 'I

240

think things are gonna get a lil warm in here.'

'Ok, but lemme shut this one and open the front one. Maybe we won't hear em that way.'

'Ethan, don't worry bout them!' she gasps. 'Get *over* here!'

Again, Felicity's warm body in waiting forces me to ignore everything else, no matter how embarrassing. I promptly return to her, reclining and waiting for me to feast upon her body, on the very bed I sleep each night. Still, the rude men carry on loudly while the blues blares on. I climb onto my bed and hover over her. I take off my shirt while she strips off her black lace bra and matching panties. In the stripe of light her skin looks as creamy as yoghurt. As I'm about to lap it up with my tongue my father bursts out, 'Ya fuckin asshole! No wonder!' It sounds like he and his crew are just right outside the window! I regroup, trying to block it out as I dive in to kiss Felicity's welcoming lips, but the noise persists.

'Yeah, kids can be a bitch, I tell ya.' my father says, intruding my room just as cold as the October draft. My lips move southward from her lips to her chin, then to her neck. My hands discover the silky-smooth feeling of her thighs and waist when my father declares, 'Look at my son, man! He works some piss poor job down at the grocery store makin beans. But he wants a car. I tell him he ain't drivin my wife's and he ain't ever gonna touch my Vette!'

'Ya got that right!' another man cries.

I stop and Felicity knows why. I look into her eyes that glow green in the dark. She says, 'Baby, ok, just shut that window and open the other one then. And turn the music up a little.' Her voice sounds less enthused and more concerned. I'm horny, but never have I been this humiliated. I pray to God that shutting the window will mute my father's rants, as my heart can't afford another devastating blow. Nor can my penis. 'Hell, he sounds like *my* dad.' Felicity says.

'I'd have a hard time believin he's as mean as mine.'

'Well, he seems pretty serious about his cars. I noticed the Vette parked in the garage.'

'Only my father's pride and joy.' I say.

'My dad has an old muscle car, too. He took some of his government payback and bought it along with that farm when I was little. Damn, that *damn GTO*.'

I get up to switch the open window and my father says, 'That wife of mine! She's something else, boy, I tell ya! She come up to me today sayin she wants to co-sign for that boy to get a car. If she's not outta her mind then I'm outta mine!'

'So, ya gonna do it?' another man asks.

'Hell no!' my father says. 'I'm not letting a seventeen-year old ride my credit rating around. He can go out n earn it just like we all did.'

'Yeah,' replies another man, 'ya can't let yer kids run the show.'

I slam the window shut, shaking with anger. Felicity heard it all loud and clear. But the *truth* of the matter is the devastating blow, not my father's words. I couldn't get it up now if Felicity clamped jumper cables to my balls.

Sex, interrupted.

I can't face her now, so I just look out the other window towards the front lawn. I watch the flickering porch lights as the second track, *'The Seventh Day'*, gives way to the Doors-y, bassless track, *'Dreaming All The While'*.

On the windowpane, Felicity's reflection rises from my bed. Her feet pitter-patter the wood floor and her breath sinks into the back of my neck. I close my eyes as her fingertips glide around my sides and across my chest. She gently pulls me back to her warmth and whispers, 'Don't worry.'

'Felicity,' I say, 'I've got to get that car.'

'Don't worry bout a thing, boy,' she whispers again. 'Don't worry bout nothin.'

I caress her comforting arms and focus on her warming breath, just like I did her first day in class. 'I need that car, Felicity. A girl like you deserves to be driven wherever she wants.'

'You'll get a car. You'll get it. Don't worry about it.' Her voice soothes my wounded mind and heart. I sigh deeply as my thoughts of my father evaporate. Felicity's touch has relit my fire. Once again, I'm anxious to experience the moment millions of teenage boys across the globe obsess about.

I turn around and say, 'I've fantasized about ya like this-' but Felicity's appearance robs my words. Her left side is in the patio light and her right is in the darkness. She wears that same emerald green gown that she was wearing at the cemetery, but it neither glows nor shines. It's tattered, torn and stained. Her arms and shoulders are patterned with bruises and blood. Her neck has gone a mix of purple and green and her face is shattered, gored and nearly unidentifiable. Her lips have rotted away to display jagged teeth. Her cheek bones are sticking through her ripped face and one of her eyes are missing. That small, turned-up nose has been ripped off and half of her skull is actually showing.

But her red hair flows just as beautifully as always from the other half of her head, but stained with blood.

I choke at the sight of her as she says, 'One day, Ethan, you'll get that car and you'll drive over to see me. We'll chase those sunsets and full moons while the wind whips through our hair…in yer car at eighty miles an hour.'

'Felicity!' I cry.

'Blazin though that golden desert as the parched terrain passes us by. As long as ya never stop believin…'

243

'Felicity! What's happened?!'

'...hope shall never fly away.' She explodes backward, as if she was shot from a cannon, into the dark tunnel that my room has become, and disappears.

'Until we meet again...' her voice rings on. 'Until we meet again...'

Darkness has consumed everything around me. I panic as I can't see anything, not even my hand in front of my face! Either the wood floor has turned to mud or I'm just not in my room anymore. And the smell, my goodness! It's absolutely rancid! I gag it's so bad!

Please, God! Don't let this happen to me again!

The faint rushing of a river is the only sound, and it's just ahead. I try to move toward it hoping it will lead me to light. 'Felicity!' I call out. My voice echoes through the tunnel as my boots squish down into this deep mud. I thrash my hands about, reaching ahead on fully extended arms in order to 'see with them' through the tunnel, or is it a cave? My heart races through my panic and I barely control myself through deliberate, deep, slow breathing. But the smell is so terrible that I can actually taste the air as I suck it in.

It's so cold! So, I try to move faster, but in doing that I sink further into the mud. I stop and hoist one leg high, then the other, to escape the depth of the sludge. But my efforts are in vain; the mud gets deeper as I move toward the river. But I must get out of here, wherever *here* is, if there's a way out?

Voices echo...

HER BLOOD

JUST A HANDBAG

BLOOD

244

A HANDBAG

BLOOD

A HANDBAG

The sound of radio fuzz is laced through the voices and come from the same direction as the rushing river…

OVER THE BRIDGE

THE BRIDGE

THE BRIDGE

There must be a way out then, but who do the voices belong to? How deep does this mud get?

Suddenly, the weakest little glimpse of midnight blue breaks through. The Light at the End of the Tunnel? I grip the blue air with my eyes, as if it will disappear if I don't stare at it. I hustle as hard and as fast as I can, taking huge, pronounced gaits forward, sinking deeper and deeper into the mud. Damn, it's coming up knee-high now! I'm out of breath, my legs are exhausted, but I don't stop.

What *is* that? Lights twirl red, white and blue. Whoopee lights. Police. More voices croon, clearer now…

IN PURSUIT EASTBOUND

IN THE WATER

PURSUIT EASTBOUND

IN THE WATER

PURSUIT EASTBOUND

245

I lose my balance in the deep mud and splatter into it face first. 'Stop right there!' one of them screams. 'Get down boy, get down now!' White torch lights blast into the tunnel, illuminating an absolute macabre scene! I try to scream but can only muster a little choking yelp. I'm on my knees in a stew of blood, guts and flesh. I bathe in the mud with hundreds of dead bodies.

'On yer knees, boy! Get down on yer mother-fuckin knees and put yer hands behind yer head!' They trounce through the human stew behind three white torch lights. They can see me but I can't see them. They march closer and closer until I feel a cracking blow over the back of my head, so hard that I don't even feel it. I'm just a dead fish of a body teetering on the edge of consciousness. These men in black uniforms, these *cops*, stuff me into a body bag and zip it up. I can't see or scream or even *breathe*, trapped as they carry me to the unknown.

The bag is unzipped and I fall out, like the yoke from a cracked egg shell, onto a muddy bank. The river rushes wildly behind three figures. I look up and see their silhouettes against the night sky. The triangle of heads stares down at me. 'Get yer last look, boy,' one says. 'Go on, she's layin right beside ya.'

Felicity lays next to me, lifeless on the river bank.

at the lockers

'It's Monday, October 11th. Welcome back after an awesome weekend! I am Justin Ronan with the Monday Morning Update!' Justin's voice travels through the hallways via Ritenour's PA from the KRHS Studio.

'This Thursday the teacher's lounge on the North Wing of the ground floor will be open for the blood drive. Any students willing to give blood should sign up in the cafeteria by Wednesday afternoon. You'll be given free orange juice and cookies for your attendance.'

'Ronan's the radio-man!' Donnie shouts at me while I rummage through my locker. 'Yer boy's talkin', Morgan! Better listen up!' he barks as he socks me in the shoulder.

'Friday night there will be another Huskies Football Caravan. Come out and support the Varsity at Normandy High School where they take on the Vikings in a Homecoming tune-up. The cost is $10.00 and will go towards RHS Athletics. Buy your tickets during lunch in the cafeteria on *Friday* and show up at the senior's parking lot after school to board the buses. Finally, voting for Homecoming Court will commence

249

today during sixth period and, as always, you can sign up for the variety of Homecoming committees in the gymnasium to lend a hand. *Ronan out!*

I shut my locker door to find Felicity's beaming face. 'Hello stranger!' Lost in her eyes, I bury my issues with the way Friday night in my bedroom ended. I smile back and ignore my anxiety for not knowing what occurred.

I watch her lips move, 'I'm really, really sorry about this weekend. I shouldn't have just up n left like that. Did ya get my note?'

'Yeah, I did. Listen, *did we-*'

'I know that I should've called ya. I got in a bit over my head with stuff. I made the girl's fall soccer team as a supplemental addition. I've also gotten myself really involved with Homecoming and...' *Muddy human stew. Men wearing black. Cops. Evil cops? Something trying to warn me? Something real? Where was I? Where's that river? Felicity was dead! She was dead...*'anyways, sorry Ethan. I hope ya understand.'

'I figured I'd see ya at school,' I lie. My brain has been throbbing in pain over this since my alarm went off this morning. Felicity doesn't seem to be good for my ever-fading sanity.

'Yeah,' she says, 'anyways, here we are.' She slides her hands around my waist and snuggles against my chest.

Ah, that's heavenly. Fine, I'll just go insane, then. 'Yeah,' I sigh.

'Yeah, so, is this locker between ours still vacant?'

'No,' I answer, 'they gave it to a girl...' and the girlish boy sabotages our conversation. He glides up to the locker between ours and twists the padlock.

'Ethan,' Felicity whispers, 'he's not a *girl*, silly. He's just...'

The girlish boy glares at Felicity. 'Howdy,' greets Felicity.

He scowls at her coldly, as if she were an insect. '*Howdy?*' he says and wrinkles his nose in disgust. Felicity glares right back, then just as coldly, back at me.

'Oh, hey! Felicity, this guy rides my bus.' I say. 'This yer locker, guy?'

'G*uy?*' he replies, wrinkling his nose again, squinting '*as if*' at me.

'*Gay?*' Felicity jabs.

The girlish boy opens it and says, 'Well, I know the combination. Who else would it belong to?'

'Oh, sorry, man. I never got yer name. Have ya had this locker long?'

'Since yesterday. I was having some-' he holds up his index and middle fingers and bends them to signify quotations, '*social* difficulties'. My counsellor thinks it's better to move me *here* than to suspend anyone.'

'Suspend *who?*' Felicity asks.

'Never mind.' he replies, rolling his eyes.

'Got it,' I say.

'By the way, I'm Tyler Keats.'

I offer my hand, 'Ethan Morgan,' but he ignores my gesture, 'and this is Felicity Farmer.'

'Ok, I'm *Tyler Keats*,' he replies, rolling his eyes again, '*remember* my name because I'm going to be famous one day.' He slams his locker shut and sassily walks away, concluding, 'Famous or *notorious*!'

'What a...'

'*Character.*' I say, saving me from hearing Felicity's first insult. I drown out the obnoxious noise of the passing students. 'Did ya have a good time Friday?'

'Ethan, I had a wonderful time! I told ya! That's why I want ya to ask me to Homecoming. Unless ya gotta a date already.'

I laugh, 'Of course I don't have a...so, yer asking *me* to ask *you* to the dance?' The first period bell rings but I ignore it.

'Wow. I didn't realise how much of a joke this would be.'

'Felicity, no! I was just...I was only laughing because I'm not really-'

'The school dance type? Well, I've must admit that it took a lot of courage to ask a guy like you. Would you even be caught *dead* at something like the Homecoming dance? As for me, I've really gotten involved as you know, and I just really wanted ya to come with me.'

'*Of course* I'll go with ya!' I say, nearly tripping over my eager tongue.

'Well, I'm not goin with ya unless ya *ask* me.'

'OK, will ya go with me?' I smirk.

'No, Ethan, say, '*Felicity*, will you go to Homecoming with me?"

I roll my eyes and smile, '*Felicity,* will you go to the Homecoming dance with me?'

'No, say it like you really, really mean it.'

'Ok...*Felicity*...will you *please* come with *me* to the Homecoming dance?'

'Yesss,' she says. She leans in to kiss my lips behind my open locker door. The world can end now. I want to keep this moment forever. Alas...it's gone. Another memory that shall live forever in the past. 'C'mon, we gotta get to class, boy!'

'Wait, Felicity…'

'Yeah?'

'It's just that…' I want her to tell me what happened Friday night. *No, Ethan. Don't screw this up* now. *You've dreamt of this moment, this feeling, all your life. But never did you dream that a girl like* Felicity *could ever want you.*

'Just that *what*?' she asks.

I recover and reply, 'It's just that…I gotta find something to wear.'

heart attack

'Ethan, I tried to get through to him,' Mom pleads. 'I really thought I was makin some progress!' She's arrived home from work and has just flown past me at warp speed into the kitchen. I abandon the television and follow her trail of panic.

I wish she'd slow down.

I scoop some ice into a glass and drown it with cold Pepsi. I take a sip, and then spread peanut butter on white bread. I wonder what my parents' conversation sounded like. Deducing from my mom's behaviour I guess that it didn't go in my favour. I was a fool to believe that it would. 'I know ya tried to talk to him. I know ya did what ya could. If there was one person in this world who could get through to him it would be you.'

Mom falls into the kitchen chair and sighs, 'I mean, he actually *did* consider it. It was the credit risk that he was worried about.'

'He chose you in life no matter how long ago that was,' I say. 'I hope and pray that he still recognises ya as his main source of trust.' After spitting those words out I have enough room for a big bite of my sandwich.

'What? Ethan, whatchya tryin to say? '

'He chose *you* but he didn't choose *me*. I was just a mistake, right? Why would he want to cater to a mistake? Why

257

should I believe he trusts ya anymore after ya had the audacity to go to him about something so *stupid?* Helpin yer mistake-son buy a car!'

'Calm down, Ethan. It ain't like that at all!'

'Yes it is, Mom! When are ya gonna realise that somethin *really bad* will have to happen? It's gonna take a *tragedy* to change him. I've made up my mind that I'd rather see things carry on *this* way and keep *any tragedies* out. I've accepted the way that things are in this dysfunctional family! Just as you've accepted it for years!'

'Ethan, honey, no…'

'He *hates* me! And I *hate him!*'

'He's ill, son. He's not-'

'He held my best friend at *gun point!* He fuckin *humiliates* me!' After my outburst I stare at my sandwich. Dropping the F-bomb in front of my mom has ruined my appetite, after just one bite. 'I'm sorry, Mom. I didn't mean to say all that.'

I have a long battle with my father on my hands that I still have the heart to fight. Mom had the heart a long time ago, but has long since submitted to him. She has given in to love. Blind Love. Love for me. Love for her husband. Love for The Right Thing. Love for who she believes she's become. Love for the fairy tale that was promised to her long ago. But then I came along. A mistake son that ruined everything. This is all *my* fault. *I'm* the reason why all of this nonsense continues.

As for *my* fairy tale, I'll just have to earn that car the hard way. At seventeen years of age, man, I'm on my own. Now that I've realised that I'll be a lot better off.

Mom isn't crying but she's never looked sadder. Her head is down as she leans against the kitchen table. Gripping its edge. She looks so tired and defeated as she tucks a few brunette locks behind her ear. 'I'm sorry I said all that, Mom. It's just that I heard him telling his friends about how stupid we were about the co-signer idea.'

Mom sighs, 'Oh, Ethan, don't worry bout those shit-bums. Are ya gonna let some low-life drunks get ya down? They've got nothing better to do than to hang out in that damn garage and watch yer dad play with tools.'

I laugh. That felt good. Now she has a chuckle of her own. Mom and I understand each other. My yearn. Her compromise. Love rules all and we are at its mercy.

'By the way,' Mom says, 'yer father and I are goin to Hannibal…*without* the shit-bums.'

'What?'

'I know, can ya *believe* it?'

'No, I *can't* believe it!' I exclaim.

'Yeah, but don't get yer hopes up too high. He says we're only gonna *look* at some property. It would be nice to move out of *this* ghetto.'

'Wow, I can't imagine you and Dad leavin St. Louis.'

'Hell, *I* can. Ya know it's what we've wanted for a long time. This town's goin to the dogs and I sure could use the wide open space to breathe again.' *To the dogs…this dying city. But why would Hannibal be any better?*

'Hannibal, huh? I don't have the heart to break hers. Not when the grass still looks greener to her, just like it does to me. Somewhere a lot further than a stretch of Missouri interstate can take me. 'When are ya goin?'

'Not til the twenty-second. Friday. All weekend.'

'Wow.'

'Ya know I'd want ya to come along but I really don't

think you'd have any fun.'

'So when are ya movin? I ask.

'What? Won't ya be comin with us?'

'Don't jinx it, Mom.'

'We're just *lookin,* son. Just *lookin* is all.'

'Thanks for the invite but I'm afraid I've got plans that weekend.'

'Plans? What plans?' she asks.

I must be careful now. Blasé. She'll have tons of questions if I don't play this off. 'That's Homecoming weekend. Lots of stuff goin on. Football game, parade, dance-'

'Ethan that's great! I never thought you'd get involved with Homecoming or anything at school besides sports!' I nod and struggle not to grimace, bracing myself for it. 'Are ya takin anyone?' *Right on cue.*

'Yes, as a matter of fact I...Mom? Mom! What's happening?'

She's slumped over the chair. Gripping the table's edge, she's gasping for breath. 'Ethan...*help.*'

'Mom, what's happenin? What should I do?'

'I don't...' She slides down the chair and onto the floor.

'Mom! I'm callin 911!'

She's on the floor, on her side, gasping and holding her chest. Her face is pure fear and tears spout from her eyes. 'Ethan, help. My chest. Help...I can't...'

'911, what's your emergency?'

'I think my mom's havin a heart attack!' Standing in the middle of the kitchen with the phone in my hand, my mother is dying at my feet, unconscious now. 'Get someone *out* here! *Hurry!*

As I pray for help to arrive I turn around to the shocking presence of the woman draped in white, just inside the kitchen entrance and levitating three feet off the floor! Now I think *I'm* having a heart attack, 'Tell me *who you are!*'

Her gigantic green eyes shine down upon us, but they're soothing this time. Her long, sparkling black hair and her luminous white gown flow behind her as she moves toward my fallen, unconscious mother. 'Who are you? *Who are you?*' The mystery woman who has haunted me, whether in dreams or reality, kneels down at my mother's side. But this is not a dream.

'Don't you *touch* her!' I shout. But she ignores me and puts her radiant white hand to my mother's heart.

'Don't worry, child.' she says, offering a confident, knowing nod. My mother breathes calmly again, still unconscious, but sleeping peacefully. She's very much alive.

Whoopee lights spin around us as paramedics storm the kitchen. The woman draped in white, whoever she is, exits through the back door…just as my terrorised father enters it. Dad staggers and grabs the inside of the doorframe to keep from falling backwards. He shrieks as his eyes roll back in his head. He's lost his breath, gasping just like Mom before she passed out.

'Dad!' I call out. I realise my concern, my fear, for the man I supposedly hate. As my fallen mother is treated I'm struck by the fact that we three are of the same blood. We're a family. Still overcome with panic, my father has caught his breath and regained his balance. He felt something pass right through him, and I *saw her* do it. The woman wearing white is a ghost!

The paramedics crowd around my mom. 'Ok, we've got a pulse…heartbeat confirmed! She's breathing…she's breathing! Mr Morgan, are you alright?'

261

'Yes, I'm fine! Now get my wife to the hospital!'

Maybe one day a *loving* family.

dim-lit crimson

Tuesday, October 12

This morning's sky is a blanket of grey ash. Its cold wind has a whisper that warns me of more than just winter approaching. As I shut my front door my heart grows heavy and my mind paranoid. I pull a wool stocking cap over my head and button my jacket all the way to the top. I can at least fight the cold if I can't fight my strange fear. Perhaps it's that I just won't rest easy until I actually *see* my mom safe at home from the hospital today. Not until I know for sure that this ghost-woman actually means *well*. But this strange fear, constricting me tighter with my every step, with my every breath, has nothing to do with any of that. There is something else…

The bus buzzes around the corner well ahead of schedule. I've missed it and that hasn't happened in a while, not since I used to hate school. Not since Felicity arrived. It reminds me…

Ignoring the tranquillity of my bedroom, I begin the long march to school. Casting no shadow through the morning's bleakness I struggle to imagine another new and exciting day with Felicity in my life. For the first time she is not clear in my mind. I can't see her beauty, smell her fruits, hear her melody, feel her warmth or taste her sweetness through this mood, this menacing mood. This routine trek to school feels like an evil trail that leads right into the jaws of a ferocious beast.

With every stride I try to focus on the new good in my

life. Sleeping well at night. Waking up energised to the sound of that alarm, knowing Felicity will be waiting for me at school. I just haven't been afraid. Mom *survived* that heart attack, for heaven's sake! But, alas, all of that is blurry. This morning I'm afraid again.

The cold wind blows hard, and the whispers dangle around my head…

PUSHED OVER THE EDGE

OVER THE EDGE

OVER THE EDGE

They weave in and out of distant howls and sudden screams…

THREE SHOTS FIRED

SHOTS FIRED

SHOTS FIRED

The oak branches above sway and creak, blending with the evil laughter that has now joined the tormenting choir. Fallen leaves bursting with colour rustle across the ground, whilst a phantom's boots crunch toward me. In the reflection of a Volkswagen window I'm alone against the daunting sky decorated with black skeletal trees. Still, his breath warms and chills the back of my neck.

Am I awake or *still asleep*? *Has* my alarm clock sounded yet? Did my mom actually *have* a heart attack? Is the woman draped in white really a *ghost*? Did she actually *pass right though* my father? Is Felicity actually *in my life*, or has she and the other new good in my life been *just part of a dream?* My concept of reality is confused. What's *real* and what *isn't* anymore? How do I know *for sure?* Am I dreaming *now?* When will this turn into *another* horrific nightmare? Or will it be *real?*

But I remember the hot blast of water hitting me on the top of the head, the smell of fresh bar soap and peach-scented shampoo, the stimulating steam that filled the bathroom as I traced a heart in the mirror. It was me in that thick steam, in that blue morning window light. *Wasn't* it?

This has all been a dream, Ethan. All too good. All too weird. All too sudden. But this right now is real. *You're wide awake, man. Feeling your cursed life. This is how it will always feel to you. You will always be cursed.*

The voices multiply, heckling louder...

HE COMMITTED SUICIDE

COMMITTED SUICIDE

COMMITTED SUICIDE

Cackling crows smear black across the sky. I stop, *dead* in my tracks you could say, and watch them.

So, try death, then. Turn back and pick the garage door open. Grab the twelve-gauge from the wall. He keeps the shells in the veggie compartment of the fridge...

That thought, that *voice,* has silenced the choir. It was *my voice,* I heard it, but my lips didn't move.

Everything is suddenly calm. The wind has ceased and the crows have perched and settled in the high branches of the churchyard oaks. But below them in their shadows, on the grass surrounding God's House, the cries and grunts of three boys crack the silence.

Yelping is the girlish boy, Tyler Keats, just a rabbit's dash from the bus stop where he usually boards his own hell-on-wheels-express to school. He's being thrashed and beaten by Donnie and Tony again and it's more violent this morning than ever before! I charge toward them across the colourful churchyard, my boots crackling the fallen leaves. The two bullies taunt Tyler as he lays flat on his chest, protecting his head with his arms. Tony dives down and thumps him good and hard with a closed fist. Tony's knuckles crack Tyler's head, loud and clear at over fifty yards away! Donnie's mad laughter is followed by his two swift kicks to Tyler's ribs, causing the struggling boy to cough and moan.

'Donnie! Knock it off!' I yell, moving closer.

The bullies whip their heads my way. They just smile when they recognise me and continue beating and kicking. Just those satanic smirks in regards. No greetings. No words. Just a 'fuck you' and a pucker of the lips.

Tony delivers another blow to the side of the defenceless boy and shouts, 'Faggot! Ya fucking faggot!' Donnie laughs even more madly and strikes Tyler with another frighteningly hard kick.

I shout 'What the fuck are trying to *do*? *Kill* him?' The bullies pause. They know I'm serious. I don't care about being on their 'good side' anymore. I'm tired of this fucked-up world that I live in! I might be a god-damned schizo because of it but I know I'm not dreaming *now*. This is *real*.

'This ain't none of yer business, Morgan.' Tony declares.

'We're tired of this fag mouthin off to us,' Donnie adds. 'Maybe a few more beatins like this will straighten em out.'

268

Tyler whimpers on the ground. The sight of him lying there in the foetal position is sad and disgusting. 'Whatchya gonna do if he goes to the police?' I cry, 'Whatchya gonna do if ya seriously hurt em or kill em? What *then*?'

Tony says, 'Morgan, we ain't gonna kill em. This is just a lesson. Why donchya just fuck off to school and mind yer own business?'

Bloodied and bruised, Tyler slithers slowly toward his duffel bag like a wounded snake. I must do something. Say something. Anything to stop this madness, even if I just shout an empty threat. 'Tyler, stay down,' I call out, 'I'm goin to the police. This is bullshit!'

'No you ain't,' Donnie says, 'I'll beat yer ass right here and now!' Donnie bought it.

'*You*, Morgan? Goin to the *cops*? Ha, that's the funniest thing I've-'

I whip out my phone, holding it out to them like a deadly weapon. Like it has magical powers. Like it can stop a tragedy. 'I've just pressed record. Smile, you're on TV.' *Another empty threat.*

Tony glares at me and then down at the state he has helped beat Tyler into. 'Donnie, this ain't worth it, bro. Morgan, forget ya ever saw this, dude. We'll leave the kid alone. Just leave the cops outta this.'

'Ya fuckin pussy, Tony!' Donnie exclaims, 'Yer pussin out *again ya punk*!'

'Donnie, I'm already in trouble, man. From the party. Remember? I can't fuck with no cops.'

Donnie gives me a death-glare and says, 'Morgan, y'ain't goin to no cops, are ya?' I just stare back at him, right over the top of my phone that doesn't even have a RECORD button.

'Well…are ya…*faggot*?

The branches overhead squeak and bend in the renewed gusts. Oh, the leaves, how they fall. The world is so beautiful as it dies…

A howling wind.

A cackling crow.

A beating heart.

A bang.

A bang.

Another bang.

Everything has stopped. Everything is silent. *Again*.

* * *

When Tyler Keats fired three shots from a 9mm Beretta pistol, the grey sky hanging over the churchyard flashed into a dim-lit crimson. The bullet that pierced my skin is lodged into a place I didn't even know that I had. I bawl bloody murder as I've *never* felt such pain. My stomach burns like Hell as the bullet feels like it's started a fire that barbecues me from the inside.

My *heart*. My *mother's* heart. Felicity's words…

'Like shards of fire burnin ya slowly inside…all the way to yer heart.'

My legs and arms go numb and I crumble to the ground like a house of cards in a storm. The church yard spins around me and the branches swirl like a black kaleidoscope around the crucifix atop the steeple. I look down at my bloody body and see a hole in my jacket right above my waist. My blue jeans and the green grass have turned red with my blood. I can't breathe…

Tony squeals in pain and fear. He's on the ground holding his bloody leg, crying out to God.

Donnie's brains are splattered all over the trunk of an oak tree much older than he'll ever be, now. His dead eyes are wide open.

Like an oncoming train in the pitch black of night, without a moon in the sky or a single twinkling star, a bright light approaches and illuminates a new setting. The churchyard has suddenly become a river bank that I now lay upon, as those hooves thunder down. A mosaic of dead, bloody bodies have washed up next to me in the mud.

There's a crackling in the woods. The smell of cinnamon is in the air as rose petals fall upon my wound. I turn my head away from the horror of three dead bodies and am awestruck by

271

the woman draped in white. Her long black locks, dancing in the wind, match the hue of the horse she rides upon. She looks down upon me, in that same calm, knowing way she looked upon my mother. And perhaps just like Mom did in the presence of this woman, my eyes roll back into a peaceful sleep.

Three tragedies

Three dead children

Three souls to be saved

'By the way, I'm Tyler Keats. Remember that name because I'm going to be famous one day. Famous or notorious!*'*

media circus (in retrospect)

A priest dialled 911. He was leaving the rectory when the three gunshots were fired. Police and paramedics arrived at the bloody scene within minutes. They stuffed Tony and me into an ambulance en route to Barnes Jewish in St. Louis City. I regained consciousness for a minute or two on the way to ER. All I remember in that ambulance was being probed by tubes and molested by blood-smeared men wearing rubber gloves. Tony was leaning up against the wall with his leg wrapped up like a mummy. His brows raised high on his white-as-a-sheet face as my eyes opened to meet his. He must have thought I was dying.

Tony's right thigh absorbed the first bullet. He was treated and released just before midnight, and subsequently mobbed by hounding local press. He was the St. Louis media's first victim in their coverage of this, as he was lured into providing a very warped version of the story just outside hospital doors. His shock-dipped replies effectively gave birth to the media circus that would squeeze the guts from this tragic event like a boa constrictor. He was horrified, had never been on the news before nor ever saw his name in print - perfect food for hungry reporters. They took advantage of him, getting his trembling lips to talk by sticking a mic in his face…

'He just opened fire...for no reason.'

The St. Louis Post-Dispatch reported consistently with the local news channels, and reported correctly, that *bullying* led to the murder. It was also confirmed that the shooter fled the scene and was considered armed and dangerous by police. Not just Tony, *many* Ritenour students lacked counsel and provided just *hearsay*, leading to several reckless interviews, published and aired by the media to fuel the hype over such a sad day. Greedy reporters chasing a buck collaborated with stupid kids chasing their Fifteen Minutes, within a terrified part of a dying city...causing widespread panic.

Donnie's side of the story wouldn't be heard, though, as he was pronounced dead at the scene from the third bullet, penetrating his forehead. He was taken to the morgue. When my shock wore off I realized just how close I came from joining him there. Reporters showed no mercy when they stuck a mic in the face of his crushed father, Reginald Applebaum...

'My son was not a bully.'

The shooter's body was found the following Monday morning in a wooded area near Eureka, six days after the shooting. Identified as Tyler Keats, he died from a self-inflicted gunshot wound to the temple. *The girlish boy.* Who knew? Detectives found his suicide note that filled three sides of ripped-out notebook paper in his duffel bag. It disclosed many allegations about himself and his proclaimed enemies, with Donnie and Tony headlining. He expressed remorse about shooting me accidentally and blamed God for the society he was born into not accepting him. The most disturbing part of the note was the final line...

276

This is goodbye, signed in the blood of a victim-

-Tyler Keats

Tyler's use of the term *'victim'* will haunt me forever, serving as a constant reminder of how life haunts me, how I'm losing control, how I'm being pushed over the edge…how *I* still might pull the trigger. And I'm no different than anyone else, as we're *all* victims for very different, personal and unfortunate reasons.

Life will haunt you.

Ritenour was re-opened the day after they found Tyler and in turn the media circus packed up and came to campus. So many students had an opinion to express and local imaginations were further stirred by more irresponsible journalism. Some kids said that Tyler only had the gun for protection and was provoked. Others believed that he was suicidal all along. A few even claimed that Tyler's actions were premeditated and I just happened to get in the way, in the wrong place at the wrong time. But I believe that *all four of us* were.

After that first day back at school, many students came to visit me in my upgraded-to-stable condition. Clearly the school organised a very artificial campaign to visit me. They just wanted to see the freak show. They just wanted to see someone who'd actually been shot. No one really cared about me. I just happened to be involved. It was just a reason to have a field trip, all part of the charade…more reporting, more news…more hype…more fear…more fifteen-minute blocks of fame being sold. A hell of a lot better than sitting in class, I agree.

I'd had enough. Concern, support and remembrance were important but overblown nonsense was ruining everything. I requested that only Felicity, Justin and James be allowed to visit me along with my parents the day before my release. However, when Ms. Keats showed up to express her sympathy, remorse and sadness I made an exception. Upon her entering my room it didn't take long for more tears to roll down. It really wasn't until *right then* that the reality of all of this crushed down on my heart.

'Do ya hate my son, Ethan?'

'No, M'am,. Tyler was a lot like me. Ya see, I used to hate myself...'

bandages

I was released from the hospital this morning. It's great to escape from that clinical, white, wretched place, now under my own warm blankets. Still, I'm confined to this bed rest. Doctor's orders. That's right. I have a bullet-wound healing. I try to focus on that and how lucky I am to still be alive. But instead here I am, wrapped in bandages and resting in the cold hands of depression, and not because of the pain from surgery. My heart hurts a lot worse than my stomach, still dwelling on not being able to escort Felicity to Homecoming. These first seven hours back at home hasn't changed that. I wish I *was* dead. Maybe that guy with my face will walk in here with that shotgun and put me out of my misery.

Mom's almost fully recovered. She was put on a strict diet and given medical leave and a bag of pills to pop for the rest of her life. Dad has looked after us. Sceptically I've appreciated his close attention. Bless him, serving up orange juice and chicken soup to the wounded around him, while dragging his most-shaken heart behind. Mom's heart attack hit him extremely hard. She's his long-time wife, the love of his life and she certainly dodged a tragic death. But he was even more affected by my being shot. That might come as a surprise to some, but a bullet-wound is of violence, not of nature. It likely rekindled his wartime memories, seeing a young man fall to a bullet, or several soldiers that he met over there and got to know. Men just like

281

him. Men that he promised he'd call or write upon returning home. Friends that would *never* return. Brothers in arms that he watched die. He sees them in me, as he sees *himself.* I'm so young through his eyes, and his only son. Despite our bad blood, flowing peacefully *for now.* So, you see, it's not surprising how hard he took my bullet-wound, just as I'm not surprised that my mind is opening up to a Dawn of a New Day for a father and son. Or is it? Sadly, my hate for him is rooted deep and he never liked me much either. With so much dark history I fear that our relationship will only return to dysfunction in due course. I won't get my hopes up.

Gazing down at my bandages I watch my past swirl into a collage of time. How old am I? Seventeen? Twelve? Nine? Five? All through my childhood this bedroom has been where I've slept and dreamt, laughed and cried...hoped and prayed. As this bullet-wound heals I realise that I don't remember the last time I truly felt safe and warm *anywhere else.* The world outside has always seemed so big and uncertain. After being shot I'm still afraid of it, but now I'm tired of being afraid. But as safe as I am in this bed, I want to run like Hell to a place where nobody knows my name. Far away from here, from this town, from this school, where my past can't find me. Where I can start new, build and prosper. Where eventually *everyone* will know my name. A place where I won't remember one damn bad thing.

Today is a *new day*, breaking within the dawn of my lifetime. I dream about where I'll be at its high noon, and what I will have accomplished by its dusk. Will I be a photographer? Ballplayer? Writer? Will I still be working at Schnucks? Married to Felicity? Will I have a son of my own? What will he be like? Just like me? I won't let this happen to *him.*

Dad opens the door with a tray of the usual. The orange juice looks refreshing and the soup is steaming. It smells delicious. The care feels great. *His* care.

'This should keep ya goin.' Dad says as he sets the tray on

the nightstand.

'Thanks, dad.'

Charlie wags his tail, waiting for a pat on the head from him. And he says, 'I had a dog when I was young. A dog and a cat, actually.'

'Yeah, a black cat.' I say.

'Funny, I don't remember telling ya about Blackie.'

'Ya must of. How else would I have known?' *That's easy. I somehow went back in time to murder you and saw that cat in an old photo.*

'Well, anyway, Blackie was hit by a car one day. I was about seven, eight maybe. Mom, yer grandma, called me in for supper and I thought that he followed me in.'

'Sorry to hear that.'

'Must've used up his other eight lives,' Dad snickers. 'So, I got a dog a couple years later. Not a Shepherd like Charlie, though, a Black Lab.'

'Spooky, though, not Blackie?' I ask. Just nervous chatter, as I remember the cat leaping off the rocking chair in that photo, then hearing the tires screech.

'No, not Blackie, yer right. That Spooky, he knew I hated school, I tell ya. Just the way he looked at me as I left the house in the morning. I had this teacher, boy, she was…well, anyway.'

'Yeah, I've had some of them,' I mutter.

'I guess I never had a chance to talk to ya about that dance ya were going to.'

I stir the hot soup, nearly salivating to take my first slurp. But I hesitate to say, 'Not a big deal, really.'

'Sure it is. I never met that Felicity until the hospital. She's a fine gal. A *real* fine gal, there.' He starts to turn away, but then he stops. 'The summer after I graduated I met a girl. Everything was great, like I never knew life could be. Then I got that letter, from Uncle Sam, ya know. I wrote Terri, that was her name. I wrote her every week or so and she wrote me back for a while. But that stopped. I never knew why. I looked her up when I got back but only managed to find her sister. She told me that Terri didn't wanna be with any soldier scum after all. She moved to California or some shit.' Dad stares at my bedroom floor, stroking Charlie's head. 'I learned a lot in that hospital, in general, ya know. I've known for a long time now that I didn't really know who I was. At least, I didn't have a clue until I saw yer mother down on the kitchen floor. I just couldn't *believe* it, ya know? But then…I *could*. Something came over me, like, something really heavy just…*passed right through me*. I could actually feel yer mother's pain and panic for…just a second. I mean, I thought *I* was going down, *too*! But then…ah, son, I can't explain this.'

'No, Dad. Please go on.'

'Well, it just suddenly felt like, after I regained my balance, I looked down on yer mom and knew she'd be Ok. And I knew that I'd been wrong all these years. Wrong about the way I'd been toward her. Toward *you*. Does that make sense?'

'Yeah, Dad. Makes sense.'

'And when *you* went down, Ethan, ya weren't talkin, ya weren't…you were just-' and he stops again.

'I was scared,' I say, eyeing my dad through the steam rising from my soup, 'in the hospital.' I look away. I'm not ready for this emotional outpour. It sort of freaks me out, as it has never happened before between us. So I focus on the soup, how good it smells, how tasty it will be…how lucky I am to still get to enjoy it.

'I was too,' Dad says. 'I was *real* scared. I didn't know that

I could *feel* that scared.' Dad's trembling, and he, too, realises what's happening right here between us, right now, on this new day. 'All those people who came to see ya. Beautiful people who care, just like yer mother and I.' His voice cracks. Tears flow from his eyes as he adds, 'And all I wanted then was my family back...'

I try to deflect the emotion by saying, 'What a circus the media turned it into, huh? It's just so crazy.'

'Fuck the media.' he snorts.

And the media circus *was* crazy, but so is watching my dad stand in my doorway, searching for the words and the time he's lost. But *that* sad circus has packed up and hit the road and there's no getting it back. Those days are gone.

Life will haunt you, Dad. Time never stops.

Still, my father's outpour is a sign...a sign that I might have a chance to have the father I've always wanted. One day...

Dad turns away again and says, 'Son, I know I've made some mistakes. I'm sorry. I don't know what else to say. I just didn't know how scared I could get til I saw ya in the hospital.' He looks back, but I'm looking down. I can feel his eyes on me, looking upon me as *part* of him. *From* him. *Him* in another body. We share a thought: Why did all this have to happen this way?

Dad walks toward me and places his hand on my shoulder. It's warm. 'Life will haunt you, son. And time never stops.' Then he leans in and kissed me upon my brow. 'I do love ya. I do,' he whispers, and retreats down the hall.

'Dad,' I call out. He returns to the doorway. 'Thanks.' I wasn't thanking him for just the juice and soup.

Oh, this life. This haunting life.

A tear rolls down my cheek...

There's dialogue coming from the living room. 'He's in his room,' my father says, 'I'm sure he'll be happy to see ya both. Oh, yeah, one more thing, I hate to sound like a jerk but do ya mind takin yer shoes off? I just installed this carpeting today and wanna keep it nice.'

Felicity enters the bedroom first with a bright and happy face. Our eyes connect and we speak in that language that no one else can hear. Then her lips move, 'How are ya, baby?' I've already answered her, though, as she's already asked.

'I'm great. The Price is Right had a perfect show today and I watched some guy get a chair across the face on Jerry Springer.'

Felicity sits at my side as the toilet flushes from down the hall. Justin storms into my room and plops down on the wooden desk chair. He says, 'Boy, don't go in that bathroom for about an hour. Don't worry, though. I opened the window in there a little.'

'I didn't hear a courtesy flush.' I reply.

'Hey, I flushed. Live with it. How ya feelin?'

I struggle to find the right words to answer Justin's question. I've thought so much about it and I know I've got a lot to say, but not now. I miss Justin. I miss Felicity more. I just want to enjoy their company. I simply answer, 'I'm feelin better.'

'When do ya get those bandages off?' Justin asks.

'Don't know. I gotta follow-up next week.'

'Yer dad apologized *again* just now,' he says, 'just like he did at the hospital.'

'At least five times,' Felicity adds, 'he pulls that shotgun on ya, and now his own son…'

There's an awkward pause. No one mentions the word *irony* but the silence implies it even harder. 'Hey, what was he talkin bout out there?' I ask. 'New carpeting?'

286

'Yeah,' Justin answers, 'bright white. Installed just this afternoon.'

'While I was sleeping? Damn, those meds are strong!'

'I just love the smell of new carpeting,' Felicity says.

'What in *Hell* happened to that guy?' I say, 'It's like he's a changed man…'

'How's yer mama?' Felicity asks.

'She's on the mend. In her bedroom restin, same as me. It's a God-damned MASH unit around here.'

Justin takes a long swig from the straw of his fountain drink and says, 'School's crazy, dude. Just ridiculous.'

'Anything that I should know that the news hasn't already told me?' I ask.

Felicity strokes my hair and replies, 'There's been talk of Homecoming being cancelled.'

'Yeah,' Justin chimes, 'the parade, the game, the dance, the whole nine.'

'That'll be good for me,' I say, 'I'll be back on my feet by the time they reschedule.'

'No,' Felicity says, 'not postponed. *Cancelled*.'

'There may not *be* a Homecoming this year,' Justin adds.

'What? They gotta have a Homecoming? Right?'

Felicity and Justin burst into laughter. Justin says, 'I never thought I'd hear ya say that, man!'

'The committee's worked hard,' Felicity says, 'But there's still a lot of tension.'

'Yeah, we've probably seen the last of the police and the reporters. But it still ain't right. I was lookin forward to the DJ gig but there are still a lot of tension.'

287

'DJ gig?' I ask. 'What DJ gig?'

'Oh, of course ya haven't heard. The day ya were shot the committee decided to have a DJ and I was nominated. It would be a big opportunity for me.'

'Ritenour should have this!' I say. 'A Homecoming event that's been worked on so hard will go great. It would be perfect for the tense times.'

'Maybe ya should call the principal.' Felicity says, 'It's his call to cancel it.'

'Look,' Justin says, 'too much has happened. There's no way they're gonna have a dance.'

'Yes! Felicity, I'll do it. I'll call up there now. The principal's office is open until five.'

'Have ya ever spoken a *word* to that guy, Ethan?' Justin asks.

'When ya think about it,' I reply, 'I'm part of the reason for this. Maybe I *can* get him to keep it on.'

'It couldn't hurt,' Felicity says, 'and *you are* one of the victims.

'I'll call under one condition,' I say, 'if the dance stays on for this Saturday night then *you two* gotta go together.'

'Ya mean as my *date*?' Felicity asks.

'Uh, yeah, Felicity. As yer date. I gotta make sure ya don't go with anyone else *but* the only guy I would *half-way* trust. If ya went with someone else I'd be forced to kick his ass. Well, not anytime soon, ya know, wrapped up in these bandages.'

Justin says, 'Only half-way trust, huh? Well, throw in yer dad's Vette and we gotta deal.'

Felicity laughs sarcastically, 'The *Vette*? That'll never happen! Not in a million years! Easy Justin, I'm still getting used to *you* being my date!'

I shake my head. 'I'm afraid I agree, dude,'

Felicity chuckles, 'Justin and I, huh?'

'It just makes sense to me.' I say. 'After all, Justin, yer gonna be in the booth. Felicity, ya worked hard on the committee and you've already got yer dress.'

'Yeah,' Justin says, 'and Felicity, yer up for Homecoming Queen!'

'What?' I cry out.

'Baby, I wanted to tell ya but it suddenly wasn't important.'

'It was announced on that Tuesday.' Justin says. 'Then all Hell broke loose.'

'It doesn't matter anyway,' Felicity says, 'it's just some stupid popularity vote-thing.'

'No, it's *mega-important*. I've heard fairy tales about high school sweethearts and game-winning touchdowns. I've pretended not to care because I've never wanted to admit to myself how much better my life would be with a spoonful of High School Glory. This is our senior year, guys! Felicity, yer gonna be the Homecoming Queen! Justin, yer gonna be the DJ! This thing's gotta stay on!'

'But, Ethan, and if it stays on then ya won't be there with me.'

'Well, Justin will just have to there. Don't worry. I'll take ya to Prom this spring.'

'*If* we're still together!' Felicity says as she kisses me.

'Hey, y'all,' Justin says, 'enough with the kissy-face, first off. Secondly, none of this Felicity-and-I stuff will fly if my girl *I asked* can come.'

289

'What?!' I exclaim. 'Who in Hell did *you* ask?'

'Deeta Von Teese.'

'Dude, shut up!' I yell and chuck a pillow at him.

'Well, I was told that Betty Page was dead.'

'Ok, Ethan,' Felicity smiles, 'I'm happy yer on board with this. But, who am I gonna dance with? Justin will be in the DJ booth all night.'

'We'll sort that out,' Justin says.

I slide my hand onto her leg and say, 'Ya gotta have a date. Ya *both* do.'

Felicity looks at Justin and asks, 'Well?'

Justin asks, 'So, there's *no* chance of getting the Vette?'

'I'd love to go with ya, Justin,' Felicity says, 'but there may not even *be* a dance.'

'Ok, assuming there *is* a dance, Ethan, is there any way we can take the Vette?'

Suddenly, a heart-racing scheme unfolds in my mind. I gulp the rest of my orange juice and say, 'Actually, my friend, there is *one* way.'

the dead of night

'So, what are ya wearin?'

'A very tight pair of track shorts.' Felicity answers.

'What colour?' I ask.

'Black. I'm squirmin in bed right now, cuz it's so big without ya in it with me, and these shorts are just really slick, satin material, they glide against my skin, ya know?'

'Oh…I do…and I don't.'

'Well, ya *would* know…if ya got off that lazy ass of yers and came over here…'

'Holy *shit!*' I gasp. In my room, in the dark, I grip my cell phone tightly. Otherwise I'm paralysed.

'Ethan, what's *wrong*?'

'There's someone in my room. *With* me.' A silhouette stands still. It could be standing on the desk. It could be hanging in the black air. As it's the dead of night, it's too dark to tell.

'What? Who? It's *3am!*'

'You'll never…*oh shit!*' I shriek. The silhouette jolts and snaps in a very inhuman way.

'Ethan, calm down! What's goin on?!'

293

'Someone's *here*! Standing on *my desk*!'

'What?'

'Holy shit!' I whimper. The silhouette swoops down to the floor with lightning speed and crawls onto my bed like a startled reptile.

'Should I come over there?' Felicity asks.

'No, I mean, maybe. I don't know. It's right on the end of *my bed!* I don't know what it's gonna do!'

'Ethan, I…is it *Charlie?*'

'No! Charlie's not in here.'

'What *is* it, Ethan?!'

'I, I don't know! It's too dark in here. Oh my God! It's *glowing*. Its face is…*ugh, it's horrible!*' The silhouette's face is defined by four dark patches on its neon-red head: two eyes, a nose and a mouth.

'What the? Ethan, tell me what's goin on!'

The eyes' patches morph into defined pupils and retinas. But the rest of its face swirls into a red glowing skull. 'Ethan,' the skull face says, 'Why are you whispering? I can hear every word you say. And *think.*'

'Felicity,' I say more calmly.

'Ethan, if ya don't tell me what in Hell's happenin-'

'I-I'm sorry. I've just been having a very bad dream. I am so, so sorry.'

'Ethan-' but Felicity's voice is muted by a few clicks…and then silence.

'The phone's dead, Ethan. Just like me.'

'Felicity! Fel-'

'Hang it up, boy.'

'Tyler? What do ya want from me?'

'I just need a place to stay tonight. I can't bear my house these days. So much sadness. But, where am I to go? How long will this last?' When Tyler speaks his head flashes, as rapidly as a strobe light, from the demonic red skull to the innocent face that I'll always remember him having. Burning red eyes alternate with soft, round, chocolate morsels. Wispy hair of the same shade gives way to a slick red dome. Ironically, though, it was that *innocent* face he wore when he pulled that trigger last Tuesday.

'Tyler, did you-'

'Didn't you hear the news?' he asks, lounging casually while his skull flashes in the dark. Definitely the strangest thing I've ever seen.

'I heard ya put a bullet through yer head.'

'I did, here, take a look.' Tyler crawls next to me like an iguana, like a spider, like a…

'Stay away from me!' I demand, but he doesn't hesitate in crawling *right through me* to sit on the other edge of my bed. 'Fuck! What on Earth?! You just-'

It only lasted a second and a half, but that's all the time it took for his entire life to flash before my eyes, for every emotion he ever expressed to flow through my veins. For a second and a half *I was Tyler Keats.*

'I just fucking passed right through you.' He says. 'I was just *inside* you, boy.'

'Tyler, that sounds…*so gay!*'

Tyler laughs, 'Very funny! Anyway, I don't have all that shit inside me like you do anymore.' He frowns in disgust and wipes his hands and arms.

295

'What shit?' I ask.

'*This* shit! *Your* shit! God, it's all over me! That human, soft, brittle tissue. All that slimy, emotional, drag-ya-down *shit* that ruined my life. Crawling through you kinda makes me happy I'm dead. But, not really.'

'Tyler, what did you-?'

'I stole my mom's car and drove out to the woods. *He knows what I'm thinking. Feeling. He answers my questions before I ask them.*

'What were ya gonna say to me that one time? On the bus? Do ya-'

'I was just going to say what I said just a moment ago. Where am I to go? How long will this last? Stupidly, I thought you might have known that morning. But, alas, you're not a fag like I was. You wanted to fuck Felicity Farmer *then*, after all, just like you're doing her now.'

'Wait, ya just said I fucked, I mean, her and I. We *did it?'*

'Sure you did it, Tiger. You came from out of nowhere this year. I didn't think you had it in ya, but after I put that bullet in my head I saw that you did. You've got a lot of…whatever you want. But you've also got a lot of problems.'

'Tyler, I…yes, I do have a lot of problems. But, if Felicity and I *did* do it, then why-'

'What you saw and felt that night in your room with her, what you remember in place of fucking that girl is not for me to explain.'

'Please, Tyler, ya gotta tell me, man!'

'Listen to you! Man? Guy? Making your demands. I'm dead now. No one owns me anymore. I'm here just because…'

'Just because why?' I ask.

'Just because you were right, what you said to my mom. We *were* a lot alike. You and I.'

'Ok, but what did ya mean by-'

'I meant that it's not my job to tell you what's been happening to you, why you've been seeing things, hearing things, missing chunks of your life, waking up on your kitchen floor. It's not that witch's either. The one who wears that white gown. *Hideous!*'

'I think she's beautiful. But how could a woman so beautiful be so-'

'Ethan, I understand you've got a lot of questions, but I can only answer what I can answer. Your life is...going to happen. Feel fortunate that you've received warnings.'

'Yes, Tyler, everything was a *warning!* But, am I going insane?'

'Ethan! I'm not *here* for that! And anyway, experts say that the insane believe their perfectly sane. But you must admit, ole chap, a dead guy with a skull for a head visiting you at three in the morning is not a very sane experience. Well, hey, I never said I was a psychiatrist.'

'Ok, Tyler. Then what the fuck are ya here for then?'

'I *told* you. I can't stand the mood at my mom's right now. All she does is cry. And, well, she just won't listen to a word I say!' he giggles. 'I thought it would be quiet over here, you know, but I didn't think you'd be having phone sex.'

'It wasn't phone sex, I mean, wait! Hold on a minute! What did ya come here to tell me?'

'Take a look. On the fourth wall of your bedroom. The wall that's always missing when you see the...ah, never mind. Anyway, there's no forest. Nothing that looks like your dream PA project. Felicity isn't out there anywhere. It's just the fourth

297

wall to your room. Now watch the movie.'

A film is being projected onto the fourth wall, but there's no projector in the room. Still, the scene in the churchyard leading up to the murder is being shown, filmed with a red filter. There is no sound, so it's just like a silent film, but without subtitles. I bask in its horrific crimson gloom while watching Donnie and Tony beat the shit out of Tyler. 'See, Ethan, look how pathetic I was!' Tyler says, wearing a black shirt and trousers, contrasting menacingly in the film's red glow. 'I was just some helpless faggot. And look at them, just a couple of lost souls, beating the shit out of me. They *beat* me. Just like *that*. So many times. And I decided to get a gun. That was the first day I ever loaded it…and took it out of the house.'

I can't control my trembling as this entire situation has become too weird, too chilling. My teeth are literally *chattering!* I never wanted to be reminded of that horrible day, especially so soon, but my eyes are glued to the fourth wall where the tragedy unfolds again.

'And here *you* come, Ethan. Yeah, this is where you tried to stop them. But, it was already decided. I already knew that I was going to kill them.' *The way he narrates it! It's like Grandma before she died, when she'd narrate old Christmas films during the holidays, around the fireplace, sipping eggnog.*

I watch the two bullies beat Tyler in a greater depth of terror now, as Tyler crawls to his bag. It dawns on me that he was able to get to his gun that morning only because I distracted them, trying to stop them! I screamed at them, and they just laughed at me in response, gloatingly waving their hands about. That morning I couldn't take my eyes from those bullies. But now I can't take my eyes from Tyler pulling the pistol from his bag.

'This is where I blow Donnie Applebaum's brains out. Watch closely, Ethan. Watch closely.'

298

'Turn this off! I scream.

<BANG>

<BANG>

<BANG>

'No!' I cry.

'Donnie's brains splattered all over that tree! Did you see that! Tony got lucky, though. But, Ethan, I never meant to shoot you…'

NEVER MEANT TO SHOOT YOU

         NEVER MEANT TO SHOOT YOU

    NEVER MEANT TO SHOOT YOU

'Tyler? *Tyler!* Where *are* you? Tyler! Where did ya *go?*' He's disappeared, but his voice echoes on…

        I KILLED HIM

I KILLED MYSELF

    I KILLED HIM

I KILLED MYSELF

        I KILLED HIM

    I KILLED MYSELF

'I'm right *here*,' he says. I twist around to see him standing on the other side of my bed, holding my father's twelve-gauge.

'What are ya *doin* with that?'

299

'Ethan, I am so, so sorry about shooting you. I never meant to hurt you. I came here tonight to apologise to you, and to make it up to you. So, here. Take it.' He holds the gun out to me, like some twisted form of an olive branch offering.

'Tyler, what are ya *doin?*'

'Just *do it*, Ethan. Stop letting it drive you *mad*. Take your father's gun, stick the barrel in your mouth and...'

IT'S YOUR DESTINY

YOUR DESTINY

YOUR DESTINY

'Tyler! Tyler where *are* you!' He's vanished and left me with the disturbing vision of my father's gun on the edge of my bed. I pick it up and handle it, wondering if I'd find any ectoplasm or some other supernatural substance. I study the long black double barrel, the trigger, the butt. I crack it open to discover that it's actually loaded! I've got to get this thing back into the garage!

But the fourth wall now portrays something I've never seen. Tyler hikes through a dark forest carrying that murderous 9mm. Has someone *filmed him*? It looks like someone actually followed him in *Blair Witch* fashion. Tyler hikes so deep into the woods that the screen goes black, or perhaps night had fell.

A red glow bleeds onto the screen and shows Tyler standing against a tree, his frothy short locks blowing in the breeze, leaves falling all around him. He's reading a note. *His suicide note.* But, like I said, it's silent. I can't hear a word he's reading. His visible breath blasts from his lips and dissipates into the night. He smiles then grimaces, and a tear rolls down from one of his big brown eyes, all the while waving that gun about like some madman.

Tyler drops that note from his fingers and it falls out of view, and he just stares back at me with that gun held to his temple...

I turn away and close my eyes. I'm crying, holding my father's loaded twelve-gauge...knowing that it's too late.

Sobbing...

Is it too late for me?

It seems like an hour's passed. It must be safe now. I open my eyes and turn around to face that fourth wall, that 'movie'...

Tyler mouths, 'Goodbye', and pulls the trigger. Blood splatters from his head. He, like his suicide note, falls out of view.

There's scratching on the outside of my door. 'Charlie,' I cry as I set the gun down. All I want to do is hold my dear friend, stroke his fur, and let him comfort me as only he can. My dear, loyal friend, the way he whimpers in my ear to express his concern, wagging his tail all along to remind me that everything's going to be alright. Charlie knows...

I rise from my bed as the burning red light goes black. The room is dark again as the fourth wall has gone blank. It's as if Tyler never visited tonight. Everything, minus Charlie's scratching, is calm again.

'Charlie, stop it!' I scold. I turn the doorknob and yank it open. It's not Charlie.

A white wolf growls at me in the doorway. Gnashing its carnivorous teeth and flashing its red gums, canine saliva splatters on my feet. It's a killer. A beast, eclipsed by the long shadow of a silhouette. Someone is coming, from around the corner, from the kitchen, down the hall toward me...toting a shotgun. I slam the door shut in the wolf's face. I twist that lock on the door and dart to my bed for *my* shotgun...but it's not there. It's disappeared! As the wolf outside my door snarls and barks ferociously the man with the shotgun says, 'Ya can't run forever. And you can never hide.'

the wolf and boy

Thursday, October 21

The morning storm thunders down. Rain slashes against the other side of the panes, blurring the outside world.

I feel safe in my bed, but how safe will I feel if I…when I…?

There's still some physical pain as I rise and put my feet down on the rug. I stand up in the grey light and can't twist or turn like I want to. I walk towards the door, and as I shuffle my feet across the floor I'm discouraged that nothing is routine. The pain is so…*real,* underneath these bandages. Even now that I'm alone I'm still too conscious and embarrassed of my crooked posture and sloth-like movement. I'm so fucked.

The pops.

The colours.

The splatters.

The screeches.

The darkness.

All of it inside a black and red minute in the churchyard.

'It plays back in my mind like an old movie, whenever it wants. The flashbacks control me, like they'll control you

305

someday. Life will haunt you, son. Time never stops.'

That minute of my life plays back over and over again. I'm a slave to the memory. I'm alive but I'm scared. I'm alive but I'm scarred. I'll never forget how we all fell down in that crisp October air.

Like fallen leaves.

I phoned the principal even though my fears and memories told me not to. I just wasn't ready to speak to anyone at the school, but I called anyway knowing that Felicity and Justin and everyone else *wanted* Homecoming. They need it after all that that's happened.

As the Principal's Office phone rang and rang, it dawned on me that this was a long shot. I was naïve in thinking I could just contact our principal and start a conversation that would somehow lead to Homecoming staying on. He's full of his own importance and stays behind the big curtain where he pitches his announcements over the PA and calls his shots in secret. He seems to be just a voice and a signature. No one ever sees him in person unless he's giving a speech at an assembly or standing down on the field with the Varsity football coach on a Friday night. He's untouchable otherwise.

The principal's secretary answered, though, and treated me like a celebrity on the phone. It was as easy as a summer breeze. She told me I was 'very sweet for caring so much about my fellow students, considering the state I was in.' She then broke the news to me that it was already decided. Homecoming and all its events, including the dance, *would* stay on after all. This Saturday, as originally planned.

I turn the knob and pull my bedroom door open an inch, letting a laser of bathroom light shoot in. Someone left it on. Normally I'd be inclined to step out into the hall and flip the switch down. Especially since *I* usually get blamed for wasting our home's electricity. But as I open my door all the way I am overcome with strange fear, just like on the morning of the shootings. 'Mom? Dad? Anybody home?' The only sound is Charlie's claws.

<click-clack, click-clack, click-clack>

He stops in the hallway and stares at me, cocking his head to the left and coughing out a whimper. Charlie knows…

'Come on, boy,' I call out and shut the door after he slips inside the safety of my room. He jumps into bed with me but I don't scold him for taking up too much space this time. It's just good to feel safer.

* * *

I spy out the front door and notice that the rain has stopped. As the sun warms my chest through the screen door my eyes feast on the glorious afternoon. My pain is less and my confidence is more. Maybe tomorrow I'll sneak out for a walk, if this weather holds. I surely could use it with the mental tug-o-war of Homecoming both exciting and depressing me. I'll be staying home, but what a night it will be for Felicity and Justin. Now that my parents have embarked on their trip to Hannibal the stage is set. The key to my father's Corvette glistens on the kitchen table, waiting for Justin to stick it into the ignition, jagged edge down, and turn it clockwise. The black panther will then glint her chrome fangs and roar, before growling all the way to the gymnasium. Justin and Felicity will be the hottest shit at Ritenour, just as I always knew I'd be if my old man ever let me drive it.

The Post-Dispatch has been delivered, shoved in a condom-tight raincoat and thrown in the front lawn. In the Homecoming spirit I want to read about how the football team played last night. I open the door and march down the porch steps, crunching the colourful fallen leaves, still damp from the showers.

And I finally notice it. My pin oak tree is gone! I move toward where it used to stand, slightly downhill just three feet from the curb. As my eyes take in the vacancy of where my tree has stood for over ten years, my mind processes it. I put my hand over my mouth and feel my knees buckle. My tree is now just a stump. The Law must have cut it down sometime between my parents leaving and my waking up. Mom and Dad would've protested even though City Hall declared we didn't have a case

308

and that the tree was indeed a road hazard. Despite my being laid up with a bullet wound, *I* would've protested, but I didn't know when they were coming.

So here I stand, in the same place that I stood ten and half years ago after planting a mere twig into the zoysia soil. That pin oak was growing up so fast, just like I have. But now it's gone, just a memory, just like my childhood.

And now one of the weirdest sights I've ever seen freezes me before I even have time to shed a tear. It's absolutely uncanny, how that wolf stalks Bataan Drive in the broad daylight! A *white* wolf. At this very moment you could knock me over with a feather, or even a dead leaf. That wolf just stares at me from a stone's throw-distance, panting calmly in the warm sun with those deep wolf eyes gazing right through me. But not even a *trace* of a wolf can be found for one hundred miles, let alone here in the St. Louis suburbs. What on *Earth* is it doing right here on my street? My street, where I live…spinning…tilting…I'm so dizzy…and I've collapsed to my hands and knees on the damp grass. And as that wolf intensifies its stare, licking its chops at my downed state, those same old voices chant…

YOU FELL IN LOVE

SHE DROWNED

FELL IN LOVE

SHE DROWNED

FELL IN LOVE

SHE DROWNED

I close my eyes hard and re-open them, regaining my focus. I grip the grass tightly as if I was hanging on to my last ounce of sanity, but a familiar sound rips it away from me.

<click-clack, click-clack, click-clack>

The first time I saw the woman draped in white she was coming around Bataan Drive's oak-lined bend. And now, from around that same bend marches a boy. A *teenage* boy. His stride is short but very quick, never breaking into a run, as if he's in fast-forward. As he comes nearer I notice his short, cropped dark locks of hair, just like mine a few haircuts ago. Now, even closer, I notice the shotgun at his side, and his clothing...fashion that I can't say I've ever seen before: blacks and greys and olives tucked into rich shades of red and blue. His collar is laced tightly around his neck like a pair of sneakers whilst his trouser legs are 'bandaged' with a sort of black denim that's patterned like a western bandana. And the strange boots that he marches closer and closer in, I simply can't describe. I must admit that I'd be deep in admiration of his look if I weren't so startled.

He stops at the beast's side. The wolf and boy stare at me from the edge of my front yard.

The voices...

IT'S YOU'RE FACE

NEVER GONNA BREAK THE CYCLE

YOU'RE SON

BREAK THE CYCLE

YOU'RE FACE

BREAK THE CYCLE

The boy has *my* face. *It's me!*

Paws scamper from behind me.

'Charlie, no! Get back here!' But my dog scorches past me toward the wolf anyway. 'Charlie! Come back here!' The wolf braces itself as its fur stands up from head to tail.

The voices whisper...

GET THE GUN

GET THE GUN

GET THE GUN

The wolf's growl matches Charlie's as its eyes turn red...

GET THE GUN

GET THE GUN

GET THE GUN

Charlie storms the wolf in the middle of the street. Gnashing his big white fangs, he goes for the wolf's throat. But the wolf, just like the boy with my face, disappears into thin air! As sure as the oak trees shiver and the dead leaves fall.

'Charlie! Charlie come!' He took a rough tumble, coming up empty on his courageous attack. Just as confused as I am, my dog shakes off the dirt and pain and trots back to me. Charlie and I scurry up the front steps and back into the house. As I slam the door shut I sigh in relief, having successfully retreated to the

311

safety of my room.

homecoming eve

Felicity enters my living room, in from the Homecoming Eve night. She wears the same smile she wore that very first day she walked into the classroom. Only, I don't just *feel* like I've known her my entire life. I *know* that I've known her forever. She's going to spend the night with me here. We'll have the house to ourselves.

In my room.

In my bed.

Under my sheets with me.

Tonight.

She follows me into my bedroom and pulls that emerald green dress from her duffel bag. She lays it out over the desk chair in which underneath she's parked her matching shoes. She looks up at me, like she's always done. Like the *very first time*. Suddenly I just know that there will be no distractions.

Tonight, St. Louis will be alive, not dying.

Tonight, the freshman year locker room attack never happened.

Tonight, I won't hate my father.

Tonight, my mother will be just fine.

Tonight, money won't matter, and I'll get that car eventually.

Tonight, Felicity is mine and everything else will work itself out.

We make love in my bedroom. There are no loud drunk men. Felicity looks more gorgeous than ever, not gored and stained with blood. We become one, surrounded by *four* bedroom walls, not three. There is no forest or river or voices. My bed is our warm cocoon where we are safe; where we exhaust ourselves but still ache for more of what we can't get enough of; where we are possessed by our teenage hormones and everything so new.

'I have these nightmares,' I whisper.

As Homecoming Eve goes by…

'My mama passed away over the summer,' she says.

We talk…

'I don't wanna hate my father.'

Our hearts spill onto our laps…

'She visits me all the time, Ethan.'

Time passes so fast…

'I believe in ghosts, Felicity. They must be everywhere.'

But we hold hands…

'I live with my aunt now. She's got problems, but she was her little sister.'

And we press against our growing love...

'I saw somethin in yer photo, Felicity.'

I want to tell her everything...

'I couldn't submit that photo. My mama was in it.'

I want to sail her seas and discover her islands...

'I knew it was her, Felicity. There are so many victims...'

We kiss...

'Everyone dies, Ethan. They serve their time in this world. Then God takes em when their time comes.'

We make love...

'Victims that couldn't see the light at the end of the tunnel. Suddenly they're dead.'

We are connected souls in teenage shells...

'But some go anyway. They're somewhere between God and Satan. They're lost.'

While life haunts us...

'Lost souls,' I whisper.

317

As time never stops…

'Ghosts, Ethan.' Felicity whispers back, 'they just wanna come back home.'

'Life will haunt you…'

She knows…

'Time never stops…'

I know…

'Like fallen leaves.'

'Where am I to go? How long will this last?' Tyler Keats will always ask.

Like fallen leaves, ghosts flutter back down here with us, trapped inside the dusks and dawns. We hear their invisible footsteps and see their glowing light out of the corner of our eyes. They slam doors shut and flicker 100 watt bulbs. Their voices are mistaken for just the wind. We see them at 3am and think we're just dreaming. That rush of a winter-cold gust on a summer night is always only just a draft…because they are supposed to be dead and there's no other explanation.

I hold Felicity close and I shut my eyes. I watch us walk through a place we all call Heaven.

Dawn breaks open another autumn morning…

318

We peacefully sleep while flying, through the blazing sunshine, down the desert highway. In my car with the top down at eighty…madly in love.

I wake up in grey daylight feeling like I haven't since I was a child, feeling like I've slept for days. I haven't felt this good, this pure, this wonderful, at least, since then. My feelings are confirmed when I look down upon Felicity, still sleeping peacefully. I can die now. I never want to let this moment go…

But there's a hard knock on the front door that wakes her. I look at the clock.

1:40pm.

'Good morning,' Felicity purrs.

'Good *afternoon,*' I reply.

bloody paws

'I'll see ya tonight,' Felicity whispers in my ear. She kisses my lips and twirls her tongue inside my mouth before walking out into the grey dusk. Justin escorts her out to the Vette, opening the passenger door for her underneath an intimidating sky. The hard gusts of wind ruffle the pair of them and the scent of a storm blasts up my nostrils. Justin shuts the door and walks briskly around to the driver's side. 'Save some of that beer for us,' he says, 'see ya in a few hours.'

'I ain't goin nowhere,' I say, pointing to my bandaged torso.

'And don't worry. I'll have her back by midnight, wearin that crown.'

'Ya better!' I smile, struggling to keep it turned up. The pain of my Homecoming Queen shoe-in going on without me sets in as Justin turns the key, igniting that 350 under the hood, and it just doesn't seem real. This is like watching a fucking cartoon! But nevertheless, there they go down the street en route to the dance. The Vette turns onto Woodson Road and Justin and Felicity disappear.

It's on...

I shut the door as raindrops start to fall, as my heart starts to break. With midnight still over five hours away I ponder what

I'll do to kill this lonely evening away. I pet Charlie on the head and stroke his soft fur. 'Just you and I tonight, boy.' He follows me into the kitchen and sits for me nicely to deserve a Milk Bone. He politely takes it from my hand and munches with all the manners a dog could possibly show. I'm entertained by how he even holds it upright to his mouth with his clamped paws. Pure Happiness. *Sigh. I wish I could be that happy tonight...*

God, this is *horrible!* What am I going to do to take my mind off the misery, watch my dog woof down Milk Bones all night?

I fetch my Vampire Bats CD and put it on in the living room. Ah, the speakers out here sound so much better than the set in my room! I bang my head to the rock en route to the fridge to fetch a bottle of Bud. I crack it open and drown my dark emotions in Beachwood-aged suds, focusing on the music that takes me back to that first night I laid my eyes on Felicity. I crank the volume up to 10 and wonder how long it will take to shatter a window, or get the cops called on me. Fuck it, I *need* this music. It's what I heard when I met her, feeling almost like that same electricity shooting up through my legs and into my chest. Maybe if I drink this fast enough and blast this music loud enough then just maybe I'll somehow go back to that raucous pit again, where she'll be waiting for me all over again. And if I get there I promise I won't let her slip away again.

I down the first bottle as fast as I can and declare that Felicity is the most beautiful girl in the world. The most beautiful girl in the world that would've been, *should've been*, my date if I hadn't been shot. I enjoy the consolation of simply *knowing* that, and knowing that I helped two of the most important people in my life have a night they'd hopefully never forget.

I crack open another bottle as Track Three begins, and another during Track Five. When Track Seven explodes from my parents speakers I decide to just keep it simple and drink one bottle per song. After all, the X-man sold me a whole case and at this rate I'll still have plenty for when Felicity and Justin arrive.

The album has ended and the living room has begun to tilt. As I stand up to let Charlie out the backdoor and into the backyard it stops tilting and starts spinning. *Jesus Christ, this is nice.* I slam the backdoor shut and just feel so damn good, wobbling back into the living room to refill the sound pool with more rock. I want to *swim* through it now and high dive into the deep end. Goosebumps rise from my skin as I replay *Tragedy*, howling the lyrics at the ceiling lying flat on my back...

Whoa, what happened? How long ago did the music stop? Oh, shit, Charlie's scratching on the door...

The voices...

SLIPPERY ROAD

SLIPPERY ROAD

SLIPPERY ROAD

The whispers...

POLICE CHASE

POLICE CHASE

POLICE CHASE

The chants...

GET YER GUN

GET YER GUN

GET YER GUN

Hooves thunder down over the phantom voices. That ghost-woman and her horse approach me as the alcohol flows faster through my veins. But I'm calm, drunk and ready for anything.

'Eee-thaan,' she calls. I twist around, anticipating her behind me on horseback, or standing, or *floating*. My stomach's stiff wound cracks as I do, but I'm pained more to not find her.

'Eee-thaan,' she calls again, remaining invisible. I take a long swig of my beer and perk my ears for more. Maybe she's not actually here and I'm just too drunk, hearing things, imagining things. But with calm enthusiasm, I want that ghost-woman to show herself right here and right now. I'm ready for her. I want to speak to her. I want to know what all of this means!

'Eee-thaan.' I *know* that I heard her that time. She's somewhere in this house.

'Where are you?' I call out. 'Show yerself!' But my demand is interrupted by another strange sound...

Drip...drip...drip...

My house has been devoured by pitch blackness and I'm in a dark, cold chasm. A huge oak tree appears, casting no shadow, as if it's rooted underneath the stage floor of a theatre. And here I am, standing right underneath it, glowing just the same.

Drip...drip...drip...

And so does a grand piano, just north of that tree. Justin

326

wears a tux and is slumped over it, his head resting on the ivory, his vacant eyes open wide.

Drip…drip…drip…

And so does a church to the east. Donnie is dressed like a Catholic priest and is standing in its yard, reading The Bible.

Drip…drip…drip…

And so does Tyler, standing in cowboy boots behind dusty chaps, the brim of his black ten-gallon pulled over his eyes to the west. He moseys toward the tree, bootheels clicking, spurs clanging. He leans against its huge trunk and pulls a silver-plated widow maker from his holster.

Drip…drip…drip…

And so does a river, rolling along to the south. Felicity in her emerald green dress stands upon its bank. She inhales, flairs the cigarette away between her fingers, and exhales a white cloud that floats up into the blackness.

Drip…drip…drip…

And so do blood drops. They fall on my head, splattering against me like thick, red rain. I look up and see the colourful leaves, soon to fall to the ground, *bleeding.*

<BANG>

Kind of like a gunshot.

Sort of like a car crash.

As the ringing sound of that bang fades away so does my…imag-

Charlie barks ferociously, bringing me all the way back. I'm home safe, sitting in the middle of my living room on this

327

new, fresh-smelling, spotless, plush white carpeting that Dad just installed.

Drunk as shit! And let's get some more music back on, for the love of God!

But what's wrong with my dog? 'Charlie! Charlie, come here!' But it's that white wolf that enters the living room, not Charlie. It stalks me cautiously, keeping its head low, piercing me with golden eyes. Its bloody paws sink silently into the brand new carpet, leaving a trail of red prints through the living room. It stops at the kitchen entrance, never taking those golden eyes from me.

'Eee-thaan,' the ghost-woman calls to me again. This time I know she's in my bedroom. But this wolf standing guard has destroyed my alcohol-fuelled nerve to confront her once and for all. 'Eee-thaan.'

Wobbling back on the heels of my hands, legs spread out before the wolf, I try as hard as I can to remain calm and not provoke it. But I can't stop staring at its trail of bloody paw prints, then into its eyes, and feeling my heart crash against the back of my throat. The wolf takes a step toward me, then another.

And another, still.

But the wolf is calm.

Head raised.

Eyes relaxed.

Tail wagging slightly.

I am paralysed. My eyes are peeled as if doing so will delay my fate and force this beast to have mercy on me. But it takes yet another step closer and sits down between my thighs. It dips its head, gazes deeply into mine. I wonder what it thinks of its reflection in my pupils, as it licks its chops.

328

The overwhelming terror shuts my eyes. My body shivers uncontrollably.

Its cold, wet nose nuzzles against my neck, then my chin, leaving a damp trail as it sniffs my flesh. Then, its rough, wet tongue whips across my lips and past my nose. I open my eyes and feel my fright melt away, just as this wolf licks my face again.

'Walter?'

Walter wags its tail hard now, up on all fours, resting his chin on my shoulder. His soft white mane feels heavenly against my face.

And as I stroke Walter's back, soaking up his silky coat with my fingertips, I feel like I've known him forever. And I remember it all backwards…

I remember saving Walter's life.

I remember jumping off the coal train near Cheyenne.

I remember hitchhiking to the Wyoming state line.

I remember walking for three days and still not making it to Omaha.

I remember almost being arrested in Kansas City.

I remember buying that Greyhound ticket.

I remember deciding to flee to Canada before I ever knew what was waiting for me out on that lonely road that might show me freedom.

I remember blowing my father's head off.

I remember wondering what killing him would be like.

I remember hating the world.

Walter knows…

But now I love this wolf, and I've come back here to tell

my father he was wrong. He *will be* wrong.

And now I love this world.

The phone rings. I let go of Walter and put the cordless to my ear, saying nothing. I hear the faint sound of the news from a hotel room television crackling through the phone and into my ear. 'Ethan? Hello? Just wanted to say we made it to Hannibal, all snug as bugs in rugs in our hotel. Honey…ya there?'

With a relaxed grip on the receiver I follow the trail of my wolf's bloody paw prints toward the bedroom, where my father slept when he was a teenager. But the red stains on the carpeting lead right into gobs of more blood, coming from underneath the bedroom door and exuding down the hallway's wood floor.

'Hello? Ethan? Honey, say somethin.'

'Hello,' I reply, careful not to slip in the blood that has turned my white socks red. I approach the bedroom as that noise persists from the other side of the door…

Drip…drip…drip…

'Is everything *alright*?' the woman on the phone asks.

'Define, *alright*.' I say. Standing in a generous puddle of blood now I push the door open. I reach my arm around and sweep my hand up to flip the light on. The bedroom is now illuminated, and there's blood *everywhere*.

'Ethan, what's the matter with ya? Are ya alright? Ya don't sound like yerself.'

'No, Grandma. Dad's not alright.'

'Ethan…why did ya just call me-'

'Stop callin me Ethan, Grandma. Dad's dead.'

'Dad? Ethan, yer dad's right here, shaving. And this is yer *mother!* What's wrong with-?'

330

'Ethan, Dad, whatever. He's dead. He's got the barrel of Grandpa's shotgun stuffed in his mouth. Ya know, he musta just blew the back of his head right out. His brains are splattered all over his bedroom wall.'

'Ethan! What in *God's name* are ya talkin about?'

'Damn. His eyes are wide open, Grandma. Just starin back at me.'

'Ethan! Honey…'

'Ethan, this is yer *father!*' the other voice said. 'What in *Hell* are ya telling yer-?'

'There's no way this is my father, whoever y'are. My father's dead. I know because I'm lookin right at him.

'Ethan, what the-'

'Look, it's late. And all of this blood and beer has made me tired. Goodnight.'

<CLICK>

<KNOCK-KNOCK-KNOCK-KNOCK-KNOCK-KNOCK>

Someone's fist raps my front door. Who is that? *Oh shit!*

I've woken up in a wet puddle of something, sprawled out on the hallway floor. The bright light from my bedroom intrudes my still-sobering eyes and identifies the wet substance I bathe in: My own beer-vomit with the Steak 'n Shake chilli that I ate earlier this afternoon floating in it. The stench is so revolting I must compose myself to keep from throwing up again. Here's to alcohol poisoning, and my body rejecting 'too much of a good thing'. At least it's not blood, but as vivid as my last recollection was, insanity must be setting in. I glare into my bedroom. No blood. No shotgun. No 'dead me'. A lot of dirty laundry but

331

nothing out of the ordinary. What the fuck?

<KNOCK-KNOCK-KNOCK-KNOCK-KNOCK-KNOCK>

Yes! Felicity and Justin are back! Oh shit! I have to clean up this mess! I whip around to open the broom closet and as I grab the mop I hear another voice. A familiar voice.

'Open up. Police.'

An unexpected voice.

I open the door to the officers' glares and the cold wind.

'Ethan.' His nametag reads *Stephens*. He and another officer stand sombrely in the flickering front porch light. A miserably wet night weeps beyond them.

'Yeah?' I tremble.

'Yer daddy here?'

'No.'

'Where is he, son?'

'My parents are up in Hannibal.'

'Well, we found his Vette eatin a guardrail down on the Jefferson Barracks Bridge.'

I stand in the doorway unable to pick my chin up off the floor while my eyes fill with tears.

'Ya let a couple friends take yer daddy's ride out tonight?'

I just look out the door and watch my beer breath dissipate between the cops into the cold night. I don't reply. Either I won't or I just can't.

'Justin Ronan and Felicity Farmer, right?'

Stephens saying their names jump-starts my voice. 'Yesss. Where *are* they?'

'Justin's in serious but stable condition at Barnes Jewish. Felicity's gone. We can't find her.'

My phone rings over and over. Countless rings. Right now I'm too fucked to answer it.

'Son, we know yer upset,' Stephens says, 'but yer phone's gonna be ringin all night tonight. Justin and Felicity's next of kin know the license plate is registered to this address.'

The other officer asks, 'Ya want *me* to answer yer phone, Ethan? I can see y'ain't in no condition to be talkin to people. Was Felicity yer girlfriend, boy?'

I fall to my knees, numb.

'Naw, we should make Ethan pick up every call tonight. It'll make em think about why he ever was so stupid to give his daddy's car away to some punk kid. Ethan, how ya gonna tell yer daddy some punk was hot-roddin in *his* ride and done fucked it up?'

'You Good Cop – Bad Cop motherfuckers!' I cry.

Some crazy woman is running at us and screaming, 'Where *is* she?! They can't *find* her! Where *is* she?!' Her panic is contagious here in late night Suburbia. Charlie joins the other neighbourhood dogs in barking and every porch light on Bataan Drive illuminates. Startled neighbours become our audience as they fill their cold front lawns. The officers take notice and size the woman up. 'Ok, now we're gonna just pretend you never said that. Now just stay inside, Ethan and get yerself cleaned up,' Stephens demands, 'What in Christ's name *is* that all over yerself, boy?' He takes a harder look at the raiding woman. 'Get him cleaned up, partner, I'll deal with her.' He twists like a crocodile and grabs his night stick. 'M'am, stop right there! Stop now!'

333

The crazy woman's rubber legs collapse underneath her and she falls to the wet grass, a sobbing basket case weeping at the boots of Officer Stephens. I recognise her as the 'weirdo' woman, my last customer at Schnucks three Saturdays ago. What is she doing here?

Another squad car pulls up, then another. Their whoopee lights make the neighbourhood look like a disco while feedback from their radios mix with the panic.

'Ethan,' the other officer says. 'That was Mr. Ronan calling from Barnes. He's very upset and wants to know why his son was driving yer father's car.'

I've officially lost it now. Tears roll down my face. My belly jiggles as I bawl like a baby. 'I told him that this ain't the time or the place.'

I collapse on the couch. I'm shivering. I'm shaking. 'What's going on?' I cry. 'What's going on, man?'

The other officer, young and delicate, reminds me of a televangelist (but I suppose his badge robbed my actually believing he was genuine). He places his soothing hand on my shoulder, squeezes gently and says, 'Ok, Ethan, tell ya what. Yer phone's ringin again but we're just gonna let that thing ring. Alright? We've got enough personnel. We'll contact those who need to know. Yer phone wll eventually stop ringin. Now just try and relax, okay son?'

'Hey Landers,' Stephens calls inside to his partner, 'I got Felicity's aunt out here on the front lawn. I'm taking her to the station for a cup of coffee and whatever else she needs.'

It's not a dream

Justin had no alcohol in his system. Authorities believe it was just a case of a kid who wanted to see what a V8 350 could do on a stormy night's slick road. On the Jefferson Barracks Bridge crossing the Mississippi River he crashed my father's Corvette into the guardrail.

He just lost control.

Found unconscious in the bloody driver's seat, he was mangled and cut up pretty badly from the impact. Jaws of Life were used to cut him out of the wreckage before he was rushed to Barnes, the same place *I* called home just recently.

Felicity's blood, hair and handbag were the only traces of her at the scene. The detectives discovered the unbuckled seatbelt and realised that Felicity wasn't wearing it. She was ejected from the vehicle through the windshield as it was busted out on the passenger side. It's believed that she went over the guardrail and plunged into the river below.

My father's pride and joy was fucked entirely, now just a crumpled piece of police evidence. The cement barrier supporting the guardrail crunched the fibre glass front end like an empty beer can. Everything under the hood was destroyed and the frame was bent like a wire coat hanger.

Justin was released from Barnes on the Monday following

337

Homecoming with miraculously just a broken arm and seven stitches in his forehead. Otherwise he was healthy. Alive. Very lucky.

The search for Felicity continued that same day. Authorities sifted through the river below the Jefferson Barracks Bridge. Since its undertow may have pulled her quite far, search parties armed with blood hounds and machetes combed the brush and banks as far as three miles downriver.

But I still had hope that she was alive. But it was all I had. The same stuff that Felicity showed me how to hold on to. Before she walked into that classroom I didn't have a hope in Hell.

I hoped it was all just a horrible dream. Hope was all I had.

Had.

As the days after melted away, Tuesday, Wednesday, Thursday, Friday, so did *my* hope. A little less each day, like a fistful of sand. I just couldn't hold onto it anymore. Still no one had found Felicity, dead *or* alive. I skipped the entire week of school, distraught, taking long walks, believing I could just walk away from it. I would always start towards school wondering if I'd have the courage to enter the double doors and actually go to class. But I'd always end up at Justin's instead. I checked on my best friend each day, staying with him as long as he'd want me there, which some days wasn't even long enough to take in a recorded Saturday Night Live sketch.

Justin's parents joined mine in taking a step back. Of course they were disappointed that their sons were so conspiring. Absolutely they were devastated that my father's car had been destroyed. But like the rest of us they couldn't rest as they were haunted by what *could've* happened to Justin and what *probably did* happen to Felicity. All bets were off. Nobody ate. Nobody slept. Nobody went to school or work. There was no sun by day or stars by night while we waited for Felicity to be found.

Still it is this way. Today is Saturday. But only just the *following* Saturday.

I visit Justin again today, but we are just like the hands on his dying Elvis clock. I'm the second hand, stuck between the **9** and the **10,** just vibrating over the "68 Comeback Special' photo. He's the minute hand, still between the **11** and **12**, just to the left of The King's nose in his 'Love Me Tender' movie promo. The hour hand is stone dead on the **7**, pointing down at Elvis in his 'Aloha from Hawaii' jumpsuit.

Justin merely lay in his bed with his arm in that sling and those stitches across his forehead, looking the same as he has all week. He's still so empty. All of his personality and character have been drained. When he does speak he sounds like an automaton, one-word answers, mumbled and whispered. He's just cold and dark, like the bottom of a well on a farm. His wild heart is down there somewhere. I drop my shiniest, luckiest coin down that well again today, but thus far it hasn't mattered. Looking at him is just like looking into the mirror. The only reason why I'm able to get out of bed anymore is because I feel closer to Felicity when I'm with Justin. Yet, at the same time, I want to be in a place where I've never spent a moment with her. I'm just looking for any way to douse the fear, pain and anxiety. Being at Justin's seems to be my only solace. He's actually *here*, in front of me where I can see him. If I stay here long enough Felicity may just come join us. Sometime.

My heart's at the bottom of that well, too.

He asks me to leave again. He wants to be alone. It's the last thing I want to do, to go back home. To have to walk the streets in which Felicity walked with me and to have to sleep in the bed in which she slept with me. But I leave him be, exiting into the night wearing maddening misery.

339

I know that Felicity is dead. It's time to go home.

I walk through the cold night, under the trees that flank our neighbourhood streets. These tall oaks were once vibrant green bursts of summertime fun and endless youth. Tonight they're rusted by autumn's tragedies. Their fallen leaves lay brittle on the cold ground, just like my hope. Summer wasn't that long ago but it's over now. Those warm, carefree days are now just faded memories.

I light a candle in my dark room and focus on the flickering light, how it dances with the gust of her walking by. Felicity's beautiful ghost. The hot wax oozes down like the tears my eyes have unwound. We had our day and tonight I must go…to sleep at last. I must sleep on our love tonight…while I slip down the mudslide of my mind with her.

But first I put pen to paper, just below my bloody heart splattered before me on my desk, pumping away outside of my chest. Still, I love her…

Felicity, my love, lost in the clouds

Felicity, my love, where are you now?

Echoes ring back for a love that was true

But where did you go? Do ghosts welcome you?

Can I buy a ticket from here to there?

Instead of this noose, poison or this gun?

Just promise to stay right here by my side

And to death I will walk, I will not run

I rest my weary head on those words, not pained enough by the hard desktop grinding into my cheek and chin, and I drift off...

A candle in the dark and nothing else...

Its wick burns sweet as it melts down slow

The ghost of her in a warm gust of wind

Jolts the flame like the love I bestow

For her...

'Get his gun,' a voice whispers.

'Yes, get his gun,' another one grumbles.

'Ya know where it is, Eee-thaan.'

'Ya know where he keeps it,' another voice croons.

I open my eyes to darkness. The candle has burned out. I lift my heavy head from the desktop and rise to my feet to turn on the light. But before I reach the switch the candle rekindles a bright flame. Its glow illuminates a big dried-up blood stain on the wall. The fourth wall. The voices cry...

GET YER GUN

GET YER GUN

GET YER GUN

It's not a suggestion. It's a command. I have no choice, do I?

341

These voices are never going to stop until I do what it is that they want me to do. I can no longer handle this life haunted with voices and murders and ghosts and victims. I don't want to meet the man I'll grow to be after all of this, let alone *be* him. I no longer believe in what Justin said to me at school…

'Our best days are ahead, man. But they ain't gonna happen if ya let this place get to ya.'

Justin doesn't believe those words anymore, either. His own words.

I go down the hallway and through the kitchen. I don't have to open the backdoor as it opens for me. I tread across the patio and the garage door opens right up for me as well. It's dark inside but I can see everything. I can see my father's gun. The voices echo…

GET THE GUN

IT'S NOT A DREAM

GET THE GUN

NOT A DREAM

GET THE GUN

NOT A DREAM

I yank the twelve-gauge from the wall and load it up. *Yes, Dad, it* is *a toy. And I'm going to play with it.* And there's that blasted red umbrella, glowing right through the darkness in the far corner.

I carry the gun by the barrel, down at my side while I rest

the opened umbrella on my other shoulder. I trounce back through the house and into my room. I shut the door.

I sit down in the chair against the fourth wall and put the open umbrella between my head and the wall to protect the room from as much splatter as possible. I cock the gun and heave the butt in-between my knees. I find the trigger with my thumb, close my eyes and take a deep breath. *Felicity, where are you?*

'She's near the river, a little ways down from the bridge.' the ghost-woman says.

I open my eyes and see her sitting on my bed, draped in her white gown. Her silky black hair hangs down and sparkles with tiny stars. Her eyes illuminate my room in an emerald glow. She's thin and white and long and beautiful. Her horse lies peacefully in front of her on the floor and dwarfs the room with its massive size. 'Yer Felicity's mother, aren't ya?'

'I am.'

'Are ya haunting me again?'

'*Life* will haunt you, Ethan.' *Life will haunt you. I've heard that before. And it has.*

'How did ya die?'

'It was a horrible fire. It was just an accident.'

'Why are ya here?'

'God. It is his will. It is the Great Mystery. The mystery of love is greater than the mystery of death. Oscar Wilde wrote that but it was Heaven to Earth. A message from the dead. That quote was a timeless message.'

'Why me? Why here? Why now? Can't ya see that I want to die? That it's my destiny?'

'Never ya mind that ridiculous notion, boy. Felicity's near the river, like I said, a little ways down from the bridge.'

343

'How far?'

'She'll be there on that muddy bank, where the police put her.'

'Police? What do ya mean?'

'She'll be there on that muddy bank, boy, where the Osage used to dwell. You'll drive down to that cave park and yer heart will tell ya where to go. She's gonna be there waitin for ya.'

'Yes, outside of a long dark tunnel. A cave. Of course it was a cave...full of dead bodies, full of ghosts.'

'Ghosts of all those battles between Red Men and White Men...from dead corpses bathin in blood.'

'I've seen it...I don't know if I was dreamin or-'

'Ethan, child, you've seen everything ya need to see in order to find my daughter. She must be found and only you can do that. By rememberin what you've seen. Usin what only you've felt. Usin what only *you* know.'

'But I want her to be alive. And what about the police?'

'Oh, she's alive, boy. She's so very alive. Her spirit is too strong to be otherwise. She can't wait to see ya. I can't wait to see her. It's been such a long time since last summer.'

'When?'

'Now. The time's now, boy. Here, take yer daddy's car.'

A draft invades behind me. I turn around to see that the fourth wall has disappeared again, leaving the familiar realm of the forest in view. But there is a road, paved and marked just like the highway that eventually crosses the Mississippi as the Jefferson Barracks Bridge. Parked on that road, just a few footsteps away from my bedroom at the edge of the forest, is my father's Corvette. There's not a mark on it as it shines in the moonlight. I move toward it and stand in its ebony dazzle in awe, admiring the way it glints its chrome. The tires are ravenous for road and the driver side door is open for me to slide in and turn the key.

Felicity's mother has disappeared. It's just me now, sitting in the leather bucket seat behind the wheel of my dad's labour of love. I turn the key and ignite the engine. It explodes into a panther's roar like a strike of lightning. I flick on the headlights and see the desolate road ahead. Just the road and me and nothing else. I crunch the gas pedal against the floor and feel the power of that 350 engine as it blasts me ahead; like a bullet through the mysterious darkness. Faster and faster…

Sixty…

Seventy…

Eighty…

Ninety…

One-hundred miles an hour!

110 mph, the thrill…

120 mph, the pull…

130 mph, the forces…

140 mph, my tongue flails out of my mouth, my nostrils flare and my eyes bug out…

150 mph, horns grow from my head, my erection throbs against the steering wheel and I taste blood…

160 mph, I cream my shorts. I came too quickly. I slow back down. The bridge is just ahead anyway, spanning over the great muddy river. But as the needle drops below ninety I recognise the flashing lights in the rear view mirror. I'm being chased by a cop. I fucking hate cops, man. That pig can suck my cock as far as I'm concerned. Those Cruisers they drive these days can fly, but I know that mother-fucker can't get up to 160

mph. So I step on it again…and he follows suit.

Ninety. The officer closes in.

One-hundred miles per hour! I still haven't shaken him!

110 mph, I'm pulling away!

The cop's falling back in the rear view mirror! With the slightest effort I tap the wheel and feel this black panther of a machine actually pounce toward my lane of choice…toward another black car that came from out of nowhere. Another '71 Stingray? How can that be? My father's was the only one I ever saw. As I pass it in a strange slow motion, yet pushing 125mph, I confirm that it's the same car! As good as a clone. And I can also confirm that Justin's driving and Felicity is his passenger! They both gaze at me in horror, certainly just reflecting the terrified look on my face. As sure as Justin's black bowtie and white gritted teeth. As sure as Felicity's red hair and green sparkling eyes (and the Homecoming Queen Crown on her head) they share the interstate's Jefferson Barracks Bridge with me in a clone Vette.

I blow right past Justin and Felicity, changing lanes well ahead of them. That cock-sucking cop is still in hot pursuit and I watch him change lanes to stay with me. The four headlights close together into an explosion of sparks and an orchestra of metal crushing fibreglass. That cop just ran my dear ones right into the guardrail!

'No! Feliciity! Justin! No!' But my scream cannot pull them out of the darkness they've disappeared into.

And from that white flash of fate is a blast of wind. Cold. Wet. Alive and howling like a wolf. Bellowing like a mammoth predator. Roaring towards me like a freight train. It attacks me through this new darkness that has removed me from the speeding Corvette and dropped me into my bed. I grab my bedpost to prevent being blown away by the most intense thrust

346

of the wind I've ever felt. Locks of my hair rip away from my scalp as I lose my grip on the slick oak finish.

The voices stereo through the violent force of the wind…

AT THE FUNERAL

        AT THE FUNERAL

                AT THE FUNERAL

They juxtapose from whispers to chants…

HE'S SEES THEM

        HE'S SEES THEM

                HE'S SEES THEM

I tighten my grip on the bedpost as my body waves like a windsock in a storm. I fear the force will yank my arm right from its socket! The pain grows too intense and I lose my hold. I'm swept away into the darkness and fall to the wood floor of my ransacked bedroom.

Suddenly, all is quiet. Have I gone deaf?

Chunks of the walls have been ruptured. My bed is on its side and the bedding is shredded everywhere, just like the rest of the furniture. The windows are just vacancies as the panes have shattered into hundreds of shards. I scan the room to digest the destruction. What in Hell has just happened?

SOUNDED LIKE A FREIGHT TRAIN

LIKE A FREIGHT TRAIN

A cold draft invades, and I shiver, because the fourth wall of my bedroom has vanished again. And through that void a forest glows red and gold, under a sky smeared a bloody tone. Beyond it all a river flows, somewhere.

A fist raps against my bedroom door three times.

'Three tragedies. Three dead children. Three souls to be saved.' The ghost-woman has spoken again, from the other side of the door.

I step over the crumbled nightstand and push the desk away from the door it was blocking. Trembling in terror, I turn the knob and open it.

The ghost-woman guides her black stallion across the gymnasium floor, illuminated by theatrical light. The steed prances away, taking her into the darkness surrounding the basketball court. 'Hey,' I shout, 'what is all this!' But without reply they vanish.

Justin appears just underneath one of the basketball goals. Wearing a black tuxedo he sits at a grand piano. His hands rest on the keys as he stares ahead at the gargantuan oak tree. It's black claw of thick roots clutch the parquet floor. The tree's branches tower into the pitch black. Its leaves of scarlet, burnt orange, gold and purple fall and decorate the court, one by one.

Is Justin alive? Is he even *real*? He sits as still as a wax figure at Madame Tousaud's, not slumped nor upright but somewhere in between. I feel like I'm in the dark audience surrounding a play that has just begun.

Footsteps hollowly click and clack from this surrounding dark. Donnie Applebaum and Tyler Keats enter the light and they've matched Justin's dapperness. Donnie's actually clean shaven and his hair is slicked into a black sheen. I've never seen him look this way! Tyler looks as highly maintained as ever with his chocolate brown tresses combed and parted on the side. Their shoes shine a luscious ebony whilst their gloves glow a bright ivory, matching the keys on the piano. The pair of gentlemen stop at centre court as the echoes of their soles clapping the hardwood fades away. Tyler politely shakes the hand of the boy who tormented him and, as a result, he shot and killed. They exchange short, subtle smiles.

Another set of footsteps sounds off and I know who they belong to before Felicity ever appears. She wears that emerald green gown with matching heels. Her strawberry hair is worn up to enhance the matching glow from her eyes. She's simply electrifying and elegantly strolls to the right of the two boys. Donnie pursues Felicity while Tyler looks on.

Justin strikes the keys and begins his performance of *'Moonlight Sonata'*. There is no doubt that he is real now. His performing grace is obvious, delicately dancing his fingers against the keys amidst total concentration. His eyes are moulded into a stare, perhaps at the beautiful old tree or its falling leaves or somewhere beyond. Thrusting his hands here and there, he rocks gently back and forth in a way that makes the musical piece appear to rise from his body to our ears. I close my eyes and take in this piano energy as it saturates the gymnasium.

Felicity and Donnie dance at centre court and after a short while Tyler cuts in. I walk around the dim perimeter, just outside the light, and view the surrealism. Closer to Justin now, I notice his deep focus. He never blinks or looks down at the keys his fingers elegantly press. His face, his mission, is stone.

'Justin, what is this?' I whisper. But my presence doesn't change anything. He carries on as if I'm not even here.

As my suspicion of being invisible takes hold there's a pause. Justin has stopped playing and he, like the others, stare at me. Right into my eyes. *Right through* me.

Felicity walks my way with bright eyes and that Mona Lisa smile. The closer she comes the more intense the scent of apples and strawberries is. She stops at the edge of the light and reaches into the dark for me. 'May I have this dance?' she asks.

I take her gloved hand that insists I step into the light with her. As I do I notice that I, too, wear white gloves and am decked out exactly as the other boys. 'Ya look so handsome,' Felicity says.

'And yer so beautiful,' I reply.

Felicity leads me to centre court where we shall perform for the thousands that have suddenly appeared in the audience that now hang on our every move. I acknowledge Donnie and Tyler on the sideline, a pair of handsome gentlemen who observe us with the masses. Gazing into Felicity's eyes, I anticipate our dance. This one last dance.

Justin begins *'Moonlight Sonata'* again from the top and I try to hold this moment still, where Felicity is the most beautiful girl that has ever lived and I'm the one she chose to dance with. With each step we indulge in our natural chemistry, knowing one another's bodies as well as our own. We're pressed together, taking each other's heartbeats as our own. She's so warm. I want to keep her right here forever. I want to always feel this natural. I know that I need her. I can't let this end!

But I can't clutch it. I can't hold it. It's passing so quickly, like that handful of sand that slips through my fingers upon my desperate grasp. And so does she, as she slithers away from my grip. She's overcome by the classical rhythm of Justin's musical performance; the sound that has been breathed into us from ghosts of another time. I feast my eyes on her moves. All of the physical abilities that she's been blessed with are displayed to me in full. She steps and pirouettes and curtsies all with a swan's grace. I'm drunk on my desire for her.

The theatrical light dims to a gloomy crimson glow. The gymnasium looks like a giant darkroom. Justin thumps a final low, crushing-down note. The piano's deep hum brings everything to a sudden stop. It's the sound of Satan himself.

Drip...drip...drip...

And as the final note fades out, the sound of dripping blood fades in. Blood drips down from the leaves above. The parquet floor collects the red splatters. The oak tree is bleeding down on us, like red rain. As the floor becomes red the gloomy crimson glow expands to reveal that all of the faces in the audience are of skeletons...and now they chant and sing and bellow in the tones of death.

Ghastly pain explodes in my stomach and I fall. Now covered in blood I look down to see that my stomach, right where Tyler's bullet pierced it, dispenses my own.

Justin is slumped over the piano, deflated with wide open vacant eyes.

Felicity and the other two boys shatter into hundreds of porcelain pieces.

I want to shout out that this is all just a dream. I want to cry. I want to scream. But nothing comes out, no matter how hard I try. I cannot speak.

'Ethan,' Justin says, 'this is not a dream.'

The other three children, Donnie, Tyler and Felicity, are dead.

'Three tragedies...three dead children...three souls to be saved'.

upon the wall in the darkness

Justin is just a shell of the guy I knew and loved. He used to talk about sunsets, girls, Elvis, God, beer, baseball, vinyl records, radio, chain wallets, pomade…and he'd just light that fire in people's minds. He'd make you feel like the only person in the room when he'd chat with you. He's ahead of his time, an old soul, mature for his age, unique in the little Missouri world we live in. But all of those personal attributes that make him such a great guy are gone now. I'm not the same either as I've got nothing left, if I ever had anything. What I love about Justin the most is that he's always been a reflection of the 'me' that I wanted to become. But sadly, at this melancholy moment, he's just a reflection of who I am right now.

I brought Justin some White Castles at 11am this Halloween Morning. It's the least I could do to thank the guy for everything he's meant to me…before I tell him that I won't see him again.

'Breakfast,' I say as I drop the white sacks of little delicious square steam-grilled burgers topped with diced onions and pickles (some with melted cheese) on his nightstand.

'Wow,' he says, 'trick or treat?'

'Dig in. Happy Halloween.'

'Thanks, man. I'm actually starvin.' He nearly stuffs an

entire burger into his mouth.

'I thought ya might be. Ya haven't eaten in, what, three days?'

'Seems like it.' Justin chews for a moment, swallows down and says, 'Ethan, look, there's something I gotta say but I don't know how well I remember it, really.'

'What's that?'

'First of all, I just want ya to know that the reason why Felicity and I took the Vette so far south, ya know, all the way down to Jefferson Barracks Bridge, is because I was just really enjoyin the drive. I was gonna replace the gas.'

'Dude, I know ya would've. And, yeah, it crossed my mind how far ya went but I knew ya were gonna get yer money's worth. I had that built into the equation.'

'Good.'

'But, ain't all that pretty much irrelevant now?'

'Well, Ok. Now the other part.'

'What *other part*?' I scowl.

'Dude, relax-'

'Relax? Relax?! Justin, Felicity's *dead*!'

'What?! Ethan, nobody knows anything yet so don't ya dare go fuckin mental on me, man!'

'Felicity is *dead*!' I declare.

'Ya don't know that!'

'Justin, God damnit! She's *dead*!'

Almost crying, Justin screams, 'Don't go fuckin' mental because I've already fuckin *gone* mental!' He throws the next burger across the room. It hits the panelled wall and onions and pickles burst from between the buns.

'Alright, Ok! Calm down, man,' I say as I sit down next to him on his bed. 'This ain't the fuckin time for this! This is the last time I'm gonna…'

'Yer gonna what, Ethan? Yer gonna what?'

'Nothin alright.' I just can't break it to him. If only I had the same conviction for *telling* him that I will put a bullet through my head today as I actually will in *pulling the trigger*.

'Ya gonna listen to me now?'

'*Yes*, Justin. Talk to me.'

'*Jesus*. Alright,' he sighs, 'I just don't think the accident was actually *my* fault! Ok?'

'Justin, man, of course it wasn't yer fault! Whatchya talkin about?'

'No, no, what I'm sayin is that I don't think it was the slick road. I still don't remember hydroplaning. I just…'

'Go on. Ya weren't drinkin were ya?'

'No, I told ya that. And I wasn't speedin either, even though, ya know, I wanted to.'

'Then what?'

'It just seems like a dream that I had,' he says, 'I can't tell if it was real. But it *feels* real.'

'A dream? What dream?' I ask.

'I mean, I was unconscious for a long time after the accident. But things are starting to, *slowly,* come back. I've had some really fucked up dreams, too.'

Join the club, Justin. 'Talk to me. What kind of dreams.'

'I think I was in complete control of yer dad's car. I even remember talkin to Felicity about Elvis, ya know, her being from Memphis and all. Everything was fine and then…'

'And then?'

'And then another car blazed right past and sort of swept us a little. Then I realised that he was being chased by police, but...'

'But what? But what?'

'But, I think the cop came a little too close to us. I think that's when I lost control of yer dad's car. I just can't remember exactly. I've been havin so many fucked up dreams since the accident that I'm havin a hard time sortin out what's real and what isn't.'

'And since it was rainin, yer jerking the car to try and avoid any contact might have just...

'Ya get it. Good.'

'So, a cop ran ya into the guardrail. Do ya believe that?'

'Maybe, I don't know for sure. I just can't believe I lost control on my own, or because of the rain. I just don't know.'

I stare into his eyes, trying to see inside his mind. Trying to read his memory *for* him. Trying to *see* what actually happened that night. Trying to set him straight before I leave this world. I can't help but harp on my dreams, or my experiences. Whatever they actually were, they were as vivid to me as Justin lays here before me now in his dreary basement bedroom.

Was he just a deer in the headlights as a cop pursued a criminal? Did a cop snarl recklessly down the highway? Did the criminal just take what he wanted? Was there any regard for the innocent on the very battlefield of those two forces? Yes, I can see it all so clearly now. Justin and Felicity were driving from the Homecoming Dance. The criminal's sharp teeth glinted while trying to escape from the cop who ran my best friend and my girlfriend into the guardrail. Justin was injured and Felicity was ejected through the windshield and into the Mississippi River below. Victims. Fallen leaves.

It's all so clear now.

As he deals with all of this in his own way he knows that I'm dealing with it in mine. After I explained that I had to find Felicity, Justin gives me his car keys. 'Take care of it,' he says, 'keep her filled up with gas. Check the oil.' But what he doesn't know is that from here I'm going home to get my father's twelve-gauge.

I start to walk up the staircase that leads to the back door.

'And, by the way, Ethan, Felicity *was* crowned Homecoming Queen.'

'Justin,' I say.

'Yeah?'

I take my last look at my best friend and tell him, 'Our best days *are* ahead.'

My obsession with having wheels of my own is justified when I throw Justin's Camaro into third gear and prowl away. But this taste I've pursued for such a long time has a bitter aftertaste. I still don't know what it feels like to step on the gas pedal in the midst of *joy*. Even though I like the fragrance of the wind blowing through the interior and the 'in-control' feel of the steering wheel, I dwell on the turmoil. Justin's at home in bed, depressed and being devoured by guilt. And when I look to my right I realise that I'll never see Felicity in the passenger side like I've dreamed. We'll never chase sunsets and full moons. I'll never see the warm breeze whipping through her hair while we share a common hope at eighty miles an hour.

Not in *my* car. Not *ever*.

359

How deeply could I have fallen in love with her while we drove through that golden desert; while the parched terrain passed us by? I'll never share that rebellion with her when the summer of my life comes. As for the summer of *her* life, I hope she felt like she saw it.

Nevada. West Texas. Mexico. Death Valley. Mars. Felicity's out there somewhere.

I pull up in front of my house and sneak toward the garage. I see my through the living room blinds as I tip-toe past. The thought of entering the house that I grew up in one last time to say goodbye is smeared by the feel of that hairpin between my fingers. I stick it into the garage door lock and jimmy my way in.

And there's my father's twelve-gauge, upon the wall in the darkness.

360

halloween at dusk

I park the Camaro at a rest stop near Cliff Cave County Park, just two miles south of Jefferson Barracks Bridge where Felicity disappeared. On this Halloween at dusk the park is painted red and gold between the dark shadows.

Have I been here before, to this place where I'll begin my search for Felicity? With hope in one hand and my father's shotgun in the other, I march into those shadows.

The river rushes somewhere down below and as I close my eyes I see it just as I've always seen it. Down the hill and through the trees. Right here. Right now. My heart now rushes just like that river, the same as it always has upon my hearing its moving waters.

And as I open them I realise I can see through the puzzling, intimidating wooded darkness. Yes, I *have* been here before. The mystery of my past month's fate will materialise, be understood and provide closure somewhere down on the river's bank. Down where I plan to find Felicity and then kill myself.

This park is known for the cave that has become a very important historical and archaeological site, also known as Indian Cave. The wooded bluffs that I hike down and through hang above the banks of the Mississippi. The deeper I go the louder the river gets, the darker the realm grows…the closer I get to her.

363

The trail is being devoured by the ominous dusk. The last few rays of the sun filter through the swaying, creaking oak and hickory limbs.

The chords of October's Song sound off: My boots crackle pretty, dead leaves that send echoes; they join the howl of the fall gusts that jolt my dark locks like campfire flames; that percussion and rhythm supports the singing ghosts and injects strange life into the autumnal death. I follow the sound of the river through October's Song and can't deny how beautiful the world is as it dies.

I look down at the shotgun and tighten my grip. Will I be just as beautiful?

I gaze through the thick inferno of trees and catch my first glimpse of the Mississippi, flowing peacefully below the edge of the cliff I hike down. How much precious life has that river supported? And as I tread through October's Song towards its muddy green flow I cannot deny how beautiful this world is as it *lives*.

As *I* live.

I detour into a six-foot drop that gives way to a lower trail. It's more difficult footing down here, much muddier and more slippery, but closer still to the banks. Nevertheless, I keep hiking down. I won't stop until I find what I came looking for.

Now I can finally see a clear path to the bank. I shut my eyes tightly and try to remember where I saw Felicity. In my dreams. In my nightmares. The voices…

ON THE RIVER BANK

THE PURPLE HEART

THE RIVER BANK

THE PURPLE HEART

364

I've been shot. Donnie and Tyler are dead. My mother had a heart attack and will never be the same. My father's Corvette is destroyed. Justin is injured and distraught. My heart has been raped.

Felicity is gone and our time together now just feels like a dream. It was such a wonderful dream! She made me feel so strong. She gave me so much hope.

But has my hope flown away?

Still I can hear those voices, spelling out the mystery of my fate.

I drop to a catcher's squat on the muddy bank and frown down at the flowing river. She's very close now. So am I. The sound of my cocking the shotgun echoes through the realm, cracking its peace while knocking on death's door. Who will answer?

Across the river on the opposite shore there is an Osage Native hunting and gathering before the long American winter ahead. Dignity and survival battle inside of him. He's regarded as just a wild savage now that The White Man has arrived. French fur trappers have rolled through and settled, having built cabins and turned his people's sacred cave into a tavern. They invade the Osage homeland barbarically using gun powder and fire arms, hell-bent on clearing the land in the name of Freedom and God. Life for the Osage will never be the same. Blood will be stained on this land forever.

Life changes.

Life is unfair.

Life will haunt you.

Time never stops.

I think about the ghosts.

The Osage called them *Wakon*.

The spirit is eternal. No one can ever take it away from you.

My life, my experience, my pain, my mind, my heart, my visions, my spirit...all of those things contributed in leading me here today. I breathe the crisp air into my lungs and am overwhelmed with curiosity about acceptance. I know that I'm standing here not *only* because of hope. I know that there is a little thing, perhaps a mosquito that zips around a place like this all summer long. That little mosquito is still here, sucking my blood and won't stop until I accept all that has happened. That little mosquito has already sucked so much of my blood.

Recently, living just hurt too much. But I'll give acceptance this one last chance. I put all the despair behind me and take a step forward just to see how it feels. I'm so close to the river's edge now that the muddy water splashes my boots. I teeter on the bank, gripping that hope tightly in my hand. I hold it out and compare it to the cocked shotgun in my other, ready to fire.

Acceptance.

All that was lost now finally feels *real* to me. I weave my first thought of letting it all be. It's sinking in so deep and fast that it hurts like Hell, but that pain is the hope. *Felicity's gift to me.* And whether she was a dream or not, I can always keep that gift.

Justin leant me his car so that I could be here today, just the same as I gave him the keys to my father's. We were there for each other. Tragedies had to occur for my dad to realise and show his love for me. Now my parents *both* love me. Yet, here I am, willing to throw that away as I intend on using this gun. *His* gun. What will my parents' life be like if I go through with this? What would Justin think if I pull this trigger? What would Felicity say? Now I know what the world really is…

I had it all wrong. What rotted will always rot but what shines won't always shine. What shines is precious. *Life* is precious, just not fair. I must cherish what shines in my short life in this little world…

Stop crying. Finish that thought…

Felicity's rotting corpse floats up against my boot and flails in the muddy water. I look down upon her saturated shell and find myself somehow prepared for this grotesque moment. *This is just like in my nightmares that led me here to her.* As the sight of Felicity's bloated carcass sinks in I finish my thought underneath my tears…

Life…precious life…

I wipe my cold, wet eyes and kneel down, breathing in the stench of what's left of Felicity. Her green dress is stained by mud and blood and slick with Mississippi slime. Her hair is still intact, still shining red. But it floats around her blue and grey half-gone face. I look into her eyes, those glorious green eyes one last time. They're just cloudy orbs now, glazed into an eternal stare.

I'm numb. My long-awaited date with finally *accepting* this thing called life has me somehow ready for anything. My life has come to *this*.

I don't frown, tremble or flinch. I just ooze down to her slowly and calmly. My body splits into two entities and I watch

367

myself look down upon Felicity's dead state in this river, in the last phase of twilight. I shut her eyelids. I watch her sleep.

The peaceful moment is interrupted by the sudden crunching of fallen leaves. The slow thumps of hooves approach. The scent of roses with a hint of cinnamon sweetens the air and leaves absolutely no uncertainty that the horse and ghost-woman, Felicity's mother, are *really here*. They always *have* been. The trail they've left for me ends here at the bank of this river.

'In her hand, Ethan,' Felicity's mother says. 'Take it.'

I open Felicity's clutched hand and take the Purple Heart medallion. I grip it tight and close my eyes, faintly hearing the whipping blades of the Huey. I see her father again on the movie screen of the back of my eyelids, in that chopper high above the Siamese jungles. His terrified eyes beg at me from under the brim of a war helmet.

I secure the medal in my jacket pocket and will head back to Justin's car with a shotgun that I've decided not to use. I've no choice but to go to the police now. But first I take one last look at Felicity's corpse, resting peacefully on the muddy bank.

'I love you Felicity. I'll always have hope.'

I walk away. *Don't look back again, Ethan.* As I start back up the hill I hear more crunching footsteps through fallen leaves behind me. I turn around and adjust my eyes through the darkness to witness something breath-taking. Something supernatural. Something heart-wrenching. Something…

Felicity's mother has dismounted and has lifted her daughter's body from the muddy bank. As her horse follows close behind she cradles Felicity against her bosom and carries her into the river.

'Stop!' I cry. Where are ya takin her?'

The woman draped in white stops, right there, knee deep

in that river. She turns to me and replies, 'Yer mother was yers, child. Felicity's mine.'

There's an explosion inside of me. Never have I felt such rage. And I roar, 'It was *you! Nothing* bad happened until *you* came! *You* killed her! You killed *everyone!'* I blast back down the hill toward her.

'No child, she says, 'everything is inevitable. After I burned to death in that fire I could see everything down here. *Everything.'* Her words stop me. I grab hold of a low branch and swing the barrel of the shotgun onto my shoulder. 'I couldn't let happen to my daughter what happened to me. Being dead and not knowing it, well, is just a little higher and a little cooler than Hell. But not much. Life will haunt you, son. Time never stops…and our fate is *arcane* fate…but fate nonetheless.'

The woman in white, with her horse close behind, carries her daughter into the river and submerge into its rushing waters. Black and red ribbons of hair and mane, just for a moment, flow south with the muddy green waters before sinking beneath.

And in my awe I lose my footing…

And my balance…

Then a deafening sound…

<BANG>

Smoke dances away from the end of the barrel and the bang's echo scatters through the realm. I pulled the trigger.

Accidentally.

Ironically.

I missed killing myself by just an inch and a half. The blast has deafened me. Fate nonetheless.

YOU CAN'T SLEEP

But if this is my fate and I am deaf, then why am I still hearing voices?

YOU'RE JUST GOING A LITTLE INSANE

BECAUSE YOU HATE THIS TOWN

Through the high-pitched ringing in my ears the words are crystal clear. *Their* words. The same voices that have been speaking to me all this time...but never showed their faces.

HIGH SCHOOL SUCKS

YOU WANT TO KILL YOUR FATHER

Just the voices and the ringing in my ears. Nothing else. But I can still *feel* them approach.

ONE OF THESE DAYS

I CAN'T STOP NOW

Their voices, their energy, come from three sides, like a triangle in these woods surrounding me and closing like a claw. I peel my eyes as thin as I can, struggling to see through the dark. Suddenly, I not only feel them, I can *see* them. In the opposite extremities of my peripheral vision, two white shadows zigzag, dance and glow against the darkness where the river flows. And

370

as they quickly approach I hear another voice just behind me...

YOU CAN'T STOP NOW

I spin around to find the third side of the triangle, the third man, just ten feet away. He wears a white sheet over his head with two eye holes cut. *Like trick-or-treating ghosts on Halloween Night. Like in the locker room.* He speaks again...

YOU WANT TO DIE

Now the other two points of the triangle speak...

GRAB DAD'S SHOTGUN

STICK THE BARREL IN YOUR MOUTH

I twist around to find them wearing the same damn sheets as the first, flowing past their knees just the same. But this time I notice that they're splattered with blood. *My* blood. Yes, from three years ago. In that locker room after practice.

Terror.

DON'T WORRY

Embarrassment.

JUST KILL YOURSELF

371

Anger.

A fourth rises from the river and marches toward us. He wears a football uniform; pads, helmet and all. He stops between the other two and I wait for him to speak. But instead he extends his arm and points past me toward the white-sheeted one behind me. And when I turn around to face that one he pulls up his sheet and yanks it off the top of his head. Long dark hair flails against his *white* skin, not black. I pivot to watch the other two follow suit and again dark hair falls against *their* white skin.

I scamper backward, creating more distance and more time while my heart crashes against my chest. It's their faces that have rocked my world! They're all the same!

Now the fourth removes his helmet to reveal that his face is identical to theirs…and to *mine*. He is me. They are me. I am them. From the very first time I heard the voices, they were only my own.

And the fourth one says…

I AM THE FOURTH WALL

JUST KILL ME THEN

I raise the shotgun, aim and pull trigger…

<BANG>

Pump. Aim. Pull.

372

<BANG>

Pump. Aim. Pull.

<BANG>

Pump. Aim. Pull.

<BANG>

Gun smoke fills the air and rises up with the vapours of my vivid imagination that I mistook for my insanity. Now that I've blown my demons full of holes I suppose it was just like suicide after all. And my fate, my *arcane fate*, was to commit it and live on. So I have, and so I will.

Now there are just two of us here and I'm the only one with my face and my voice. The other one is that corpse on that riverbank. But it ain't Felicity anymore, it's just her body. She's with her mother now, somewhere out *there*.

the funeral

It's an unusually mild November morning, but the falling mist is cold. I close my eyes and feel it collect on my lips, on my cheeks and on my sunglasses that I wear to hide my tears. I try to take myself away from this most sombre setting, Felicity's funeral, by trying to see her walking at my side, smiling as we parade through the bustle of Delmar Boulevard. I remember the way the sun set behind her and the starry lights twinkled around her head that night. Yeah, she's still sipping that latte.

But my eyes open to the reality of her casket dressed with a rainbow of flowers, blazing brightly in contrast to the greyness, just as *she* always did. Felicity is each and every one of those flowers to me, as she certainly brightened my glum world. As I stand here I promise that I'll become more like her and live the rest my life in colours. The colours of her hair, her eyes…the colours of the flowers on her casket ready to be lowered into the soil next to her mother. This is the very spot where the student-photographer dropped to her knees in finding what she was looking for. Her mother's name was etched on that headstone.

IN LOVING MEMORY

MARILYN TREADWELL-FARMER

BORN DECEMBER 6, 1958

DIED JULY 31, 2010

As tears roll down my misty face I'm dressed in black. So is Tobias Farmer, Felicity's father and my dad's Vietnam comrade. Wheelchair bound he's right next to me, resembling a Southern Gentleman if I ever saw one just as he did in the photos. As I watch the ceremony in the reflection of his lenses the priest's words sink into us.

'The Lord is my shepherd; I shall not be in want. He makes me lie down in green pastures, he leads me besides quiet waters, he restores my soul. He guides me in paths of righteousness for his name's sake. Even though I walk through the valley of the shadow of death, I will fear no evil, for you are with me; your rod and your staff, they comfort me. You prepare a table before me in the presence of my enemies. You anoint my head with oil; my cup overflows. Surely goodness and love will follow me all the days of my life, and I will dwell in the house of the Lord forever.'

Two tears fall from behind Tobias's lenses, provoking my deepest realisation that Felicity is really gone.

I crane my neck to send Justin an acknowledging glance. But Justin's eyes are on Tobias in that wheelchair, likely overwhelmed with wonder about what could've been, would've been, and should've been. Caught up in wonder about ghosts and victims. Caught up in wonder about every step he'll take for the rest of his life, as he knows he's lucky. Tobias was not.

Funerals can and will bring anyone together no matter how long it's been. Tobias and my dad are reunited today despite the circumstances. Now that the funeral has concluded, my parents and I will take him back to our house. He's staying with us tonight before flying back to Mississippi in the morning.

My parents walk back to the Corolla but I just stand still and watch Tobias. He wheels himself to his late ex-wife's grave and lowers his head. Now he turns to the casket that his daughter rests in and gazes through it. I follow Tobias's lead and pay my last respect.

I've just woken from a long nightmare. But this tornado of tragedy has renewed me somehow. Tobias comes out of his gaze and asks, 'So, what's this city life like for a young guy like you?'

'City life?'

'Well, this is city to me.' he says as we move together toward the car. 'I never thought Felicity would like livin away from the countryside. Still, I got a letter here from her saying she did.' I look hard at the sealed envelope he's lifted from his jacket pocket. 'All so strange, with how long I've known yer daddy.'

I point to the letter and ask, 'Felicity wrote that?'

'All thanks to you, so it seems. Here, take it.'

'No, Sir, I can't. Ya gotta keep this. It's from yer daughter.'

'Son, don't be silly, now. I got other letters from her. Ya need to read what she wrote in there. Ya need to always remember what ya meant to her.'

I take the letter from him and study it, as if I could read Felicity's words through the envelope if I stared hard enough. 'Ya put that thing away, now, son. Ya open that up one night when yer down.'

But, I'm down now.

I stuff the letter into my inside pocket and am reminded of

379

what I want to present to Tobias. 'C'mon Ethan. Yer parents are waitin for us.'

'Mr. Farmer, this is yers.' I dangle the Purple Heart medallion from the ribbon and rest it in my palm. His eyes light up, as if he can see his entire Vietnam experience pass right through George Washington's head.

'Where did ya get this from, boy?'

'Felicity wanted ya to have it.'

'No, boy, no,' he cries with wild eyes, 'this blasted medal was destroyed in that fire!'

'What?'

'This can't be, Ethan! It was destroyed! All my valuables were...but, it looks *so real*!' He takes the medal of high prestige from me and presses it to his face, then to his lips. He closes his eyes and sighs deeply. 'I'll be God-damned!'

I tremble and say, 'Mr. Farmer, *what fire*?' And I remember what Marilyn, the woman draped in white, had said...

'It was a horrible fire. It was just an accident.'

Tobias looks up at me with tears in his eyes. 'Ethan, there was a fire in the wee hours of July 31st this summer. Felicity's mother, Marilyn, *died* in that fire. I married her when she was just *Felicity's age*, in 1976! That home we purchased on the outskirts of Memphis burned to the ground. I lost my photo albums. *All* my photos of my mama were lost. I lost my vinyl collection. I lost my *horse*! My beautiful black stallion! *Everything* was destroyed in that fire! *Marilyn died in that fire*! Felicity *started* that fire when she fell asleep with a *lit cigarette*!'

A gust of wind blasts against me, blowing my hair into my face. I nearly lose my balance as I can't believe what Tobias has just said! 'Mr. Farmer, I-'

'Tell me now, boy, where did ya get this from? Where did

ya get my medal?' *I can't. You'll think I'm crazy.* 'Tell me!' *And if I lie, you'll wonder why Felicity never gave it to you.* 'Boy, cmon now! I lost that medal in the fire!'

The wind is really rocking now, drawing the urgent call from my Dad, 'Ethan, Tobias, c'mon, we gotta get outta here!' A bad storm's comin'!'

Saved by the bell, I start away from Tobias. But he grabs my arm with a fierce grip and says, 'Ethan, was Felicity still *alive* when she gave this to ya?'

'Mister...Mr. Farmer, I-'

'Or was she dead?'

I feel myself turn white. My heart jumps into my throat and my knees buckle.

'Was Marilyn with her?'

'She was-' I can't speak. I feel like I've just seen *another* ghost.

'C'mon!' Dad yells, 'We gotta go!'

'Alright, we're comin!' Tobias calls out.

The wind is as violent as I've ever seen in my life as the tornado siren sounds. Under a sky now blackened with storm clouds I wheel Tobias as fast as I can toward the Corolla.

'One last thing, son!' Tobias cries as I wheel him through the weather, 'Don't ya worry yer head about yer daddy's Vette! I'll have it shipped down to my body shop just outside of Biloxi! My boys will have her lookin as good as new in two weeks! I want ya to know that I've talked to yer daddy and he don't really care bout that car too much no more! He was just gonna let her go until I insisted! Said he just wants to sell it, anyway!'

'He shouldn't sell it! It's his-'

'He's really shaken up about what's happened in the last

381

month! Damn, this wind!'

'Yeah…we gotta get outta here!'

'Yer father's a good man!'

'I know, Tobias! I know!'

My dad and I strain to get the 6'3', 250-pounder into the back of the car then we fold his chair down to fit in the trunk.

'Hey Ethan!' Justin calls out. I slam the trunk door down and turn around to see him and Justin standing there. 'James and I are goin to Steak 'n Shake! Wanna come with us?'

'Boys,' Dad replies, 'we're gonna get a hell of a storm through here! I suggest ya'll get home! Come over to the house after it passes if ya want!'

We pile into the car and my mom steps on the gas. But she struggles to drive in a straight line. 'Oh, Hell!' she cries, 'The wind is blowin this damn car all over the road!'

'Just keep yer pace slow there, darlin,' Tobias says, 'easy does it.'

But the wind is getting stronger and thunder follows lightning all over the land.

'From KMOX weather service <CRACKLE> the tornado watch has been upgraded to a *tornado warning* for the bi-state area. Tornados have touched down in Osage County, Gasconade County, Franklin County and St. Charles County. <CRACKLE> Please bring the pets in and take cover in the basement. If you don't have a basement <BZZZ> move to an enclosed centralised room of your home. Stay away from any windows, exit doors or perimeter areas-'

382

'Shit, St. Charles County!' my dad yells.

'That's just the next county, ain't it?' Tobias asks.

'Yep, this is gonna be one hell of a storm!'

sunsets and full moons

Mom swerves the Corolla into our driveway through the brute winds. My dad and I carry Tobias into the house and down to the basement where we take cover, settling on redwood patio furniture that lives down here in the cold months. 'Sorry, Tobias,' but I'm afraid that our home's not very wheelchair friendly.'

'Aw, don't worry bout that, Robert,' Tobias replies, I'm used to it after all these years. Anyhow, it was all too kind of ya'll to let me stay here while I'm in town.'

'It's the least we can do.' My dad fetches three ice cold Budweisers from the fridge and distributes them to Tobias and me. I crack mine open and watch my mom and the two soldiers share smiles, as if what we'd all been through has made this storm trivial.

'Why are the sirens still blarin?' Tobias asks. 'It's calm out there now. Look!' We all look up and out through the basement windows set just below the rafters.

'The calm before the storm,' Dad warns before taking a long swig of his beer.

'But it's November time. Ya'll get tornadoes this time a year?'

'In my experience they can happen anytime,' Mom replies.

'All ya need is the right combination of weather and warm air,' Dad adds.

'I suppose it *was* rather mild out there today,' Tobias says. 'We get the odd tornado back home, but in Mississippi it's all about hurricanes, especially in Biloxi.

'Tobias, are ya ok with discussing this court case coming up?' Dad asks. 'I bring it up because yesterday we received a subpoena.'

'Well,' Tobias replies as he strokes Charlie's fur, 'I'm happy ya did bring it up to be honest. Ya got that subpoena cause there will be questions about the Vette. They'll wanna hear from Ethan about how Felicity and Justin got access to the car. They'll wanna know that ya'll were out of town when it all happened.'

'Oh, Tobias, we understand all of that,' Mom says, 'but we just wondered if ya knew why it was all going to court if they've already proven that Justin wasn't drinkin. Was Justin speedin or something?'

'Of course he wasn't speedin!' I cry out.

'The boy's right. He wasn't speedin.'

'Well, what in God's name happened then?' my dad barks.

Tobias replies, 'The detective that's liasin with me is cocksure that a St. Louis County Police officer was in hot pursuit of another car after he ran the plate and it came up red.'

I close my eyes and feel my heart race. I remember what Justin said to me on Halloween. The truth is coming out...

'The detective believes this cop and two others tried to cover it all up.'

'Cover it up?' Mom gasps.

'Yep. I'm afraid so. He thinks that this cop in question flipped his siren lights on and the suspect, if ya like, smashed the gas pedal down and turned it into a high speed chase. It's alleged that the suspect whipped right past Justin and Felicity, who were in the wrong place at the wrong time. When the cop tried to follow he lost control and clipped yer Vette. Two other St. Louis County cruisers came on, but by the time they got to the bridge my daughter had already gone through the-'

But Tobias can't finish, overwhelmed with a sneaky moment of grief.

'Easy, Tobias. Easy.' My dad says. But Tobias shivers and whimpers as Mom consoles him by caressing his back. Tobias's bawling is contagious. Mom's tears give way as Dad conceals his, just walking back underneath the window, looking out at the eerie calm. I watch the outpour in silence. I'm numb. Have I got anything left?

'Don't worry about court, Tobias,' Mom says. 'Our main concern before getting that subpoena was the family counselling sessions that we three had set up.'

'Also there'll be a psychiatrist,' Dad remarks, 'for Ethan and me. But this court date is job one right now.'

'I see,' Tobias replies.

'Tobias,' Dad says, 'we'll be there for ya every step of the way.'

Charlie's ears perk and he scampers underneath the stairs and cowers down. I take notice of my dog and his whimpering. Now I realise the dark-as-night sky that warns out the window.

'The windshield was already smashed out,' Tobias recovers to say. 'He told me that at a glance it certainly does look like what was originally thought...that Felicity was ejected from the car.'

'But why would-'

'I don't know. I suppose all those answers are gonna come

389

out. But, I do hope y'all will cooperate anyhow.'

'Of course we will.' Dad replies.

Suddenly I hear it…that freight train.

Far away…coming on strong.

It's rushing towards us.

An explosion of wind and rain hammer into the house. I take a long gulp of my beer and stand up. The bright one hundred-watt bulb light flickers and goes out briefly before re-illuminating my parent's and Tobias's concerned faces. The weather is no longer trivial. There is a crash and a flash and the basement stays dark this time, just as it has outside and it's still the early afternoon. And the freight train, Mother Nature's angry wrath, is coming hard and fast. It sounds like it's an express right down Bataan Drive! The sixth sense within us as beasts of the world kicks on, just as it already has for Charlie. In unison and we all know what is about to happen. There are more rumbles, bangs and booms. It's all happening so fast. So *incredibly fast*!

<Flash>

Bleak silence, but somehow it's deafening.

<Crash>

I've been having these dreams, these visions, of freight trains blasting through my soul.

<Crack>

Life has haunted me. It has warned me. Time never stops. Time is now and always…and everything before.

<Nothing>

I've never seen a freight train in my life, nor have I ever really *heard* one.

Everything is in slow motion. I trounce my heavy feet up

the basement stairs, like I'm climbing a steep mountain, and open the door. Darkness welcomes me, floating with dust and debris. The electricity has been knocked out. A cold draft raids in and I follow it across the kitchen.

There's that black cat again on the back porch. It still twirls its tail calmly on the rocking chair. Its eyes glow brightly through the plume of dust. I struggle through the darkness down the hall toward the bedrooms, passing that black and white photo of my father as a child. He rocks away in that chair just staring back. *But this is* my *house, not Grandma's...*

Mom, Dad and Tobias are yelling at me not to go further, but I ignore them. I know where I'm going and I know what's happened as I've been warned of this for the past month, just the same as I'd been warned about everything else.

The dust and debris come from my bedroom, the only room with the door left open. Inside that door it's wet, cold and covered in grey daylight. I march ahead, abandoning the warnings of danger, with hunger to confirm another vision's meaning.

Growing up in the Midwest I've heard so many stories and legends of tornadoes that have made them one of the most mysterious and fabled weather events. Like the one about the two houses on the same street that were absolutely levelled, but the house just in between them remained unharmed. It was as if the twister just picked and chose which homes it wanted to attack. There was also a cow that was reported missing by a farmer after a tornado swept right across his land. The next day that cow was actually found alive and well, eating grass by a neighbouring farmer over a mile away. Dorothy and Toto were carried away with one from Kansas all the way to the Land of Oz, and the little farmhouse landed on and killed The Wicked Witch of the East. During countless news channel interviews, folks from Kirksville to Springfield reported, 'It sounded like a freight train.' And indeed it did this afternoon.

I walk into my bedroom littered with fallen leaves. The tornado has ripped away the outer-wall cleanly - the *fourth* wall - along with most of the roof. Chunks of wood, shingles and fibreglass are strewn everywhere. Paperwork has blown all over the place and dirty laundry has shifted and soaks up rain. But all of the furniture remains in its place and undamaged. Wet, but undamaged. I look up at the grey sky where the ceiling should be and watch birds fly across. From high above a soldier in a helicopter can see me. Perhaps a high school student gazes down at me in wonder of what fate the next month will bring him. All the while I stand down here in this three-walled solved mystery. A tornado was coming, and it indeed came. In more ways than just one.

Ghosts: Messages from the Dead lays underneath my bed. But I thought I left it in my locker at school. I squat down to pick it up and give it a dust-off as debris sticks to its damp cover. I thumb through the moist, yellow-edged pages and know that I'll give it a good tending to and start reading it right away, after all that's happened.

In the middle of the book I find three photographs. The first one I shot of Felicity in the Delmar Loop.

'Felicity, smile!' Felicity poses, flashing a coy smile. Her green eyes sparkle right on cue, just before the camera flashes.

The photo reminds me of love and happiness. But I didn't put it in there.

392

The second one is the mysterious cemetery photo that Felicity didn't want to submit.

'So why aren't ya submittin that photo?'

'It's just...special. It reminds me of things.'

It reminds me that there is death and there are ghosts. But I didn't put that one in there, either.

The third photograph is of Felicity and her mother, Marilyn. They kneel on either side of that beautiful black horse, lying in an emerald green pasture that blooms red roses; a pasture they tend together. It looks magical, mystical and dreamy. They look so happy, calm, and content. They look like angels in Heaven, probably where the photo was taken. This photo reminds me that Felicity will always be with me and one day I will join her there. I turn the photo over and read what has been written in green ink…

fallen leaves

I plop down on the damp wooden floor spotted with rain puddles and pull Felicity's letter from my jacket's breast pocket. At the foot of my bed I read her words...

Dearest Ethan,

We will chase those sunsets and full moons. The wind will whip through my hair...eighty miles an hour in your ear though the golden desert...while the parched terrain passes us by.

I can't wait for us to meet again but, no matter what, I'll always be with you as long as you never stop believing that we one day will. Always follow your heart, Ethan, and hold on to your hope.

And until we meet again...hope shall never fly away.

Love,

Felicity xxx

A startling rustle distracts me from the letter. Outside, in the void of the fourth wall, that white wolf stalks me amongst the rubble, crunching the fallen leaves. It stops and stares and disappears as his master's footsteps approach...

<click-clack, click-clack, click-clack>

A shadow is cast upon me. 'Dad,' the boy says.

Slowly I turn around, wiping the tears away that Felicity's letter jerked from my eyes. The boy I see, he is the spitting image of me, as if I'm looking in the mirror! My son stands in my bedroom doorway with a shotgun at his side. I say, 'Go on, do what ya came here to do.' I hand him the letter Felicity wrote. He takes it from me and upon her words he casts his eyes.

My eyes.

'Go on, son,' I say, 'I don't wanna become the man ya hate.'

I watch him read the letter. He raises his eyes and stares into mine, lying his weapon down on the bedroom floor. I approach him carefully, knowingly. I close my eyes and kiss him upon the brow. 'I do love ya, I do.' My eyes open and my son has vanished, back to where I pray he will wait for me in peace.

And as for his weapon, this twelve-gauge, I'll put it back on Dad's garage wall where it belongs, if the tornado spared it.

the end

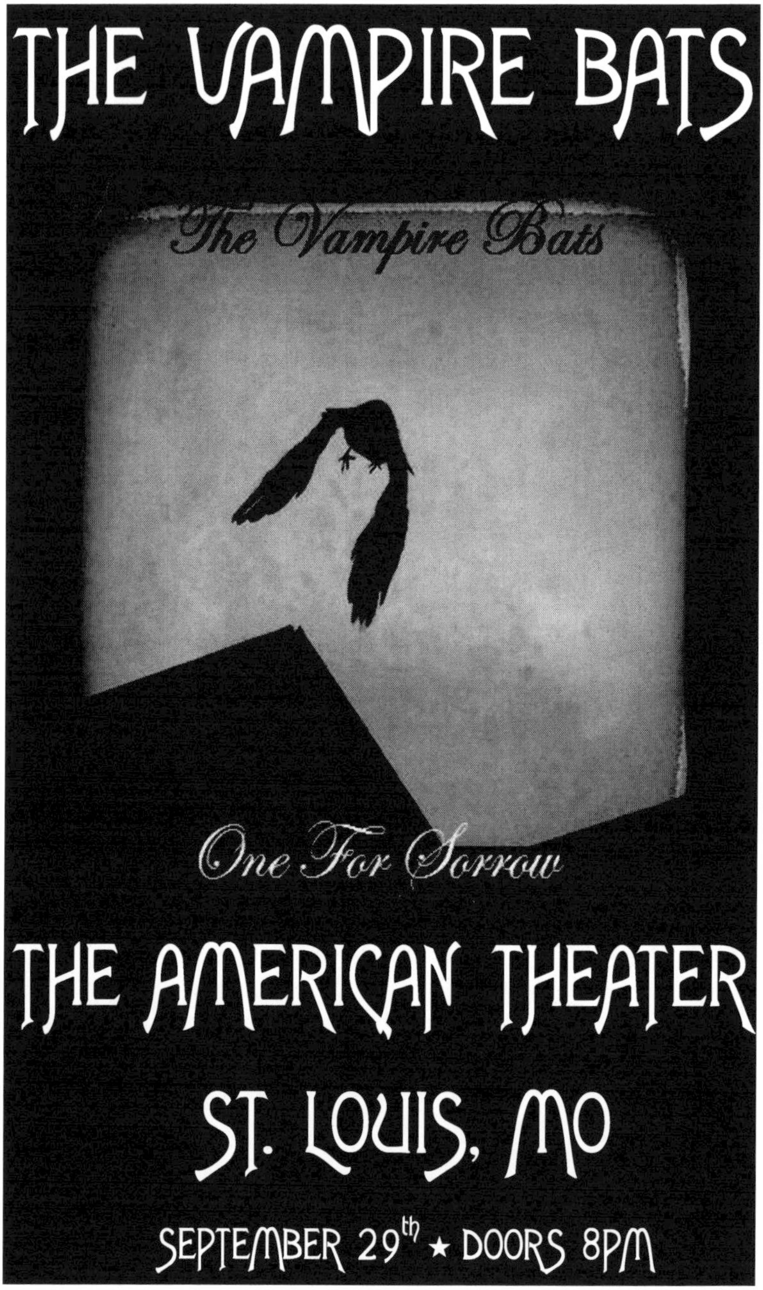
THE VAMPIRE BATS
The Vampire Bats
One For Sorrow
THE AMERICAN THEATER
ST. LOUIS, MO
SEPTEMBER 29th ★ DOORS 8PM

erickoppitz★com

2394122R00218

Printed in Great Britain
by Amazon.co.uk, Ltd.,
Marston Gate.